Deadly Vicious Lies

The Realm of Farehail

Deadly Vicious Lies

The Realm of Farehail

Emma Lynn Ellis

Cover Art by Katie Youngblood
TikTok: @katiespodsandpores
Cover Design by Jasmine Bender

Print ISBN-13: 979-8-9889673-5-4
Digital ISBN-13: 979-8-9889673-6-1
Youngblood Publishing LLC
Youngbloodpublishingllc@gmail.com

For the girls who looked
at their brother's friend
and thought…
Yes.

Prologue

"Tynan. Ty-nan."

I repeated the name over and over again. My name. The mantra gave me something to focus on as my arms barked from the strain of rowing for…

How long had I been out here?

I was so thirsty. Ravenous. So tired.

"Tynan," I said again, keeping myself awake. I couldn't fall asleep again. It was hard enough to tell which way I was going, and I could easily get turned around if I didn't remain focused. If I lost consciousness out here, I would die—lost at sea forevermore.

The skin on my arms and the back of my neck was searing in the hot sun. Blisters were beginning to form, large red swells erupting from my normally smooth, brown skin. Luckily the sun was dropping behind me now, though my eyes still strained, and my head still pulsed from the days staring into its rays. My face felt tight, and I swore it would begin to melt off with how burned it was getting.

How long had I been out here?

Water sloshed as my oars dipped repeatedly into the sea. I was going to be sick. If only I'd had something in my stomach to retch. All I could see was an unending expanse of blue. At times, I couldn't even discern the water from the sky. I felt so small, nothing but a speck of existence in such a vast place. A speck that was about to be wiped out.

My tongue was sticking to the roof of my mouth, and I opened my stiff jaw slowly to peel it away. A bad idea, because the air hitting my tongue just reminded me of how thirsty I was. A dry, tacky film was beginning to develop over the surface of my mouth, my lips, and I was tempted to drink the seawater just to wash it away.

My foot kicked the now empty pouch of water I'd pilfered before boarding the small craft. I should have grabbed more provisions. But I didn't think I'd be out here this long.

I wasn't supposed to be out here at all, actually. Things didn't go as planned. They had turned on me. All of them. I could feel it happening, too. So slowly.

It had started with a look from one of the deckhands. He looked at me as if I was some creature not fit to lick the dirt from his boots. I could feel the whispers as they tittered while my head was turned. From him, it spread like wildfire.

My back twinged in pain from the idle thought—almost imagining the feeling of flames licking at my skin—but I rolled my shoulders to try to forget about it.

I had no remorse for fleeing when I did. I'd surely be dead if I hadn't. Honestly, it was a miracle I had scrounged up as many supplies as I had before they came for me.

Those provisions were long gone by now.

How long had I been out here?

I was going to die. It was a truth I had been trying to swallow down for a while now. Since I had run out of water, the food long gone before that even. I wasn't going to make it to land. My body would shrivel up in the heat or collapse from exhaustion. I would turn to dust beneath the excruciating heat of the sun, forever floating aloft on my stolen craft. Forever lost at sea.

It was only a matter of time.

"Tynan." I repeated my mantra, reminding myself of—

What was I reminding myself of?

My hand spasmed, and I cried out, the sound a gnarled hiss. The cramp cascaded pain up my arm and into my neck. My jaw tensed and tightened over a curse I could not utter even if I wanted to.

I flexed my fingers one at a time, each digit throbbing as they cracked from the handle.

And then my oar slipped from my grasp. I lunged for it, my boat swaying in protest as I tried to reach over the edge. But the wood was just out of reach, floating away without a care in the world. I watched it bob over the light waves and pulled my remaining oar in for safekeeping. I didn't trust my limbs to obey me right now.

My body became very cold and very quiet all at once. It had never felt this quiet. My power always had something to say, some sort of protest. But I hadn't felt anything from it in…

How long had I been out here?

I slid onto the floor of the boat. My shoulders rested against the seat, and I ignored the stabbing pain it caused the tender skin along my back. My head lolled back, and despite the harsh sun looming behind me, my eyes drifted closed. Exhaustion enveloped me, and I couldn't pry them back open. I almost didn't want to open them ever again. It would be easy: falling asleep and never waking back up. I didn't deserve it, honestly. This death was too easy. Too peaceful.

"Tynan," I whispered, but no sound reached my ears—my mouth was too dry. My last thought before I succumbed to darkness was that I was slowly dying, and there was nothing I could do to stop it.

I woke up.

Which was a miracle in and of itself. My body was stiff, the feeling liken to being asleep for days. I wouldn't have doubted it in the slightest if that was the case, either. There was no way to mark how much time had passed out here, so I had no way of knowing for sure.

And it was dark when I awoke. Another blessing.

I was so hot, my skin radiating heat from the deep burns marring its surface. It was beginning to shed layers—not unlike that of a snake. I stretched out my arms and my legs, rolling my neck each way. Pain lanced through my tight muscles as I worked them free of the knots. At least enough to settle myself back up onto the seat of the boat.

Thousands of stars glittered above my head, which I would have regarded in wonder on any other night of my life. They were the only light in an otherwise black night. Still, I couldn't see where the sea ended, and the sky began. Couldn't tell which direction I faced. If I had turned around in circles while I slept.

I was so thirsty.

But my mind was clearer now than it had been. A sort of fog had lifted while I slept, which wasn't necessarily a good thing. If I had thought my prospects bad amidst my delirium, I felt worse about them now. I knew there was no getting out of this mess, not with how weak I was. Not in the absence of food, least of all, water.

My chances of stumbling upon land or another ship were next to none, not without knowing where I was and what direction I needed to steer myself toward.

I should have just stayed on that ship. Being a prisoner and alive was better than dying alone on a scrappy boat in the middle of the sea. And all of this for what? It was for survival, yet I wasn't going to be surviving anything much longer.

Staring my own death in the face sent a chill down my spine. I wasn't ready to die. That was the reason I was out here. I escaped so that I could live.

I began to cry. Or at least my body tried to cry. My eyes burned; my throat constricted as raspy, silent sobs tore from it. But no tears wetted my lashes.

Not a good sign. My body was so dehydrated and dry that I couldn't even make tears.

Hopeless. If only my father could have seen me.

Cool dread skittered along my skin and nestled into my chest. I shivered again from the cold feeling of it. How could I be so cold when my skin felt like it was on fire? Another chill skated down my back.

Wait.

That was a cold breeze I was feeling.

I stood almost too rapidly. The boat rocked abruptly, and it took every bit of my fast-fading strength to keep my body from tumbling into the water. I lifted my chin, scanning the expansive stars—searching.

One by one the stars behind me began blinking out and I nearly howled with joy. Storm clouds were rolling in.

Water. It was about to rain, which meant I would have fresh water. I fell to my knees, my body shuddering in relief. In reassurance, I felt the first drop of cold water sizzle against the back of my blistered neck.

I tilted my head back once again, holding my mouth open, this time for the onslaught of rain as it began pouring from the clouds above. The first drop that hit my tongue had my body going lax as a gratefulness I had never experienced crashed inside of me.

And there it was.

A writhing inside me, almost so slight that I could have missed it. My body sagged further as more droplets met my tongue. I let them slide down my cracked throat. It wasn't until I tried to swallow that I realized just how thirsty I truly was.

I had undoubtedly been moments from death.

The rain began beating down harder, nearly drenching my clothes. I welcomed the cool embrace on my hot, aching skin. I was shivering, but I didn't care. Water began pooling on the floor of the boat, so I cupped some within my hands and sipped up the life-giving liquid. I drank again and again, unable to quench that undeniable need.

My body was so dry.

The rain was nearly deafening as it beat against the sea. Thunder rolled, the sound reverberating off the water and making my ears ring with the impact. Light flashed briefly, and it wasn't until then that I realized I was in trouble.

My boat was bobbing up and down over ever-growing waves. The wind from the storm was blowing across the water, coaxing the tide into turmoil.

Yes, I was no longer thirsty. But I was still about to die.

Thunder boomed even louder overhead, the water pounding against my skin. It was stinging now, the force of it smarting against my blisters and burns. I sat back onto the seat, grabbing my one oar and beginning to row forward—flinging that bit of wood from one side to the other between forceful strokes. In the hopes of what, I wasn't sure. There was no outrunning this storm, but I'd be damned if I went down without a fight.

My boat reared up, the movement sending the sickening feeling of falling spearing through my gut. The power inside me lashed around in protest, but I ignored it. With how weak I was, it was useless to me right now anyway. The waves were cascading around me, the sound deafening in combination with the storm. My craft was pushed this way and that, and I could do nothing to fight against the will of the storm.

I screamed, but the sound was swallowed up by the frenzy. It tore through my dry and damaged throat, regardless, as a wave crashed into my boat this time. The salt water stung my eyes as it splashed onto my face—into my mouth. I sputtered, hacking a cough that sent water spraying back out.

Another wave crashed, sending me flying to my knees on the bottom of the boat. My clothes were soaked, and my knees barked in pain as wave after wave slammed into me. The boat was swaying, tipping from side to side, and I was flung against the wall of the vessel, my head smacking into the wood.

Ringing sounded, and for a moment, everything around me was drowned out. But then I was enveloped in water, my lungs filling with the burning of salt as I swallowed another scream. I had been thrown overboard.

I kicked and clawed my way toward the surface, but I couldn't tell which way was up. Everything was so dark around me, the water shuffling my body and turning me head over heels. I twisted and flailed, searching for the surface—searching for a mouthful of air.

But I found none.

Chapter 1

Kaya–Six years ago

D isposable.

That's what we were. The lot of us. We were hundreds in number, but not one of us mattered. What mattered was protecting our secrets.

Protecting *their* secrets.

They had given us this power, and using it to protect them was the least we could do in thanks. At least, that's how we'd been trained to think.

Not everyone in Farehail was blessed with power. No. Only some of us were. The lower families who had children blessed with power were the unlucky ones. Those children were taken once they showed potential. They were ripped from their parents' arms and thrust into the bosom of the guild. They were trained not only in their abilities but in bloodshed and deception as well. The guild was ruthless.

The higher families, those with sway and money, were lucky. They were usually able to stay together, even with that power flowing beneath their skin. Especially with that power. They ruled this land.

It wasn't as cut and dry as that. Everyone did their part. Everyone valued the contributions put forth by others. Without one group, the other would fall. We needed each other, and we all knew it.

The rain was cold as it beat down on our heads. I was chilled to the bone, sopping wet and almost shivering. But I wouldn't show that weakness. None of us would.

We stood in rows, listening to the orders as they were shouted over the sounds of thunder reverberating off the surrounding wall. Lord Holden was demanding, but he was thorough. We had never been so safe as we were now with him as our leader.

Our scouts had sent word that there were intruders on the island, and they were to be found and dealt with. We were to be sent out in groups of four—our normal groups—to sweep through every inch of the island.

Nash, Finn, and I had been together for years—since we were children. We made the perfect unit, especially for how young we all were. Our mentor and superior, Shepard, was reserved and aloof, but he handled us well enough. He valued what each member brought and encouraged our independence as well as our teamwork.

"Shep!" Holden's growl caught me off guard. I turned toward Shepard, shooting him a confused look. He rolled his eyes and stomped forward to see what Lord Holden was on about. The rows dispersed, and Nash came to stand with me.

"What do you think he wants? Shouldn't we get going? We're losing valuable time," I ranted to Nash. I hated waiting. I was always biting at the bit to go out on these missions. It was the only time I felt like I actually had a purpose here. I loved being beyond the wall, surrounded by the trees.

"Finn's sick. I assume we're getting a stand-in until he gets over it." Nash was so nonchalant as he spoke, as if his best friend being left behind was no big deal. Though, it wasn't to them. They didn't feel the same about these things as I did. They didn't feel the pull that I often felt to scurry beyond the city. I was sure Finn was sound asleep right now, warm and dry, not a care in the world.

This was my entire life, though.

I smothered my annoyance. Water trailed down my cheeks, but the rain was beginning to let up. Shepard stood talking to Lord Holden, boredom almost leaking from his pores. I huffed a short laugh before noticing the silhouette standing off to one side.

Cillian.

Shepard turned and assessed Cillian, sensing where my own eyes had gone. The younger man was standing with his hands tucked into his pockets. He held himself in such an assured way that made me jealous. He was lethal—skillful—and he knew it.

The lower half of his face was covered by a piece of solid black cloth, as always. Only his striking gray eyes were visible beneath his charcoal hair and the barest hint of dark skin. Shepard gave him a curt nod, then inclined his head back to where Nash and I stood.

He couldn't.

My heart skittered to a halt as Cillian fell into step behind Shepard—a shadow flitting in tandem with its owner. I felt Nash pull his pack from the ground and toss it over his shoulder. I dipped down to do the same, unable to take my eyes from Cillian.

"Since Finn's out, we've been assigned Cillian. Let's move." Shepard always had a way with words. Straight to the point. I tried to ignore the delight emanating from Nash as we leapt from the rise and onto the sodden ground with little more than a splash.

Without a word, we moved as a unit through the archway of the city wall to the tree line just beyond the border. Under the canopy, we were protected from the pelting rain. I wiped the water from my face with the back of my arm, trying as I might to clear my blurred vision.

"We've got the northern, outer quadrant. We'll comb through slowly, double-checking the areas as we make our way out. We don't want to miss anything." Shepard disappeared into a tree, getting swallowed up by its dark void, and each of us followed in turn. Nash, then me, then Cillian taking sweep. Emerging somewhere it wasn't raining, I gave thanks to the Wildewood for the small blessing.

"What are Ezra and Wren doing since you're with us?" I asked Cillian.

"Well, Holden only sent the novices out today. So, I assume they're somewhere warm." Cillian sent me what I could only assume was a half smile. It was hard to tell beneath the mask, but his eyes sparkled slightly with playfulness. "I was just unlucky enough to be available as stand-in."

"Lucky for us," Nash practically sang. I shoved him in response.

"Your brother will be happy I was sent with you. You know how he worries." Cillian stepped around me as he spoke, heading to where Shepard studied a map.

"Ezra needs to relax." I grabbed Nash and pulled him alongside me, my fingers digging into his flesh slightly harder than necessary. We hovered over the map together as Shepard marked our destination.

"Kaya doesn't need anyone's protection," Shepard mumbled, but he didn't take his eyes from the parchment. I smiled, knowing this was likely the only compliment I would ever get from Shepard. Not that I needed it. As long as he wasn't berating me, I knew I was adept. He wasn't one to coddle his inferiors, and he did not hesitate to give us a good smack every now and again if we failed to follow his instructions. My corrections came fewer and farther between than either Nash's or Finn's, thankfully. Shepard had trained me well.

"Ezra still sees her as a child. I don't know if that will ever change." I watched as Cillian spoke, noting how his eyes darted to me sidelong.

"This wasn't his idea, was it?" I demanded, annoyed by the idea of Ezra sending a chaperone to look after me.

"No." Cillian didn't elaborate more, though I felt like it wasn't entirely the truth.

"I think the best approach is to split into groups of two. Our quadrant is one of the largest. Two of us need to sweep from the left while the other two come in from the right." Shepard dragged his finger along one of the many trails we'd traveled along countless times before. "We'll meet in the middle." Shep rolled the map up and shoved it back into his pack. "Nash, you're with me."

"Why can't Kaya go with you?" Nash almost whined as he said it. I rolled my eyes, knowing he just wanted to be alone with Cillian. His crush couldn't be more obvious.

"Because, as I said, Kaya doesn't need as much backup. She and Cillian together are as strong as me alone. You'd drag her down and probably get her killed, and he'd leave you tied to a tree."

I bit back a laugh. Cillian just stood there, impassively staring at Nash with his hands tucked into his pockets once more. Obviously, Shepard wasn't far off from how Cillian felt.

"We'll make our way to the edges tonight. Make camp and get some sleep. Once the sun is up, drag the area back until you hit the middle. It should be around early evening at that point. If we find nothing, we'll head back and give the all clear." I nodded to Shepard, my silent acquiescence to his orders. The chances of the intruders being in our quadrant were slim. There was no port on the northern end of the island, and they would likely stick to an area they could easily board a ship and flee from.

Shepard and Nash parted from us, disappearing through a tree to their destination. Nash threw me a sullen glance before he sank through the bark, bitter about being stuck on his own with Shepard. He didn't enjoy Shep's tough love the way I did.

Cillian stood motionless, his eyes never leaving my face. I could feel my cheeks begin to redden under his gaze.

"He really didn't send you to keep an eye on me?" I asked if only to fill the silence.

"No."

"Good. Because I'm fine on my own," I snapped. "He needs to quit mothering me." Cillian didn't respond. He narrowed his eyes slightly, searching me for lies.

We set out in the opposite direction from Nash and Shepard. The trees allowed us passage, drawing us deeper into the forest. The sun was coming out, causing the birds to begin swooping down in search of a meal brought out by the rain. We were silent as we moved, staying hidden within the underbrush and branches. Our presence would easily go unnoticed by everything within the forest—especially someone who didn't belong here.

Cillian wasn't a talker. He never had been. Not even during our weekly family dinners. Ezra and he had been friends since childhood and made it a point to keep close into adulthood. My brother insisted I join them, even though my presence always seemed to make Cillian uneasy. He had been a recluse most his life.

The day passed with nary a word between us. Night fell, and he took the first watch while I slept. We were perched in a tree, my back resting against the trunk—legs tied to the branch so I didn't tumble out during my slumber—while Cillian's legs hung loosely over the branch. I trusted in the trees to keep me safe while I slept, though, that, and Cillian. Ezra would kill him if he allowed me to fall from this height.

My eyes grew heavy. I was being lulled to sleep by the music of the forest, the pulsing undercurrent emanating from the power here. The chirping of the bugs was rhythmic and soothing. My body went limp; then everything turned to darkness.

Sunlight pierced through my eyelids, and I awoke with a start. Cillian was still perched in the same space, alert as ever. He assessed me as I loosened my neck and yawned.

"Why the hell didn't you wake me?" I snapped, stretching my arms out to each side.

"You obviously needed the rest."

"Yeah, but so did you. You can't do that, Cillian."

"I'll be fine. I've lasted a lot longer than one night without rest." Cillian dropped from the branch and onto the ground. The movement made no sound, and I was a bit jealous. I untied myself and stowed away my rope, dropping after him and landing in a crouch at his side.

"Are you sure? We could always get a late start while you take a nap," I suggested.

Cillian walked off without sparing me a glance. I let out a groan and chased after him. It was almost as if his feet were floating over the ground with how silent he was. I felt like such a child following after him. Not that it was a far-off assessment. He was five years my senior, but all that meant to me was that he had five years of training on me. I was a novice compared to him, and his abilities made that obvious. Made me envious.

"You're trying to take care of me."

"Why do you say that?" He still didn't look at me.

"Because you let me sleep through the night."

"Don't read into it."

"I am not a child."

"I didn't accuse you of being one."

"You're *treating* me like one."

He sighed but didn't falter in his steps. "No, I'm not."

"You and Ezra don't have any faith in me, do you?"

"Kaya, like it or not, he is always going to take care of you. Maybe that's rubbed off on me in some way, but just know it's for his sake, not yours." He adjusted his grip on his pack, and I ignored the pang his words sent through me. "He doesn't like you being put in dangerous situations like this."

"Well, he can't do anything about that. So, he needs to get over it and trust that I know what I'm doing." I was practically running to keep up with him. He was fast, his legs much longer and more graceful than mine.

"He knows that, but he still feels helpless and protective. What's wrong with that?"

"You know, Cillian, I don't think I've ever heard you talk this much before. It is quite a nice change of pace." Finally, he stopped and turned to face me. He shot me an annoyed look that made me laugh outright.

"Can you please stop talking? We're supposed to be covert right now, and you're doing a good job at blowing our cover." I snapped my mouth shut with a bit too much force, almost biting my tongue in the process. He wasn't wrong, but that didn't quell my annoyance. Cillian rolled his eyes and continued walking.

"Sorry," I whispered, scanning my surroundings. The forest was clear. There were animals skittering about, birds flying above. "I think we're alone, though."

Neither of us spoke again for hours. We walked on, then doubled back and retraced our steps, checking in valleys and caves, on riverbanks, the shoreline, and throughout the surrounding foliage. No space was left unturned in our search. The quadrant was clear.

I opened my mouth, ready to suggest we head to the meeting place since evening was closing in, when a twig snapped. The sound dried out my tongue and raised the hairs on the back of my neck. My eyes shot to Cillian instantly, hoping he heard the disruption as well.

He was frozen, eyes already scanning the surrounding trees, searching for the origin of the noise.

Nothing. There was nothing around us. We were alone. It must have been some animal passing by, though the hair on my arms began to stand on end.

Our eyes met. His held a question just below the surface, but before he could voice the words, his eyes flared in horror.

His dagger was flying at my face before I could suck in a breath or turn around. I was frozen in place, watching in terror as the blade soared directly for me. I squeezed my eyes shut, bracing for the slicing pain.

But it never came.

Instead, I heard a guttural noise and felt the ground rumble at my feet as something heavy fell there. Prying my eyes open, I looked toward the dirt.

Blood pooled around my boots, leaking from the body now lifeless beside me and seeping into the ground. A sword was discarded just out of reach of the corpse's hand.

He had meant to kill me, the fucker.

"You thought I was throwing that at you, didn't you?" Cillian's voice held a hint of amusement. "Pee yourself a little?"

"Shut up." I kicked the body over, unveiling his face. His features were ruddy and plain. It wasn't anyone I knew. "Well, I think we found our intruder." I looked back at Cillian just in time to see someone lunging at him, emerging straight from the tree just to his left and into an attack.

I didn't think; I just moved. Cillian dug for his dagger when he saw me careening toward him, unaware of the person intent on maiming him. He would be too late. The assailant had his sword raised, a dagger poised in his second hand. I slammed my body between them, bringing my blade up and connecting with the sword, the force reverberating down my arm. Without any other choice, I threw my other arm up, blocking the dagger from piercing into Cillian's skull.

The sharp pain pulled a deep grunt from my throat, but I didn't relent. I punched my blade forward, knocking his sword to one side. Before he could steady his arm, I plunged my dagger into his throat. Ripping the blade sideways, crimson began pouring from his neck. His grip fell from the dagger still embedded in my arm as he brought both hands to clutch at his wound. I dropped my blade so I could pull his free from my flesh. It seared as I slid it free, the flesh pulling against the metal.

Arms wrapped around me from behind—nearly cradling me—hands began clutching my wound together. I heard shouts from above, then the clashing of metal as I was dragged backward toward one of the trees. Before darkness enveloped me, I glimpsed Shepard and Nash slicing down more assailants. Where they had come from, I couldn't begin to guess. They had been silent in their assault.

When I emerged from the darkness of the tree, I was dropped gracelessly onto the dirt—far away from the chaos. Sounds of ripping cloth greeted the ringing in my ears, and then Cillian was kneeling before me, wrapping my forearm in a makeshift bandage. The fabric from his shirt was tight as he wrapped it around my seeping wound, and I winced from the pressure. Cillian tied it off and grabbed my face harshly between his hands.

"Are you alright? Are you hurt anywhere else?" I could only see his eyes, but they held so much worry within them. I watched as his pupils bounced across my face, searching for something in a panic. His fingers tightened, digging into the flesh of my cheeks. His heat sank into me through the pads of his fingers.

"I'm fine. It's not that bad."

"Can you heal yourself?" His hand was like a vise under my chin.

"It's not that bad," I repeated.

"Kaya. You need to try and heal it." It was useless telling him my power didn't work like that. The cut was too deep, and my power only worked so well on myself, not like it did on others. I humored him, though, placing my palm over the wrapped wound. The cloth was already soaked through with blood. I reached into myself, searching for that power lying within.

Heal.

I felt the light tingle of my power, searching for the wound. The heat was soothing, though I could tell it only partially healed the gash. It was good enough for now until I could find another healer within the city to tend to it.

"Better?" I asked, annoyed.

"Yes."

Shepard and Nash appeared from a tree a heartbeat later, blood spattering their clothes and skin. Shepard assessed me, his eyes lingering on the wrapped wound. He gave me a curt nod. The only praise I'd receive. I glanced away, my gaze landing on Cillian, who was still crouched on the ground beside me. Beneath the torn section of his shirt, I could make out a section of dark, muscled skin on his lower abdomen. My cheeks heated.

"There were five in all. We finished them. We'll need to double back just in case, but I think that was it," Nash said, surprising me with how well he was taking charge. A slight smile played at the edges of Shepard's lips in pride. Nash asked, "You good, Ky?"

"I'm fine. Just a scratch." Cillian was still holding my face. He must have realized it a moment later because he abruptly released me. Getting to his feet, he offered me his hand. I allowed him to pull me the rest of the way up.

"Let's go home. We stick together, and we'll make camp once we get far away from this place," Shepard said.

"The bodies?" I asked.

"Let them rot where they lie. The ground will claim them soon enough," said Cillian.

Chapter 2

Cillian–Six years ago

How had I been so slow? How had I not *sensed* them there? Ezra was going to kill me.

Kaya was more skilled than I gave her credit for, though. If she hadn't been so fast, so alert, I would have been dead. That dagger was meant for my skull. Yet she took it for me.

The *idiot.*

Shepard led us through the trees. Darkness was closing in, and we'd have to make camp soon. Nash practically danced along, hyped up from the killing frenzy. That was probably the most action the kid had ever seen.

The silence in the forest was almost eerie. It was not like the silence of last night, so full with the songs of insects and the skittering feet of creatures. No. Something was wrong.

I turned to Kaya just in time to see her drop to the ground. I was at her side in a flash, rolling her onto her back. Her copper eyes remained closed, and her thick lips were slightly parted. Her face had gone pale—a stark contrast to its normal honey brown—and sweat beaded along her forehead.

"Kaya. *Kaya.*" Both Shepard and Nash immediately stopped walking when they heard my calls. Dirt shuffled beneath their boots as they hurried back toward us. I shook her gently by the shoulder, still calling her name. I shook her harder.

"What's happened?" Shepard was beside me now, leaning over Kaya. He pulled her eyelids back, checking her pupils. Her copper irises rolled back into her head. His fingers lingered on her pulse for a moment. Grabbing her arm, he ripped the makeshift bandage from her flesh.

The wound was swollen, the skin so puffy that the split was being pulled farther apart. Purple veins riddled the skin, the gash weeping a yellow pus. My stomach knotted, and my mouth went dry as bile roiled in my gut.

"Poison." Shepard let his pack drop from where it rested against his back. It thumped to the ground with a thud, and he tore through it quickly and with ease. Procuring a tin from the depths, he scooped a generous amount of salve onto his fingers and slathered it across her skin in a thick layer.

I wasn't moving. I wasn't breathing. Frozen, my hand still gripped her shoulder, feeling as her pulse waned and fluttered beneath my fingers.

"She needs a healer faster than we can get her to one." Shepard's tone was emotionless.

I wanted to strike him.

"I'm on it." Nash was gone before I could even look up. I felt his essence disappear in an instant.

"We need to get to shelter." Almost on cue, thunder blasted through the trees. "Can you carry her?" I hadn't noticed the storm rolling in—too focused on Kaya's waning life force.

I didn't answer, instead lifting Kaya from the ground and cradling her in my arms. Ezra really was going to kill me.

"There's a cave just to the south of us. Nash will know where we've gone," Shepard said.

We ran as the rain broke from the clouds looming menacingly overhead. I shielded Kaya as best I could, trying to keep the cold water from chilling her further. Shepard ran slightly ahead, scanning the surroundings for any unwanted guests. He disappeared into the cave just moments before reemerging, signaling the area was clear.

In the cave, I lowered Kaya onto the roll Shepard had already laid out for her. I dug through my own pack for another blanket, gently covering her with it.

She was so pale.

Logs clattered onto the stone floor, dumped gracelessly from Shepard's arms. Stacking them quickly, he said, "Light it." Heeding his command, I reached deeply for my power.

Please.

Flames burst from the wet logs, uncaring of the moisture. The logs hissed with steam, but the cave warmed immensely in an instant.

"I'll keep watch for Nash and the healers." Shepard disappeared through the cave mouth. I settled onto the ground beside Kaya, unable to take my eyes off her face. Unable to keep my hands from reaching for her—running along her clammy skin—as if they could hold her waning life within her body. She had been fine only moments ago. What sort of poison acted so fast?

The light shining into the cave from the forest diminished as the time ticked by so slowly. The flickering flames glowed ominously, casting shadows across Ky's pale skin. Her color drained further with every passing moment. Still, there was no sign of Nash.

Lying back, I tucked her into my arm, absently brushing the black hairs from where they were stuck to her face. The pads of my fingers tingled as they moved along her cheek. Unease gripped my heart as I felt how shallow her breathing became. An amused huff from the mouth of the cave had my head snapping up.

"Fuck off," I bit out toward Shepard.

"I didn't say a damn thing." But he smirked at me as if this were the right time to find something funny.

Rustling sounded from outside, and I let out a breath. Nash. I could feel him approaching with two others. Healers from the city.

They wasted no time, coming straight for Kaya. One placed hands on her chest, and even I could feel their power sinking into her. Her heart rate spiked, causing her skin to bloom with color—easing the constriction in my chest. The fear clutching at my heart. The other healer uncovered her arm and placed a palm over the seeping wound, which was even more purple now than before. I watched the healer close their eyes as they dug deep for that power within.

A moment later, they both let her go, sitting back on their heels.

"She needs rest, but the poison has been removed." The first healer, Rose, looked at me as she spoke. "She should be fit for travel in the morning. It seems you could use some rest as well, Cillian."

I only nodded, too enraptured by Kaya's flushed cheeks. My body began deflating with exhaustion almost instantly, that distress having taken so much out of me. The healers rose, departing without another word. I hoped they wouldn't say anything to Ezra before I could.

"I'll take first watch. You three go to sleep." Shepard was gone before my head hit the ground.

"I don't think you're ready to be out here like this."

Kaya could have killed me with the look she threw my way, but I was only grateful for the life her eyes held. We were halfway back to the city, sloshing through the sodden ground in the early morning.

"Excuse me? I saved your ass back there," she scoffed.

"Yes, and nearly died for it. If you had been a bit more prepared, you would have drawn your second dagger and used *that* to block the blade.

Not your *arm*." The advice came out dry, uncaring, and harsh. "We could have been home last night and avoided the entire headache."

Kaya stopped and whipped around, nearly colliding with my chest. She shoved her hand into my collarbone, causing me to relinquish a step. "A *thank you* would suffice, Cillian."

"If you don't think my training is adequate, maybe you should take over." Shepard's voice carried over the wind, even though he was many paces ahead of us.

"That's not what I'm saying," I protested.

"No, really, Cillian. Be my guest. You are extremely talented. She could learn a lot from you. And if it would give you and Ezra the peace of mind you two so desperately need, then it's for the best." Shepard didn't even so much as turn back to look at us. Kaya was still blocking my path, staring daggers into my soul. "She'll be out here with us regardless."

Kaya's eyes flashed with something before she turned away and followed Nash and Shepard. She dragged her boots through the mud, like walking was still too much effort.

"I'll run it by Ezra," I mumbled, annoyed at myself for the fluttering feeling my power gave off at the idea of spending more time with Kaya.

We were silent the rest of the journey. When the stone archway into the city was finally in view, Kaya's gait quickened, a new energy taking over. She nearly bounced into the perimeter, looping her arm through Nash's. She steered him off into the crowds without a goodbye to either me or Shepard. Though, the group leader did much of the same. He meandered off toward his home, not sparing me another breath.

I made my way to Ezra and Kaya's home. It was midweek, which meant our routine *family* dinner would be tonight. Ezra would appreciate the help cooking, while Kaya and Nash did who knows what together—hopefully steering clear of Asher.

She often spent time with the other fire wielder of the city. He was also one who liked to keep his distance from others. Something about Kaya must have been magnetic to that flame in each of us. Though, the guy was bad news. A possible murderer, or just someone with very, very poor luck. No one could rightfully say.

Ezra and Ky weren't really my family, though they were the closest things I'd had to it in a long time. Most of us were all taken from our true families at young ages. I had been different. I was born to a couple within the guild—both adept fighters themselves. Both died when I was six, however.

Ezra was with his family until around age nine. Kaya had been four.

I remember how small she was, even now. Both Ezra and I had been the same age when she arrived, though I had been with the guild for three years at that point. Kaya was brought in only a couple of months after Ezra. I think that wound of separation was still fresh for him, and when he looked into Kaya's tiny brown, upturned eyes, he was putty in her hands. He felt like he needed to protect her. He threw a fit until Lord Holden finally let them live in the same house.

He had taken care of her ever since.

Ezra and I hated each other initially. It wasn't until after two years in the same group that we were finally able to tolerate each other. It took many years after that for me to call him my friend. Now, at age twenty-three, he and our other group mate, Wren, were the only people I even talked to.

Other than Kaya, but that was by default. Where Ezra was, she was bound to be.

I didn't knock when I reached their small cottage in the middle of the city. I slinked through the front door, shucking my shoes in the entryway. My pack thumped to the ground, and I headed for the sitting room. Ezra was in a chair, reading. He didn't look up as I fell onto the couch and covered my eyes with my arm.

"Kaya got hurt."

The book snapped shut, but I didn't turn to look at him. "I assume she's fine since you're showing your face here."

"Yes. Shepard suggested I give her more training, though, since I think she's lacking."

"Is she?"

"Well, if she wasn't, she wouldn't have been hurt. It was a stupid mistake, really, and she could have died." I didn't bother to add that she had saved my ass. No. I'd let her be the one to tell her brother about it. I could see that wide grin of hers behind my closed lids.

Ezra was silent for a long moment. I almost expected him to come over and throw me onto the floor for letting anything happen to her, but judging by that silence, he remained in his seat. Unconsciousness began dragging me down before he finally answered. "I think it's a good idea. Are you okay with it?"

"She could have died."

Chapter 3

Kaya–Six years ago

Y ou two are overbearing." They were both waiting for me when I got home, and honestly, it felt like an ambush. We had just sat down for dinner when they told me what was happening. "I am just fine on my own."

"Cillian told me what happened," Ezra chastised.

I glared at Cillian. He sat back with his arms crossed over his chest giving the semblance of being bored. "Shepard has been just fine as a mentor."

"Shepard is the one who suggested it, Kaya." Ezra stood, clearing the table of dishes. Since he cooked dinner, it was my turn to wash up.

"So, who's training me? You?" The question was more of an accusation toward Ezra.

"No. Cillian is. I'm too busy lately with the extra job patrolling the docks. Cillian has more free time." Ezra placed the dishes into the sink. Cillian sighed audibly in response as if this entire situation wasn't his fault.

"You know if you don't want to, he can't make you," I said in Cillian's general direction. I could tell he was annoyed by just the idea of the task. He had a hard time saying no to my brother.

"I already agreed. Besides, I've seen you out in the field more than Ezra. I know what you need to work on, and he doesn't." Cillian placed his mask back over his face before standing from his seat. "I need to get home." He looked utterly exhausted—as if he hadn't slept the entire time we were in the forest.

"When do we start?" Though I was annoyed, the prospect of training with Cillian grew on me with each passing second. He was one of the most skilled fighters in the city. Even if I felt I was adequate, I couldn't deny there was so much more I could learn from him.

"I'm thinking we start tomorrow at dawn. We'll meet three times a week if you aren't called out for other jobs. The other days, you should keep up your normal routine with your group." My jaw dropped, but Cillian was out the door before I could yell my retort.

"When am I supposed to have free time?" My voice was shrill.

"You'll have every evening." Ezra cleared the remaining dishes.

"Yeah, unless they give me other jobs. I have friends, you know. Unlike Cillian."

"It won't be the end of the world, Kaya. You'll have time for other things. And it's for your own good." Ezra came over and gave me a hug. He squeezed my body so tight it was almost painful. "I don't know what I would do if anything happened to you." He planted a quick kiss on the top of my head. "You are the only family I have."

"I know." I wrapped my hands around him and gave him a squeeze in return. "I'll try not to kill him. I'm sure you'd be sad to lose him too."

Ezra laughed before pulling away. "Yes. I would be sad." He disappeared out the door, leaving me to tidy the rest of the mess on my own.

"You're late."

My feet dragged over the grass, my body still weighed down with sleep. The sun was barely peeking over the horizon as I made it to the clearing just south of the city. This was only one of the many training grounds around the city. We were surrounded by them, and they were greatly needed. With so many of us living in the city, we needed ample room to train not only our bodies but our powers as well.

"It's still mostly dark out," I complained, and didn't miss the way it sounded like a whining child.

"I said dawn." His arms were folded over his chest, and I wanted to knock him over. I couldn't stand how aloof he acted. Did nothing faze him?

I gestured wildly around us. "The sun is right there. If this isn't dawn, then we will have to agree to disagree on this."

"Warmups. Now."

I gaped at him. "Well, good morning to you, too," I said, rolling my eyes.

"*Now.*"

I didn't have time to argue before he sent a ball of fire directly at me. I ran, narrowly avoiding being singed in the process. Growling to myself, I did laps around the clearing for what felt like hours—until Cillian barked at me to start on laps of lunges. I could kill him, but my muscles burned so badly I could barely keep upright. I kept going, though, if only to prove to him that I didn't need these training sessions.

"Rest."

I toppled to the ground, albeit a little dramatically. Focusing on my breathing, I pulled in slow, deep breaths as I grounded myself. I could feel my body relaxing into the earth. Its energy radiated back into me in response. The buzzing of insects became a song around me as I leached what I could from the forest, taking all the Wildewood offered.

"Ready for arms?"

My eyes snapped open to see Cillian hovering above me. I nearly screamed, not expecting him to be so close.

"What did I do to you?" I asked, breathless.

"Risked your life for me. This is your punishment. Arms. Now." His boot nudged into my ribs, encouraging me to roll over onto my stomach. I obeyed, only because I didn't have the energy to tell him off. I knew it was easier to just give him what he wanted, so I went through the arm exercises, silently cursing his name every second.

"Okay. Rest again for a moment, then we start hand to hand."

"You're joking, right?" I whined from where I was sprawled in the dirt.

"About?"

"I have to do *more?*"

"Kaya, that was literally just the warmup. What do you even *do* with Shepard?" His eyes were wide, and I could almost see how his mouth gaped open beneath his mask.

"Nothing, apparently," I mumbled under my breath. No wonder he was the best if this was a normal workout for him.

The time he gave me to rest was not nearly long enough. I grunted as I pulled myself onto my feet, heading to where he stood with his hands in his pockets. His face was void of emotion from what I could see above that stupid cloth. I wanted to ram him into the ground.

"We won't be using weapons yet. We'll start with fists." He sounded almost monotone. Detached.

I wasn't sure if it was the exhaustion from being poisoned or my annoyance from him running me ragged, but I careened into him as hard as I could before he could give the signal to start. Tackling him to the ground, I brought my arm back to slam my fist into his face. Before I could, however, he flipped me over and had me pinned into the dirt.

The breath left my lungs on impact, causing me to emit a choking noise.

"Don't act out of passion. That only gets you hurt." He breathed the words mere inches from my ear. "Or pinned," he hissed.

I slammed my head into his, ignoring the cracking pain that lanced across my own skull as we connected. He jolted back, and I took the opportunity to shove him off me. Before I could regain control over him, he was on his feet—stomping a boot onto my back.

I yelped, sinking once more into the dirt.

"What did I *just* say?" he barked, and I could feel his exasperation oozing from him.

"Get off me," I growled through gritted teeth.

"Say please," he taunted back.

Anger flooded me. I thrashed a bit for show to hide the fact that my hand slithered down into the waistband of my pants and unsheathed the dagger I kept there. Thinking I was trying to throw him off balance, he chuckled softly to himself. In a swift move—too fast for Cillian to realize what I was doing—I flung my arm behind my back and slammed the blade into his ankle.

"*Fuck!*" Cillian yelled, falling hard onto the ground as I pulled my dagger free. I took my chance, flinging myself onto him. I straddled his waist and brought my bloodied blade up to his throat.

Pressing gently into the soft skin against his jugular, I asked sweetly, "Are we done?" I batted my eyelashes for emphasis.

"I said no weapons." His brow furrowed, anger contorting his features. But there was something like smug satisfaction behind the disdain and pain there.

"And any adversary won't play by your rules. There's a lesson for *you*." I pressed my blade harder into his skin. Scarlet began beading where my dagger connected with this throat.

His face softened a fraction. A spark of arrogance overtook me.

Then, Cillian knocked the blade from my hand and threw me backward onto the ground.

"We're finished. Go home." Cillian stood and began to hobble out of the training field.

"Let me at least heal your ankle," I said. Now that we were finished and I had the promise of a warm bath in my future, I felt a bit remorseful about stabbing him. I couldn't let him walk back to the city in pain.

He said nothing, only stopped and extended his leg toward me. He waited, his hands in his pockets once more, acting like the wound didn't bother him. Though, maybe it didn't. I'd heard of the injuries that had been inflicted upon him in the past. This was only a scratch in comparison.

I stood and slowly brushed the dirt from my clothes, making a show of taking my time. His eyes rolled back, obviously annoyed by my antics. I chuckled to myself before skipping to where he patiently awaited me and kneeled before him.

I dipped both my hands beneath the fabric of his pants, then wrapped them around his ankle, which was now hot and wet with blood.

Heal him.

The tingling in my palms began seconds before the heat left me and dove into Cillian's skin. It took only the blink of an eye before his wound was fully knitted back together. Still holding his ankle, I snuck a look up at his beneath my lashes.

My heart skipped a beat when I saw him gazing back, a near indiscernible look on his face. He was studying me, or so it seemed.

My mouth went dry at the sight of him.

I looked away quickly, fighting back the blush that was threatening to stain my cheeks. "I hope I have the day off tomorrow?" I asked, turning away from him to collect my dagger from the ground.

"Yes. You're supposed to be with Shepard and Nash tomorrow. I heard Finn is still unwell."

"Okay." Dirt shuffled as he turned and started to walk away. Before he could get too far, though, I added, "Thank you, Cillian."

Chapter 4

Cillian—Six years ago

The sight of her kneeling before me…

The ground beneath my feet was silent as I ran through the forest, not caring where I ended up. I really needed to clear my head. I obviously wasn't thinking correctly. Kaya needed training; that was it. That was why we agreed to this. I wasn't doing this for any other reason but to give Ezra some peace of mind. To ensure she could protect herself better than she did on our assignment.

Ezra had forced her to come. That was the only reason she showed up. She was there to keep her brother's mind at ease as well. I knew she also wanted to learn from me, even if she didn't want to admit it to herself. It was obvious she was envious of my skill; I had seen the way she watched me when she thought I wasn't looking.

With Holden as my trainer growing up, I had a leg up on everyone else in the city. He was the best of the best—that was one of the many reasons he was now in charge. Only the most skilled of our kind could run the guild, and rightfully so. Without strong leadership, everything we built would crumble easily.

My ankle didn't so much as twinge from where she stabbed me. I couldn't keep the smile wholly from my face as I thought back to this morning. It had been funny, really, the way she defied my one and only rule. She hadn't been wrong. The people we would come up against wouldn't play by any rules, after all.

I didn't understand why outsiders chose to come to our island. We made sure others saw our land as lacking—we had been in ruins at one point in the not-so-far-off past. For all that the other realms knew, that was how our small island remained.

It was a lie, of course—a well-protected lie—as anyone who so much as set foot on our land without permission was cut down almost instantly. That was why so many of us were stationed at the docks, to keep an eye out for unwanted guests who thought it would be a good idea to go exploring on their own.

This had happened too many times for me to count within the last five years. It seemed someone was getting nosey, trying as they might to figure out what we were hiding.

"How was training?"

Nearly tripping, I stumbled to a stop beside Ezra. "Were you waiting for me?" I asked.

"I came looking for you after Kaya stormed through our front door." Ezra wore a bemused expression.

"Was she pissed?"

"Oh yeah. She called you a few colorful names before sequestering herself back into her bed." He came closer, crossing his arms over his chest before saying, "Didn't take it easy on her, I gather."

"You know me," I said.

"Good." He looked as if he had more to say but slipped his hands into his pockets without another word. I quirked an eyebrow at him, waiting for him to spill it. He gave me a half smile before finally continuing, "I know it's asking a lot of you, but you're the only person I trust."

"I don't like where this is going." Leaning against a tree, I let my head relax back against the rough bark.

"I'm going to have to spend more time at the docks. I just got the order from Holden."

He didn't go on, so I just stared at him. My gut turned over, knowing what he was about to say—what he was going to ask of me.

"Would you keep an eye on her? During the times I'm away?" His brow scrunched, eyes pleading. I could tell he was waiting for my inevitable denial.

"You realize she isn't a little girl anymore, right? If she knows I'm keeping tabs on her, she'll kick my ass. Then yours." I definitely sounded annoyed.

"Don't tell her what you're doing. Train her like you arranged. Make sure she's staying out of trouble."

"You've got to be kidding. I'm not going to follow her around. She'll know."

"No, she won't, and you know it. You can make yourself nearly invisible." He wasn't wrong, but that didn't quell the unease I had about keeping track of Kaya behind her back. Not after today, when she had looked up at me with those eyes…

"Ezra—"

"It would give me some peace of mind. I don't expect you to watch her every hour of every day. Just make it a point to check in every now and again. If there's anything I need to know about, you can send a message." I chose not to answer because he wouldn't accept my refusal. What he didn't know wouldn't hurt him. I could easily lie and tell him I'd done just what he asked.

No, I couldn't. I hated myself for it. Hated that he knew me well enough that if I agreed, he knew I would follow through.

"How long do you think you'll be gone?" I asked.

"I head out this evening. Instead of three days at a time, he wants me out there for an entire week, then I'm allowed reprieve for a day or two before going back."

"Are there new threats?" To have them out there for over double the time...

"He wouldn't say. But I would assume as much. I mean, those intruders the other day. You said there were five. We've never had that many at one time. They're searching for something, it would seem. That, and there seems to be something else going on entirely." Ezra tapped his foot against the dirt, and I could tell he was uneasy thinking about it.

"I'll keep an eye on her. But only while you're away."

"Thank you, Cillian. Really." He turned, heading toward the tree now that he got his way. Presumably, to head back home. Or to Wren. "Oh, and don't stop family dinners on my account. I'm not sure when I'll be back, and I want to keep the tradition alive."

I kept my curse to myself as he disappeared through the bark, leaving me alone.

Spy on Kaya without her knowing. What was Ezra thinking? I understood how protective he was of her, but this was a little out of hand. Unless...

Unless he thought she was in some sort of trouble.

Surely, he would have heard something by now if she was into something she shouldn't have been. Though, I couldn't be so sure. The elders liked to keep personal matters secret, and only doled out information on a need-to-know basis. Perhaps Ezra knew something about Kaya that he couldn't tell me, and this was his way of filling me in on the problem. I hated myself for it, but the stray thought was enough to get me wondering.

Chapter 5

Kaya—Six years ago

If I had been born without power, I would have gotten to stay with my family.

At this point, I didn't remember my family and only knew what others had told me throughout the years. I was the youngest of four children—the only one blessed with power. My parents had been without power as well, so that made me a sort of anomaly. It wasn't every day that someone like me emerged. Usually, power flowed through familial lines.

It must have been easy for them to give me up. I was a burden, just another mouth to feed. I was also different—something they hadn't been expecting. It was the way of things here, too. They wouldn't dare question the law of this land.

If I had been born without power, I would have lived in one of the smaller villages on the outer edges of the city.

I was forever grateful to have been born with power. Learning to use it had come naturally. The gift flowed from me with ease, requiring little effort to heal those around me.

I had always known my place within our guild. I had always known my purpose. I was to be a healer—something highly valued amongst the guild, as someone always got into some sort of trouble. I greatly surpassed my only purpose when I learned how to fight and how to do it well. I was welcomed within the city with open arms.

Because I was useful.

I loved the city, though. I had met so many people here that I never got the chance to feel lonely, even on these long days without my brother by my side. I had Nash and Finn. I had Shepard. I had so many acquaintances that I never grew bored and could always find something to do with my free time.

However, that free time was less now that I was training with Cillian. Ezra had been gone for half the week, and I'd had two more strenuous morning sessions with Cillian. His unbearable warmups were beginning to get easier for me, though I was excruciatingly sore almost every day afterward. I often had to take a nap to recuperate after soaking in a warm salt bath.

Today was one of my few days off, and I was forever grateful for the short reprieve. I weaved through the bustling bodies of the crowded pathways. Shops lined either side of me, overflowing with trinkets, clothes, savory-smelling foods, and so much more. The city was abundant and plenty, and no one within its wall ever wanted for anything.

We welcome outsiders to the city as well. People from the outer villages traveled to us often, either on day trips with their families or just to shop the many fine goods we provided. They would also bring their own goods, to sell or trade with the many shop owners. The people of the smaller villages didn't want for much, either.

I often found myself wondering on days like today if I had ever passed my own family within the streets. Did they journey here frequently? Had I run into a sister, a brother, and not realized it? Had I been unwise to the conversation I had with a stranger when all the while it had actually been my father?

I would never know.

I tried not to ruminate on those ideas, flinging them from my mind as I finally made it to the bakery where I was meeting Nash and Finn. I could see them through the open window, sitting at a small table and waiting for me. They had three mugs of tea already before them, as well as a hefty pile of sweets. My mouth watered as I weaved through the chairs—the restaurant being overly crowded today—and took my place between the two boys.

"How're the scones today?" I asked, snatching one from the towering pile before me.

"I wouldn't know. Finn made me wait until you arrived to start," Nash said, sounding annoyed. I grabbed my mug and took a swig. The hot, spicy liquid trickled down my throat, warming my insides.

"It's called being polite, Nash," Finn reprimanded. Finn was nicer than either Nash or I, considering I'd already scarfed down my first scone and was onto a delicious-looking tart before either had reached for a sweet themselves.

"You don't need to wait on me. Eat before I finish off the plate myself."

Nash lunged for the remaining tart before Finn could even lift a finger. He opted for a muffin instead and nibbled between sips of tea as he watched Nash and I ravage the food before us.

"You two act like starved animals," Finn mused. He shook his head, deciding to let it go as I reached for my third helping.

"We have to eat to keep our bulk up. We don't want to get lanky like you, Finn," I teased. Finn was lean, but he was swift. Both Nash and I had a bigger build, our muscles showing starkly beneath our skin.

"Don't cry to me when either of you gets a stomachache."

Nash kicked his leg beneath the table. I stifled my laugh, not wanting to poke the bear that was Finn. He was usually easygoing, but when he got angry, it was hard to calm him back down.

Today, he must have been in a good mood. He didn't kick Nash back. Instead, he rolled his eyes and continued working on his muffin. Nash went to take a sip of his tea but was met with a block of ice instead.

This time, I didn't suppress the laugh. Nash dropped the mug back onto the table, the contents staying wholly in place as the cup spun on its side.

Finn sniggered and asked, "Is something wrong, Nash?" He batted his eyes innocently at his friend. Darkness swirled around Finn's mug causing it to disappear then reappear within Nash's hand in the blink of an eye. Nash drank deeply, draining the mug in one swallow.

"Nothing wrong, Finn. Nothing wrong at all." The two laughed in unison, and Finn collected Nash's discarded mug, returning the contents to steaming liquid.

I leaned back in my chair, utterly content being in my two friends' presence. Days like today made everything worth it. This was what our people fought to protect. Our peace. The safety of our people. There was no realm quite like ours, but our secrets were what made that possible. Without them, we would have been susceptible to power-hungry souls who wanted to take everything we had. We might have had an obligation to the guild, we might have been stolen from our families, but it was all to keep the peace.

I stretched an aching arm above my head, cocking my stiff neck to the side. That's when I noticed charcoal hair in my periphery.

I whirled, spying Cillian almost instantly. He stood in line as if he was there to order food. I had never seen him out in the city like this, mingling with the people. I knew he preferred to keep in the shadows or out of sight in his own home. He would never come into a shop if he didn't have to. What was he doing here now?

Nash must have noticed my shift in attention because he turned almost completely around to see what I was gawking at. He asked, "Is that Cillian?"

I drew my attention from that dark hair—that lean body clothed in black—and turned back to my friends. I shrugged my shoulders, pretending I hadn't noticed.

"What's he doing in here?" Finn asked, genuinely curious. Everyone knew Cillian was a recluse. He sent out for any items he needed, having one of the messengers fetch his goods and leave them on his doorstep. If he wasn't at home or on a mission, he was training or holed up in some meeting with Holden.

"I don't know, but it's weird, isn't it?" I asked, furrowing my brow.

"Maybe he came to see Nash," Finn teased as he waggled his eyebrows. Nash shot him a harsh look, begging him to shut up. "Maybe you won him over on that mission together." Finn's voice had gone dreamlike as he rested his chin on his hand. He gained a far-off, whimsical look.

I tried not to laugh at the look of mortification cutting through Nash's features.

As if he heard our entire conversation, Cillian's eyes flicked to our party. They didn't linger long, but I felt their hot weight rove over my body. I focused on keeping the heat I felt beneath my skin from staining my cheeks.

"I'm out of here," I said. My chair nearly toppled backward, startling the woman sitting behind me. I offered her an apologetic look as I righted it once more, shoving it beneath the table with a bit too much force.

I had been seeing glimpses of Cillian a little too much lately. I knew in my gut it was no coincidence.

"Wait up," I heard Nash call as both he and Finn collected our remaining pastries, stuffing them in their bags and pockets as they fumbled after me. I didn't slow my steps, knowing they would catch up with me in no time after they'd woven through the maze of people within the establishment.

"You seem on edge." Finn fell into step beside me, nudging my arm and staring down at me expectantly.

"I think he's following me," I confided, voice low. He quirked an eyebrow at me. "Ezra," is all I said in response.

He smiled slightly at that. "That checks out."

Nash came clambering up behind us, trailing closely while still crunching into a croissant.

"I don't know why he can't just trust me to take care of myself." Acid coated my tongue. My brow was tense, the annoyance eating away at me.

"Well, not to make matters worse," Nash began. I spun, not liking his tone. I saw the figure trying to blend in to the crowd as Nash continued, "But he just followed us out the door."

"Does he think he's doing a good job?" Finn asked, nearly laughing as I rolled my eyes.

"He must," I said. "I'll meet back up with you in a few. I have to take care of this." I veered off, not watching to see where the boys took off to. I set my path on the southern gate, leaving with a nod toward the guards stationed there. I wouldn't receive any questions from them, having left through here too many times to count on my way to the training yard beyond the stone wall of the city.

I slipped into the closest tree, knowing Cillian would be able to track me with ease. Emerging farther south, I strode toward one of the trees and leaned casually against it.

I waited.

Three heartbeats passed before Cillian stepped out from the peeling bark. He came up short, eyebrows shooting toward his hairline as he processed the look of annoyance and anger I felt on my face.

"Seriously?" I asked by way of greeting.

"I don't like it, either," he said.

"Is that why you're doing such a poor job?" I asked. "You couldn't have been any more obvious."

"Well, I figured if you saw me, I could tell Ezra, and he'd let me off the hook." He leaned against the tree at his back, crossing his arms over his chest as he continued. "Let us both off the hook."

"Well, when he comes back tomorrow, he's going to get an earful from me, so don't worry about it." I pushed off the tree, stalking closer to him. "I don't need you watching me like I'm some insolent child."

"I know."

"Good. Now, if you don't mind, my friends and I had plans for our day off." I pushed past him, ready to slip into the tree.

"Have fun," he mockingly huffed. "I'll see you tonight."

I paused. "Excuse me?"

"Family dinner?" One eyebrow lifted, his eyes sparkling beneath. He really looked like he enjoyed messing with me. "I was also instructed to keep that tradition going so that we didn't get out of the habit."

"Oh, for the love of—" I snapped, but my words were swallowed up by the darkness as I continued into the tree.

Chapter 6

Cillian—Six years ago

The fact that I was nervous should have been the first warning that this was a bad idea.

A very bad idea.

I unlatched the gate and stepped through, securing it back into place behind me. My body trembled, actually trembled, as I walked up the path to the front door of Ezra and Kaya's cottage.

What in the Wildewood was I doing? Promise or not, this was a terrible idea. But I could see Kaya through the glowing window, stooped over the stove as she idly stirred something within a brass pot. Steam billowed up, the dew sending her features glowing under the dim candlelight. Her dark, heavy waves were swept over her shoulders, falling down her back—a dark current that I often found myself drowning in.

Hand lifting to grab the doorknob, I finally pulled myself out of the spell she had me under. Squeezing my eyes shut as tightly as I could, I sent my thoughts running, shoving them so far down where they should have stayed locked up tight. I gripped the brass and turned the door handle. I heard the latch snick free, just as I was sure Kaya had.

When the door swung open, she was facing me—her eyebrows scrunching her face into a scowl.

"You get soup. Then you leave." Her arms were crossed over her chest, highlighting the curve of her breasts. I noted the flames scattered about the small space jump ever so slightly higher.

Get it together, Cillian, I thought to myself, willing them to diminish slightly. Nodding my thanks, I shrugged out of my jacket and hung it on the hook by the door. I hooked a finger under the fabric over my face, slipping it from my chin and letting it rest around my neck. Kaya's eyes flashed minutely before she quickly turned back to the stove. It still surprised her: seeing my entire face. I liked keeping it covered. It was like a second skin, another layer shielding me from those around me—a barrier to keep others at arm's length.

I walked toward the table in the center of the room. Pulling back the chair with a scrape against the floor, I sat myself down and rested my elbows on the table. Steepling my fingers, I pressed my lips into them as I watched Kaya work.

She bent over to retrieve some bowls from a cabinet, and I averted my eyes, squeezing them shut to block out the image—but it was stamped behind my eyelids. Dishes clattered against the counter, drawing my attention back to her. She ladled the steaming liquid into two bowls, then plopped the spoons in after.

A smile tugged at my lips as she twisted in my direction, nearly splashing some of the soup onto the floor in the process. Her scowl remained in place as she chucked the bowl in front of me, taking her own seat to my side.

I watched her for a moment as she took her spoon and began eating, not bothering to wait for the contents to cool. It smelled divine, and my stomach grumbled in response. I hadn't eaten today—too nervous about being alone with her to manage choking anything down. Finally, I unlocked my muscles enough to begin eating my own dinner, pleased that it was as good as it smelled.

We ate in silence for a long time, the only sounds being the clicks of our spoons on porcelain. I kept my eyes focused solely upon my food, not daring to look up at her. But I felt the weight of her gaze on me more than once.

When I felt it again, I finally met her striking copper eyes head-on.

"Good soup," I said. Words must have been failing me because, apparently, I couldn't even form a full sentence in front of her. I watched as a blush crept along her neck, lightly staining her skin a deep burgundy. I took another bite, swallowing my embarrassment.

"Thank you," she said, averting her eyes once more.

"Is my company so abhorrent that you can't even have a conversation with me without Ezra here?" My stomach fluttered, not reflecting the confidence I feigned with my jab.

"I just don't know why you went along with his idiotic idea," she said. She pierced those eyes once more into mine, an edge resting within them.

"It eases his mind, knowing someone is here to look after you when he can't."

"Then lie."

"I respect him too much to be dishonest. He's a good man, and his heart is in the right place." It was all the truth. Ezra was the one person I trusted and respected above all others. "And you know he'd pry his way into my mind to make sure I was telling the truth."

Kaya grumbled under her breath, but I couldn't make out what she said. She sat back in her seat, apparently done with her meal. I continued eating, ignoring her sour mood. I didn't care what she thought about it; I refused to go against her brother's word. Whether she liked it or not, he was right. Someone needed to look out for her. There was so much more happening lately than Holden was telling us, it would seem. Ezra knew something that we didn't. I was almost sure of it.

"I'll quit following you, but we aren't stopping your training." She looked away from me, her eyes trained on the bookcase leaning against the wall. "You're still young. You have so much you still need to learn."

"I'm not a child." Her arms crossed over her chest again as she leveled a steady look at me.

"You don't need to convince me," I breathed, exasperated and leaving the rest unsaid. "I'll clean up." Standing, I collected the dishes and placed them into the sink. Her chair scraped backward, signaling to me that she was at my back. There was already water in the sink, so I grabbed the soap and scrubbed it against a sponge, working up a lather.

"You don't have to," she protested.

"You cooked, so I clean. That's the deal." She didn't respond, instead leaning against the counter next to the sink. Her hands were folded over her stomach as she watched me work—cleaning the dishes, rinsing them, and setting them to the side to dry.

After drying my hands on the towel, I leaned my hip against the sink, facing her. Her eyes were unfocused, head tilted toward the floor. Lost in thought like this, I couldn't keep my heart from fluttering at her beauty.

I cleared my throat.

"It's late. You should go." She didn't look at me. Turning away, she disappeared into her room without another word.

I felt my body deflate, knowing she was pissed off at me for taking her brother's side on things. But she was so untried in her skills, no matter what she thought of herself. And having someone else on her side didn't mean she wasn't good enough. It meant people cared for her.

If only she knew that when her brother asked me to look out for her, I had already planned on doing so anyway.

"I assume she gave you quite the tongue-lashing when you got home."

Ezra fell into step beside me as I headed toward the training ground on the east side of the city. It was still nearly black outside as we weaved through the trees. I got an early start, hoping to set up the course I intended Kaya to run through well before she arrived.

"You are correct." Ezra's tone was clipped.

"I told you she wasn't going to like it." Normally, I liked being right, but I knew Ezra was warring on the inside about what he thought was best for his sister.

"I know you told her you'd stop following her, but I would appreciate it if you didn't." He looked at his feet as he spoke. I stopped walking.

"I'm just going to piss her off more."

"I'd rather her be pissed than dead. And with what I've been seeing out there, Cillian…" He didn't finish his train of thought.

"Is there something you know that I don't?" I prompted.

"There's been quite a few invasions on the shore as of late. We don't know if they're coming from the North or the South. Most of them flee when they realize we're coming for them." He blew out a breath. "The ones that aren't fast enough get dispatched, per Holden's orders. I think we need to detain them. Figure out what they know. What they're looking for."

I considered. "I agree. Then we can be on the offensive."

"And the uptick in husks is a whole different story."

"What?" I rubbed a hand along my jaw, calluses snagging on the fabric there. How had I not heard about this yet?

"Well," he began. His mouth tightened as he leaned against a tree. Crossing his arms over his chest, he skewed his lips to the side, chewing on the words. "We've seen some of them wandering the forest as of late. Some have been completely gone—those people completely drained of power—just left to rot above the ground. I know command thinks they're being dumped here, but I'm not sure that's the case. I think they're being created here."

My insides went still. "You think it's one of our own?" I breathed.

He nodded, not risking saying the words aloud.

An ominous glow emitted from our surroundings as the sun began its ascent over the horizon. So much for setting up before Kaya arrived.

We stood in silence for a long moment before I relented. "Alright," I whispered. "I won't follow her, but I'll be sure to take note of her actions. So, if there's trouble, I'll know right where she is."

"You're the only one I trust, Cillian," he reiterated. Swallowing, he pulled his eyes from the ground to meet my own, and I realized I could suddenly make out the blue of his irises.

It was sunrise, and I was late.

Chapter 7

Kaya—Six years ago

I was nearly nineteen and in no need of a babysitter.

I had told Ezra as much the second he arrived home from his mission. However, I could tell my complaints went in one ear and out the other. He wouldn't take any of my pleadings seriously.

I could have a worse babysitter, I supposed.

I believed Cillian when he told me that he knew I could handle myself. I also believed him when he told me that he would quit following me, no matter what Ezra wanted. Though, I had no doubt in my mind that the two had reached some other agreement on my behalf.

Cillian no longer trailed me when Ezra was away, but I could tell he kept note of my comings and goings. He had even gone so far as to ask Shepard to report to him when we were on watches or missions of our own.

I couldn't change clothes without him knowing about it, it seemed.

But at least he was keeping his distance, save for our *family* meals— meals that were becoming more and more just dinners between me and Cillian.

Ezra had attended only once since Holden had extended his stays on the docks. One time in the last month. That left three silent meals between me and Cillian. Sometimes, I cooked; other times, he arrived with dinner in tow.

No matter who was cooking and who was cleaning, my stomach was always twisted into knots before his arrival. Despite having been basically raised with the man. Despite him practically living part-time in our house when Ezra was around more.

He was a staple in my home, yet things felt different between us now that Ezra wasn't here as a buffer. He had always been Ezra's friend. But now Ezra's friend felt more like *my* friend with my brother not around.

I enjoyed Cillian's company—more than I used to—even though our meals were quiet, to say the least. Like tonight.

Cillian had brought over a dish of garlicked potatoes, steamed greens, and smoked rabbit. Everything was seasoned perfectly, so it was easy to keep my focus on the meal and not on the handsome man beside me.

I did love it when he took his mask off. It was a rarity, saved for moments like this—away from prying eyes. Saved for moments when he felt most comfortable. I tried not to blush thinking about it, how he felt comfortable enough with only me here to show his true self.

It was hard to keep my eyes off him, but I didn't want the blush that accompanied my staring to deepen. If he had noticed his effect on me, he hadn't let it show. But sometimes… Sometimes, I would catch him looking at me in the same way I looked at him.

Perhaps it was only wishful thinking. Something I had dreamed up and projected onto him. He was only here because he gave my brother his word.

And Cillian was not a man to go back on his word. He was honorable. Sometimes too honorable.

"How is it?" he asked softly, his voice gravelly from disuse. The sound sent my pulse skittering.

I took my time chewing a mouthful of potato, chasing the swallow with a sip of tea. "It's delicious. Thank you for bringing it."

"I don't mind cooking. Especially when it means you'll be the one cleaning up," he teased with a half smile. His voice was just over a whisper.

I smirked back at him almost too easily.

"Training hasn't been as grueling, has it? You seem to be recovering quicker." He watched me, assessing my response for any sign of a lie.

"I can feel myself getting stronger."

"You're getting much quicker, too." The side of his mouth tugged up further, and I tried not to look too long at the dimple that appeared.

"So, does that mean we can call off the extra training?" I asked, feigning more hope than I truly felt. I already knew his answer without him having to say it. And if I was being honest with myself, I had started looking forward to our sessions alone together, though they left me sorer than I had ever been before.

"No." He set his fork down next to his plate and wiped his mouth with a napkin. "It means I need to push you harder."

I nearly groaned, but I wouldn't give him that sort of satisfaction. "Can't wait," I said instead. His smile broadened, and I had to look away as I felt heat begin to sting my cheekbones. Begin to pool somewhere much lower.

"Are you finished, or would you like some more?" Cillian asked, reaching for my plate as he rose from the table.

"I think if I eat another bite, I might vomit."

His soft chuckle met my ears and sent a shiver down my spine. I followed him into the small kitchen area, sliding in front of him to begin washing up. There were fewer dishes than on days when I cooked, so I didn't mind doing the washing one bit. I stretched out my arms and rotated my shoulder, trying to work out the knot that had been tensing my muscles all day.

He lingered next to the sink as I worked, a little too close for me to be able to relax. His proximity had my muscles tightening even more than they already were. I could smell his scent—like earth after a fresh rain. I detected soft notes of pine and some sort of spice that must have been the remnants of the soap he used. And the heat that radiated from him. That fire in his veins was evident just by standing close to him.

I kept my eyes on my task, not daring to look at him even as he said, "I rather enjoy our meals together. I wasn't sure I would, but it's nice not being alone with Ezra and Wren gone."

The thumping in my chest had my head feeling light, making it hard to form a response. "Yeah, you're much nicer to be around without Ezra here. The two of you can't gang up on me." I smiled. It was the truth. They had both always dug into me about something or another when they got together, feeding off one another.

"It's because we care about you, Kaya." His voice was low, lightly reprimanding. But I didn't miss how he said *we*, and not just Ezra. "Is your shoulder bothering you?"

My heart dipped, and I glanced over said shoulder to look at him. "It's been a bit tense all day. I assume I pulled something during training." His eyes narrowed on me. I could feel the beating of my heart as it nearly exploded. His hand rose, and my mouth dried out as he carefully began to prod my tender muscles. I tried to hide the shiver it sent down my spine.

Cillian began kneading my shoulder, his fingers deft and smooth across the pain. The pressure from his touch pulled a moan from me, and I tried to swallow the noise before I embarrassed myself further. Apparently, he didn't notice because he kept at it, rubbing small circles— slowly coaxing the knot from my shoulder.

My traitorous body tightened beneath his touch, completely inappropriate for the context in which his fingers danced across my skin. A light swirling of power bubbled beneath my ribs. My eyes closed, head tilting back as Cillian pressed the pads of his thumbs into my shoulder blade. Another low moan rattled in my throat, but this time, I didn't care. I could feel his breath as it brushed across my neck. My thighs pressed together as bumps erupted along the sensitive skin beneath his exhale.

I forced myself to pull away from his grip.

Turning to face him, I set the wet dishes on the towel he had laid out for me. I dried my hands on my pants, not wanting to get water on Cillian. Placing my hand on his shoulder, I pressed firmly—hoping to stave off the tremors in my fingers. My eyes connected with his, noting that they weren't just merely gray.

No.

Blue swirled around his pupils, light and almost undetectable. I held his stare as I said, "Thank you. For caring."

"It's hard not to when I see how much Ezra loves you."

The saliva soured in my mouth. I definitely made up those suggestive looks earlier and read more into that touch than what was intended. I was seeing things, wishing things into existence that weren't there. He was doing this for Ezra, I reminded myself. He cared for me because Ezra would be devastated if anything happened to me. He was being a good friend to him. Not to me.

I let my hand drop back to my side and gave him a tight smile. His expression changed, dropping immensely almost as fast as mine had. I stepped around him and into my room.

"Good night," I called over my newly relaxed shoulder, too embarrassed to see him out.

Under the open night sky, I felt like anything was possible. It felt like there was no end, no beginning. Like time stood still under those twinkling stars, and I savored every second I got to spend beneath their flickering light.

I walked on the edge of the wall that surrounded the city, nodding to the many guards stationed there to keep watch. I was looking for one in particular but enjoying the hunt itself. I was in no hurry to get back home— my mind was too awake to even attempt sleep.

Ezra had been back for three days, his longest stay in the past month and a half. He seemed exhausted and overworked and fell asleep early every night.

Yet, it was hard for me to get any rest with him there. I had grown used to being alone after so long with him out of the cottage. Just sensing another presence in the house with me had my power on edge. It was as if it knew something I didn't and kept me awake because of it.

I was almost to the watchtower on the western corner when I finally found him. Ahead, in that tower, he leaned against his elbows and scanned the expanse beyond the wall.

I quickened my pace, fueled by excitement at the prospect of catching my prey. Taking the stairs two at a time, I made quick work of the tower's looming height. Making sure my feet were silent, I slowed when I had nearly reached the top.

"Figured you'd show up."

"You always know me best," I responded, a bit annoyed I hadn't been able to startle him.

The tower itself felt warm, even with its many open windows and the chilly night air wending through. It must have been warmed by the fire in him, I thought to myself as I skipped closer to my truest friend. The one I tried to keep mostly secret since he was a pariah within the city.

Asher didn't leave his post to greet me. No. He was ever the perfect guard—poised and ready to sound the alarm should something arise. He was faithful to his realm. I just wished everyone else could see it as easily as I did.

I slipped beside him, nudging beneath his arm and pressing myself into his embrace. He tightened his hold around me, planting a kiss atop my head.

"Can't sleep?" he asked, the sound rumbling against me through his chest.

"Unfortunately, no. And I'm exhausted, too."

"Cillian still running you ragged?" He smirked down at me. He and Cillian had trained together for a while, so he was no stranger to the man's favorite form of torture.

"Yes. He made me stay longer this morning to perfect my form at knife throwing." I huffed in annoyance. "I'm a perfect shot. I think he was just trying to piss me off."

Asher only laughed quietly.

"Why do you think Holden keeps Ezra out so much?" I asked, knowing Asher might have had more insight than I.

"I think your brother is smart, and Lord Holden knows that. He brings strategic value to the watch on the shore." His eyes remained glued to the forest, even still. I leaned my head into the crook of his arm, breathing in his scent. He was so familiar to me, and we were so comfortable in each other's presence. I knew I could do or say anything to Asher, and he would never balk at it.

"I wish they'd chosen someone else. My power is used to him not being around, and I hate it. I hate that I'm on edge when he's near me." I leaned forward, resting my own elbows against the stone ledge before us.

His hand stroked my back, fingers scratching lightly.

"Change is hard, Ky."

I snorted. "Thanks for the almighty wisdom, Ash." But that's what it was. He had always seemed wise beyond his years.

I stayed in that watchtower for most of the night. Asher and I talked sparingly, mostly just taking in each other's comforting presence. When my eyelids finally began to feel heavy, I bid him farewell and made the journey back to my cottage.

Instantly, I fell into a deep, dreamless sleep.

Chapter 8

Cillian—Six years ago

Ezra and I sat in the training field, resting after a harsh workout. Wren sat with us, legs stretched out before her as she worked to loosen the muscles. Our trio had been together for so long that a sense of ease always befell us when we were with each other, even if I saw less of these two lately.

The field was busy today, which was anything but comfortable for me. But Wren and Ezra insisted, arguing that we needed to rotate out with more partners than just the three of us.

They had a point.

The more people I fought against, the more well-rounded I became. Everyone had their own way of fighting—of coming at an opponent. The more I knew and experienced, the more I could defend against.

That was important, now more than ever.

"Another one was found today," Wren whispered from beside me.

"Where?" Ezra asked, startled.

"Down south. It was completely drained, though. No life left at all." Her voice lowered even further, knowing that if she was overheard, a panic would take hold amongst the kids that were lurking around. Watching. Learning.

"Any leads on who it is?" I asked casually, trying not to betray how I truly felt. Dread coiled in my gut. What was happening—it was the nightmares of other lands. It wasn't something that had happened on our island, not since the beginning of our realm. Someone was draining people of their powers and leaving what was left for us to clean up.

"That's the thing. Holden and the rest have no inclination of who's behind it." She glanced around her before continuing. "No one seems to be having a surge in power, and no new powers are manifesting from what he's seen."

"How is that possible?" Holden was perfect for the position he was elected into. He had the ability to detect the powers within others. He could sense them—tell what it was lurking beneath their skin. If he hadn't noticed anything different, then perhaps...

"I think it's one of the villagers hiding out, away from Holden. Or." Ezra paused, turning contemplative. "Or maybe someone has gotten onto the island without us noticing and has been evading us ever since." He opened his mouth to say more but was cut off by one of the guards plopping down into the dirt beside him.

"So, your sister and Asher," the guard—Greyson—said in lieu of greeting.

"What about them?" Ezra quirked an eyebrow.

"I didn't realize they were together. I'm surprised you're allowing it, honestly. He isn't exactly what I'd call—"

"Kaya and Asher aren't together," Ezra cut in.

"They looked pretty cozy last night in that watchtower." I tried to ignore the pang of jealousy the image brought forth. I could still feel the softness of her shoulder beneath my fingers. I flexed them.

"Tell me what you saw before I kick your ass, Greyson." Ezra looked livid now, sizing up the guard. He knew better than to test Ezra's ability to follow through.

"I was on the wall last night when your sister crept out of nowhere. Anyone not on duty isn't supposed to be up there. We weren't going to rat on her, obviously, because who really cares. But she went to the tower that Asher was manning without saying a word to any of us. She stayed there for hours." Greyson stretched out his arms, a crack emitting from his joints in the process. "I wasn't going to say anything at all, but I thought you should know. Especially with the way they were all over each other."

Icy rage consumed Ezra's features, and I tried not to let my breathing change because I mirrored that same feeling within myself. I tried to calm my racing heart as I waited to hear what Ezra would say.

"Show me," he commanded.

Ezra's eyes took on a far-off look as his power plunged into Greyson. Wren braced her hands behind her back and leaned into them, silently waiting for Ezra to rifle through the memories of last night. She looked annoyed.

If he had been angry before he saw into Greyson's mind, he was feral now. His jaw was tense as he said, "Thank you for letting me know."

"I don't see what the big deal is," Wren mused. "She's almost nineteen, Ezra. And she's gorgeous. I'm surprised no one has tried to get with her before now."

"I think they're too afraid of what he'll do to them if they try anything," I offered. Ezra shot me a look that had me biting back my next words.

"I know that," he ground out. "But it doesn't need to be him."

"You can't judge him on speculation." Wren shot Greyson a look that had him clambering to his feet and scurrying away.

"He had not one, but *two* units disappear on missions."

"And each time, he had a plausible explanation." She rolled her eyes. We'd had this debate before. The circumstances surrounding Asher and his teams were suspicious, to say the least.

"Nothing that could be proven. We have only his word to go on, and I don't trust it." Ezra stood and stretched out his back, a dark shadow hovering over him.

"Holden is the one who questioned him," I said, trying to be impartial. Wren had a point, but honestly, I didn't trust the man either. And I really didn't like the idea of Kaya being alone with him.

Especially late at night.

"You're just going to make her resent you. I get you want to protect her, and you feel like being in control is the way to do it." Wren also got to her feet. She dusted off her pants before sauntering off into the tree line. Before she was out of earshot, she said, "You need to give her the space to find herself. Even if that means she makes mistakes."

Now standing, I stared at my feet in silence. Ezra wasn't going to give up control so easily, not after everything we'd all been through. I understood his overbearing attitude toward Kaya. I truly did, even if I resented it a little myself.

The way he reacted to Kaya and Asher wasn't just because of Asher's shady past. It was the idea that he would eventually lose her to someone else and would no longer be in charge of her safety. If he wasn't in charge—in control—then he felt at risk of losing her altogether.

Not that she couldn't handle herself, especially after all the extra training I had been putting her through.

Ezra's reaction also told me everything I needed to know about how he would react to the thoughts I'd been having about his sister.

I sighed inwardly.

"What?" Ezra demanded.

I blinked. Apparently, I had been a little too obvious with my self-pity.

"I just see both your sides. I get not wanting her near Asher, but at the same time, you need to let her spread her wings."

"Has she said something to you?"

I toed the dirt at my feet, crossing my arms over my chest. "Oh, she's very vocal about how you're suffocating her." I gave him a smile before I remembered he wouldn't see it beneath the mask.

He understood regardless. "I want her to live, Cillian."

I knew what he meant.

There had been another husk found that morning. Another body drained that Holden still hadn't officially briefed anyone on. Rumors would start flying soon. Surely, he knew he should get ahead of that before anyone did anything brash.

It made me wonder if they were trying to cover something up. He should have already told the guild that there was a threat to the land. We should have been hunting it down and dispatching it. Yet it wasn't even on our radar.

We started walking back toward the city. Ezra was no longer paying attention, far too focused on the issues with Kaya that had been ungraciously dropped into his lap. I didn't bother trying to press him further on her behalf. He would do what he thought was best.

Even through all the guilt, I still couldn't wipe the feel of Kaya from my fingers.

Chapter 9

Kaya—Six years ago

S weat trickled down my back as I crunched through the fallen twigs and branches littering the forest floor.

It was excruciatingly hot out. The sun's piercing rays beat down on the back of my neck as I trudged behind Shepard and Finn. Nash followed closely behind me, and I could hear his panting breaths over the sounds of the wilderness.

Normally, I would be panting along with him—begging Shepard for a break, even. But ever since I'd started training with Cillian, my stamina had greatly increased.

I needed to thank him.

He stopped by early this morning to collect Ezra for training with Wren. I had my own assignment, so I declined when they offered for me to join.

We'd been sent to the south of the city to do a thorough sweep of the forest. What we were looking for, Holden didn't say. Only alluded that we should be looking for anything unusual—that we should report anything out of the ordinary.

I hated training runs like this. Undoubtedly, that's what this was: a way for Holden to gauge how well we observed, how detailed our reports were.

So, we kept our eyes peeled, searching for anything that shouldn't be here.

Shepard didn't even bother to look interested as he led us further from the city, unworried about whether or not we completed the menial task. I knew he couldn't wait for the day Holden deemed us skilled enough to be sent out without him. He hated being a mentor and babysitter.

But most of all, he knew we were ready to continue on our own.

"Let's stop for lunch," Shepard said as he dropped his pack to the ground, directly beside an oak. We followed his lead and began digging in our own bags for the food we'd brought with us.

I pulled out a chunk of bread and strips of dried meat before sitting next to my pack on the ground. My stomach rumbled as I chewed, so I didn't hesitate before inhaling the morsels. Between Nash and Finn, I contemplated what would happen when we truly did satisfy Holden's requirements.

The three of us would be forever grouped together, but dynamics would change without Shepard leading us. And where would we be stationed? On the docks with Ezra or some other port? Would we be assigned to one of the many small villages as guards? Perhaps we would stay here, manning the wall and training our own groups of recruits one day.

When I finished eating, I lounged against my pack and waited for the others. It was hot, but the bright canopy above was gorgeous, swaying in a soft breeze and emitting a quiet melody, almost like it had its own pulse. Critters skittered about the branches, birds swooped through the sky, and I could hear the buzzing of insects a little too close to my left ear.

"What do you think we're looking for?" Finn asked before taking a swig of his water.

"It will probably be some sort of artifact hidden away somewhere. He'll want to see how well you guys can search. I'd check the caves, tree hollows, and other such places." Shepard stood and swung his pack back into place.

"Should we split up to knock it out faster?" Nash asked.

"No, because if there's something to find, you guys should all be there to see the environment around it. There will be a lot to learn." Shepard said no more before sauntering off between the trees, not sparing us another glance where we still sat on the ground.

We groaned in unison as we pulled ourselves up and lugged our packs back onto our backs. This time, I took the lead with Finn and Nash following closely behind. We weaved through the trees in the direction Shepard had disappeared into.

We were coming up on one of the southern caves, which would be a good place to start searching for whatever it was we were supposed to find. Shepard was nowhere in sight—probably off lurking in the trees, waiting for us to comb through the cave and head on to our next destination.

"I'll check inside. You guys, search the surrounding area," I said to the boys. They grumbled their agreement as they started shuffling through the tall underbrush. I headed straight for the cave. The surrounding air emanating from the cave mouth chilled my body as I entered the stone depths.

Bumps erupted along my skin, the coolness leaking from the cave so at odds with the hot summer air that had been stifling me moments before. I shivered as my feet connected with the stone floor and I rolled my shoulders, trying to ebb the gnawing feeling I had in my gut.

If my instincts were right, whatever we were searching for was in here. Something was disturbing the eternal peacefulness of this space, and I could feel the difference held within the air.

Darkness was closing in the further I walked, so I dropped my pack onto the floor and rifled through it in search of the small lantern I always carried with me. It had proven useful on more than one occasion—well worth the extra weight.

I found the matches soon after, tucked delicately within a scrap of leather. Pulling one free of the ties securing them, I struck it on the rough stone of the ground. It ignited, and I held it to the wick before the light breeze could extinguish it.

An ominous glow cast shadows around me, and it took a moment for my eyes to adjust in the small space. I decided to leave my pack on the ground, making it just a bit easier to squeeze through the cracks cutting into the sides of the cave.

I found nothing to the left, so I ventured right. Around fallen boulders, underneath pointed pillars, I plunged deeper into that ancient darkness. My footsteps echoed through the empty space, giving the illusion that someone was following me.

The hairs on the back of my neck stood on end, causing me to pause and check my surroundings.

Just in case.

If anyone was here, it would likely be one of the boys or Shepard, checking to see what was taking me so long. But there was no one there.

I stepped to the side, turning back around once more. Out of the corner of my eye, I saw something tucked discreetly behind a mound of rocks. Extending my lantern, I squinted, attempting to make it out.

Whatever it was, it nearly swallowed my light entirely. A void. At least I had found it, and we could go home, I thought. The exercise hadn't been as trying as I'd expected, honestly. Perhaps Holden was getting lazy or running out of new ideas.

"Nash! Finn!" I yelled toward the mouth of the cave, now a distant dot of light behind me. "I found something." I projected my voice, cringing at the echoes reverberating back at me. They'd hear me—I was sure—and come running any second.

I decided to investigate without them, my need to be the best outweighing any ideas of teamwork I might have had. Sometimes, I felt as if they held me back. Not that they were lacking by any means. I just worked better alone. Because we were too good of friends, we let that friendship and the fun we had get in the way of our work. It was too easy not to take things seriously when I was around them. I also often felt my power pushing me for *more*—like I was meant for something bigger.

I stumbled, the object fully resting within my light now.

No.

It wasn't an object at all, but a person.

Or it *was* a person. My body went cold, and not from the chilly wetness within the cave. A lead weight dropped into my stomach as I stared down at the husk, dried up and discarded like trash.

I didn't even hear Finn and Nash as they approached, the blood pounding in my ears far too loud to register any noise they made on the journey. Finn stumbled into me when he noticed what I stared at. His hand was suddenly on my shoulder, dragging me away so he could get a better look.

"What the hell is that?" he asked, bewildered. He crouched down closer to the body, hovering just over its torso. Luckily, it wasn't anyone I recognized.

"A husk."

His head turned slowly back to face me, his eyes wide and mouth gaping. "Are you sure?" he nearly whispered. It wasn't concerning that he didn't know what it was. Most people on the island had never seen one before. The only reason I knew without a doubt that this was, in fact, a husk was that Ezra had shown me. He had floated the memories into me, just in case.

I never expected to need that information.

"I'm positive," I said as I heard Nash vomit somewhere behind me. Another set of footsteps sounded, and I recognized they belonged to Shepard.

"Find it?" he called from a short distance away.

"No," I mumbled, unable to move from where I stood. He made it to me, halting almost as fast as Finn had.

He swore under his breath before saying, "Nash, head back to the city and find Holden. Report this to him *now*."

A whimper sounded from Nash's general direction as he disappeared into nothing. Finn stood once more, moving back to sling a comforting arm around my shoulders. He squeezed tightly, but I still couldn't relax—I was struck rigid with utter terror.

"This isn't what Holden meant for us to find, is it?" Finn asked.

"Definitely not. But it's a good thing he sent you out here." Shepard shuffled forward, knocking both Finn and me out of the way. "This is bad."

"How is this here?" I managed to ask, my voice breaking over the words.

"I don't know, Kaya." Shepard's voice was gentler than I'd ever heard it before. "Why don't you two wait outside. You don't need to see this."

I felt Finn begin to pull on my arm, urging me out of the cave. I let him lead me, still unable to tear my eyes from the atrocity discarded on the stone. Eventually, the darkness consumed us, and I could no longer make out the husk or Shepard still kneeling over it.

The sun blinded me, the heat of the air weighing me down as we stumbled into the awaiting forest.

Nash reappeared before us, with Holden clinging to him as his shadows slithered away. Nash still looked green in the face, but Holden's expression was set in stone.

"Go back to the city. Tell no one what you saw." The command was barked between clenched teeth as the lord of our guild stomped into the cave. Nash lunged for us without skipping a beat, grabbing Finn and me and whisking us away into darkness.

My hands shook as I chopped vegetables for our family dinner. The images from earlier in the day still plagued me, especially as I stared at the gray skin of the mushrooms resting atop the counter—the same color as the husk that was hopefully resting peacefully beneath the earth.

Cillian and Ezra chatted amicably, unwise to the anxiety I could feel eating me from the inside out.

When I had returned to the cottage hours after Nash brought us into the city, Ezra seemed to be in a foul mood. I let him stew, opting to hide in my bedroom and avoid anything that might bring up the horrifying events. Holden gave the order to keep it silent, and I had to obey, even when it came to my own brother.

My eyes kept going bleary as my mind repeatedly dragged me back, back, back to the image of the dried-up body, broken and hollow, lying on the cold, hard—

"So, what's going on between you and Asher?"

I jumped, startled from thought by the seemingly nonchalant question. Ezra was watching me as I turned from the counter. Cillian was doing his best to pretend he wasn't listening to every word being said.

"What?" I blinked back at him, unable to decipher what he meant through the fog shrouding my mind.

"You and Asher. Are you seeing each other?" His jaw was set, obviously not pleased by whatever it was he thought was happening.

"Why are you even asking me that?" I turned back to my task, shoving the mushrooms farther out of my sight.

"I was informed that the two of you were looking pretty cozy together last night up in the watchtower." There was an underlying edge in his tone—like a razor slicing the skin at the nape of my neck.

"Asher is my friend."

"Since when?" Ezra demanded, pushing up from the chair and coming to stand next to me. I didn't hear Cillian so much as readjust from where he sat by the bookshelf.

"Since five years ago."

"Why haven't you told me?"

"I know how you feel about him, and I didn't think it was worth the fight." I chopped the potatoes with a little too much force. "I know what you think of him. You're wrong."

"You can't know that." It almost sounded like he was pleading with me.

"I can, and I do." I dropped the diced vegetables into the sizzling pan. They hissed as they fell into the oil.

Out of the corner of my eye, I watched Ezra's fist ball up. This was exactly why I never mentioned the friendship to him. He always thought the worst of people and hated when he didn't have control. I braced myself for the reprimand that I knew was about to be thrown my way. I could feel my shoulders tensing with the weight of his disappointment.

"Just be careful, Ky." His hand fell from the counter, and he returned to his chair across from Cillian. I whirled, unsure of what was happening. My eyes found Cillian's immediately, and his shock mirrored my own.

"I wouldn't hang out with him if I thought he was dangerous." I didn't know what else to say, but I had the urge to quell any unease I knew Ezra harbored. An urge to continue my defense of Asher. He nodded, then plucked a book from the side table and began to read.

Cillian glanced at me again, and the shrug of his shoulder was almost unnoticeable. Apparently, he was just as confused as me. I wondered if Ezra's time on the docks hadn't changed his ways if only a little. Perhaps he didn't want to fight during the small amount of time we now had together. I was grateful for it.

Chapter 10

Cillian—Six years ago

I never thought I would be uncomfortable in my own home, but now it felt too big. Too open and exposed. A shell of what it once was.

Of what it could be.

I could still remember my parents, though only in flashes now and again. We were happy. When they passed, I was allowed to stay in my family home—Holden would check in with me daily, ensuring I was cared for and safe. He became a father to me, in a way.

I stared up at the ceiling, unable to quiet my swirling thoughts long enough to fall asleep. Ezra had listened today. Either to Wren or me, I wasn't sure, but it really didn't matter. Perhaps he was realizing how overbearing he had become.

And Kaya wasn't with Asher.

I hated myself for the spark of hope that fact left in my chest. I knew in my heart that I could never be with Kaya. I could never betray Ezra's trust in that way. We had been friends for too long. He was a brother to me as well, and I couldn't throw that away.

Not even for someone like Kaya.

No matter how much I was tempted to.

Lying here was futile. I rolled off the side of my bed and slipped back into my clothes. If I couldn't sleep, I'd at least go work out my body. Maybe I could exhaust myself enough to find sleep.

The city was silent as I left my house. Guards stood watch upon the wall, some wandering the streets as well. They nodded at me as I passed, unconcerned about my comings and goings. They knew me well enough to understand my habits.

I slipped from the east gate and stepped into a tree, emerging just outside the secluded training ground. The path was lit by the brilliant stars above, and I could make out only shadowy shapes within the plain.

It wasn't until I was nearly next to her that I realized Kaya was there, too.

"Couldn't sleep?" Her voice pierced through the blackness, halting my feet. I stifled my gasp but could tell she knew she had startled me. From where she sat, I could just glimpse the outline of a smile that began to curve her thick lips.

"It seems neither could you," I said coolly. "Did you and Ezra argue after I left?"

She stared off into the forest for a long time before she answered. "No."

"Is something else bothering you, then?" She had been distant throughout dinner, barely saying a word as she pushed her food around on her plate.

When no answer came, I sat down beside her upon the fallen log. I could feel the warmth radiating off her, and I might have moved a bit closer because of it. She was trembling, her body nearly vibrating. I could feel the tension within her as I looped an arm around her shoulders and asked quietly, "What's wrong?"

Her head dropped onto me. A sob choked from her as she embraced me and nestled her face into my shirt. She'd never touched me like this, only through strikes and punches during training. I gripped her with my other arm, holding tightly—the only thing I could think to do for her.

I waited for her to calm down, waited for the words to come to her. All the while my heart filled with dread and sank. My gut twisted, my power writhing inside me as her sobs slowly began to ease. My head rested upon hers, and I didn't remember when I had placed it there. I didn't move it away, either.

"We found something. South of the city." Her voice cracked, but she went on. "It was a husk. I'd never seen one before. I'd never…"

Breathing in sharply, I focused on what she was telling me, what this meant. Ezra had been right; more was happening on the island if even Kaya had seen something. "Where?"

"A cave. We were doing a training, and it wasn't supposed to be what we found." She held me tighter, and I cursed my traitorous heart as it began skipping. "I wasn't supposed to tell anyone. Holden ordered it. Don't tell anyone. Please."

I pulled back from her and swiped at the tears spilling down her cheeks. I couldn't help myself. "I wouldn't do that to you, Kaya. Ever." Her lip wobbled but she nodded. Seeing her like this broke my heart.

She dropped her head back onto my chest and I wrapped myself around her. Perhaps it was selfish or wrong of me, but I didn't care. I breathed her in, stroking the long waves of her hair as she held on to me.

I felt the brush of my power behind my ribs, reaching out toward Kaya.

Stop, I told it. It writhed in response, unhappy with my command.

"If Holden's aware of what happened, I'm sure he'll get to the bottom of it soon," I murmured to her. "I'm sorry you had to see that. I know it's hard."

She sobbed once more, and I felt her wipe her face on the cloth of my shirt. "I'm sorry I'm such a mess."

"Don't apologize. I remember the first time I saw one."

"How many times have you seen them?"

"Twice. Years apart as well. Both times they had been dumped here, and they were still... active." I worked my jaw, thinking back.

"Did you have to kill them?" She looked up at me, wiping her nose on the back of her hand.

"Yes."

Sitting up straight, she shook her head. "Do you think this one was dumped?"

"I don't know. But apparently there have been others as of late." I regretted it as soon as the words rolled from my tongue.

"Why haven't we been told?" she nearly yelled.

"I don't think they want terror to spread." I rubbed the back of my neck. "I only found out through Ezra. He's seen some on the coast. I assume that's why they've been extending his stays out there."

She gaped at me. "Is he in danger?"

"He can handle himself, Kaya. And he's not alone. He's got Wren and the others."

She stood and crossed her arms, beginning to pace in front of me. "I understand not telling the general public. But to not tell *us*? We're all a part of the guild. We have a right to know what's going on."

She wasn't wrong and I hated it. I was just as angry about not being told. About Holden not telling me. Of all the people who should have been aware of what was going on, I would think I should've been one of them. "I agree. I wouldn't have known had it not been for Ezra."

Kaya watched the stars in silence, and I couldn't help but study her. Her dark skin was perfect—almost glowing—beneath the sparkling sky. I could still feel her smooth cheek beneath my fingertips.

I balled my fist, trying to hold on to the feeling forever.

"I'm afraid of what's happening." Her eyes found mine then, and I could have sworn they sparkled with surprise to find me already watching her. "I don't want our land to be like other lands. I don't want to give up our peace." She resumed her watch of the sky.

I had nothing to say. No response would calm her fears, so I just nodded before gazing up at those stars too.

There was nothing I hated more than waiting.

And I had been waiting a long time already. Holden was in a meeting, so I was directed to stay outside his office. I watched the inner workings of the servants who bustled through the long corridors, all of which kept well away from me. I knew the look on my face was part of the reason. The other part was my tendency to keep to myself.

Which I was fine with.

I could hear raised voices behind the closed door but couldn't make out anything they were saying. If Holden was already in a foul mood, I was about to make things much worse.

The door banged open, wood slamming into the stone wall and bouncing away. Sloan, Holden's second-in-command, stormed down the hall and out the front door of the manor without sparing me a glance.

"What is it, Cillian?" Holden barked from inside the room. I took that as my cue to enter.

He sat behind his ornate desk, head dropped into his hand. I pulled the door shut behind me, the click of the lock jarring him slightly.

He was on edge.

"I've been hearing things lately that are concerning." Judging by the look on his face, I didn't need to explain further.

"And?" He set his jaw, rubbing a hand along the scruff there.

"I was wondering when there would be a formal announcement about it. I think the entire guild has a right to know what's happening." If I were any other person within the wall of the city, Holden would have had me thrown out for how forward I was being with him. But I would not cower.

Not when he valued my ability to stand up and fight for my beliefs, even when it involved fighting with him.

Which I did. Often.

"I'm not going to ask who told you, because I'm sure I can guess." He stood, moving around the desk to lean against the front. He crossed his arms and let out a sigh. "We haven't seen anything this bad in a long, long time. I was hoping we could get to the bottom of it before it got out of hand. But here we are."

I slipped my hands into my pockets, waiting for him to go on.

"I planned to address the situation during the weekly brief, but I feel it's time to call in an emergency meeting." He leveled me with a look. "Spread the word. We meet this evening at sundown."

I nodded, knowing that this was my dismissal. But at least the others would be told. At least they would know to be on the lookout. They would know what was coming.

I went straight to Ezra's after meeting with Holden to notify him and Kaya of the impending announcement. Kaya hadn't been home, but Ezra promised to pass along the information. He would be leaving tonight to go back to the docks, however, and was sure to remind me to keep a watch on his sister.

I agreed a little too readily and didn't miss the flash of suspicion that flickered in his eyes.

Swallowing my guilt, I reassured myself that there was no way he could know of my feelings for Kaya. He would never know because I refused to act on them. But the shame for even having those feelings was still there, gnawing at my insides.

I tried to keep myself busy for the rest of the day. It would have been much easier if I had a set job to do. But instead, I was one of the *lucky* ones who got to play stand-in all the time. I would assist on missions as needed, work guard duty, and even train young children in the fields. I barely ever ventured far from the city.

Sometimes, I thought life would be more fulfilling if I were stationed at one of the outer villages or even at one of the many docks. I would have felt more useful and less like Holden's pet. I knew that was the reason I was one of the few to have my position within the guild; he valued my being within arm's reach at all times.

Putting distance between myself and Kaya sounded like a good idea as well, even though my gut twisted at the thought. But for the sake of my friendship with Ezra, it might have been worth the pain I would undoubtedly be put through.

I really needed to stop thinking about her.

Chapter 11

Kaya—Six years ago

R ows of people stood before me, all staring up at the dais where Holden stood, briefing us.

It was about the husks, and it was much worse than either Cillian or I had known.

"It has been an ongoing issue. One that has mine and Sloan's full attention." Holden's voice bellowed loud enough for the hundreds of us in attendance to hear. "We hadn't relayed the information prior to now because we'd hoped that we had it under control. Unfortunately, that is not the case." I watched as his throat bobbed.

I glanced sidelong at Shepard, who stood behind me with his arms crossed and a scowl pulling at his heavy brow. His eyes flicked to mine briefly before returning his focus to Holden as if he could feel the pressure of my attention on him.

"How long has it been going on?" someone shouted from a few rows ahead of us. The brave soul was voicing what each of us was dying to know.

"We started finding them over a year ago." Murmurs rolled through the crowd, and even I couldn't stifle my small gasp. How had they kept this from us for so long? "Only sporadically. But as time has gone on, they have started getting more and more frequent."

The murmuring cascaded into shouts of outrage, and I didn't blame those who chose to protest one bit. I felt slighted by this omission, and it stung. We were the defenders of this realm. Something of this magnitude should have never been hidden from us.

"*Silence!*" Sloan roared her displeasure. The tumultuous crowd stilled instantly. "I understand that this is concerning, which is why we tried to get ahead of it. But it's become unmanageable."

"We are asking you all to keep your eyes peeled for anything suspicious," Holden continued, now that the crowd was under control. "We do not know where these husks are coming from or who may be creating them. If you see anything of concern, please report it immediately. We've already increased our patrols on the docks as well as in the outer villages. We will have more guards stationed on the wall, ensuring those within the city stay safe." I heard the underlying meaning beneath his last words. Those guards were also there to watch everyone leaving and entering the city at all times. They would monitor and report anything that might be amiss.

"This is an unprecedented time, so we are counting on each and every one of you to help us make this work. To help us track down the culprit and secure our realm once more." Sloan's straight red hair blew in the breeze as she spoke, near luminous in the setting sun.

"You may leave. Additional duties will be given to each of you by way of messenger by tomorrow morning. Until then, continue with your normal schedule." Holden didn't linger as the crowd once again became rowdy. No. He disappeared in the blink of an eye, Sloan following closely behind.

"Well, at least I know why he ordered you to the docks so much," I said as I turned to Ezra. His hands rested on his hips, a sour look on his face.

"Yes. I'm glad he's finally told everyone." He shook his head at the ground.

"You've recently seen them, then?" I asked, already knowing the answer.

"I have. Twice. And so have the others around the docks, which is why I had Cillian keeping an eye on you. I just wasn't allowed to say anything about it." The heat of his hand on my shoulder had my annoyance toward him melting away.

"I'm sorry I got so upset about it. I get it now."

"Cillian said your cadre saw one yesterday." His fingers squeezed, causing me to face him once more.

"We did."

"It's rough. But I'm sure with everyone aware now, something will finally be done about it." He pulled me into his arms, crushing me into him. "I have to head back to the docks now. You need to stay safe. No going out on your own. Stick with Nash and Finn or Shepard. Asher, for all I care. Whoever. Just don't go out on your own if you can help it."

"Okay," I breathed as I hugged him back. "Same goes for you. Stick with Wren." I smiled into his shirt as he chuckled.

"Always."

The sun was barely waking as I walked through the city gates and into the forest beyond. I watched as the guards atop the wall tracked me before marking my exit, all the while grumbling to myself about the eyes that never seemed to leave me as of late.

The trees looming above me blocked out any sunshine that tried to reach through, darkening this area of the forest as if it were still the dead of night.

I stepped into a tree, the void within consuming me and spitting me back out near the west training ground. I swore Cillian had some sort of schedule stamped into his mind letting him know which training field was used least and on which days of the week.

Not a soul was to be found amongst the equipment other than Cillian himself. He waited with hands in his pockets, as always, watching as I came closer with an indiscernible look on his face. Almost as if he was scrutinizing every step I made, every breath I took.

My heart pounded in my ears, and I was thankful for the darkness that hid my burning cheeks. Why did this always happen around him? I didn't say anything as I began my laps around the track, just as he always had me start my training. Today, however, he ran beside me. I tried not to let my surprise show, instead forcing myself into a faster stride.

He kept pace without faltering.

It turned out to be a quiet day with Cillian, though it was not unpleasant or strained like it had been previously. The silence was amicable as we completed laps of lunges, climbed tree branches, and threw daggers at targets. As the sun ascended further into the sky, the air heated immensely. I felt droplets of perspiration sliding down my spine, causing my shirt to stick to my skin.

"Swords."

Metal glinted in my periphery, and I whirled on instinct, catching sight of the long, heavy blade. Cillian lunged without warning, and I thrust my sword up and in front of my face before his came crashing down on me.

The clanking of metal became the only sound between us as we slashed and parried, carving out a dance between us. Cillian made to stab at my chest, but I deflected with a back swipe of my arm, sending him stumbling a step. He recovered without hesitation, parrying. My attack was quick and deliberate, and I felt the vibrations from our swords' impact sing down my arm.

We sparred for as long as my arms could stand. When I couldn't last any longer, I tossed my sword to the ground and extended each arm out to the side. Cillian lowered his blade, panting slightly. When I was certain he wouldn't make me pick mine back up and spar more, I dropped to the ground, my limbs feeling like jelly.

Lying back in the grass, I shut my eyes against the brightening sky. I focused on my breathing, drawing air in as deeply as I could, then blowing it back out slowly. My chest thrummed with the pulsing of the ground and its power beneath the surface. It hummed in tune with my hammering heartbeat.

My head was spinning slightly, so I relaxed further into the dirt. Palms falling open to the sky, I let my muscles go limp. The sensation of sinking into myself and the power of the earth felt astounding.

Shuffling grass vaguely caught my attention. Cillian must have been collecting my sword to put it away, I thought.

But then the air shifted, and I felt him lie down beside me; I felt the heat that emanated from him. His scent washed over me a moment later—an almost sweet-smelling pine. My body hummed in his proximity, and my power awakened deep within, interested in what was happening. I could feel a vibration in the atmosphere around me, the Wildewood was begging me to pay attention. To remember this moment.

I tried not to let my breathing quicken, hard as it was.

Cillian didn't say a word as he lounged in the dirt and grass next to me, unaware of my warring insides or the change in our surroundings. He didn't move an inch, though I could feel how close he was to me. I could feel his essence as if he were somehow a part of my own being.

My hand crept closer to him, some force propelling it forward of its own volition. I didn't try to stop it, though. My index finger uncurled slightly, extending out, reaching for him.

When it connected with his skin, I expected him to jerk away, to move his hand out of my reach. He was always so reserved and guarded in every aspect of his life. But he didn't even twitch at the invasion. So, I ran that finger down the side of his thumb, tracing the edge of it. The texture of his skin was mesmerizing, the warmth and roughness of it alluring.

His hand flexed, and I almost pulled away but somehow couldn't. Instead, my finger found his and curled around it tightly—linking myself to him. His finger bent around mine in response, and my heart skipped a beat. It was an anchor holding me in time. A brush along my thumb had my body tightening.

Unlooping my finger, I swept my trembling palm over his, bringing it to a stop before his fingers laced through mine. All at once, I could feel every line that etched itself through Cillian's skin, but I also couldn't decipher where he ended and I began. His fingers were warm against my own, and they held firm as a defeated sigh slipped between his lips.

My breath left me in a hiss as I was yanked from the ground and abruptly slammed against a tree. Pain lanced through my spine and flashes of light danced in my vision as I tried to choke down a breath.

Cillian was inches from me, a despondent look on his face. His forearm was braced against my sternum, pinning me into the bark of the tree. "Don't," he seethed.

I gaped at him, unable to form words other than, "Why?" I hated how wounded it sounded. I looked from his serious eyes down to where his arm was pressed against me, right between my breasts.

"We can't do that to your brother. No matter how much we might want to." He shoved away from me, and I stood there gaping at him. I was too confused to respond, too slow to process his meaning to argue. He shot me a regretful glance, then marched out of the training ground without a backward thought.

Chapter 12

Cillian—Six years ago

I t had been three days, and I had scrubbed my hand countless times, but I could still feel her there. The memory of her touch haunted my dreams and every waking moment, the sensation branded into my skin. It burned.

It burned for her.

I had been such an ass. I should have never let her touch me. I had all but encouraged it by not pulling away the second her finger connected with mine.

But I was too damn selfish.

I had to feel her skin at least once. Once was enough for me to imagine—to dream—of what it would be like to be wanted by her. To be loved by her.

That's all it could ever be, though. It could only be a dream.

I didn't have much in this life. The one thing I did have, the one thing my superiors and my friends could count on, was my honor. And I couldn't throw that away for her.

No matter how much I wanted to.

I couldn't do that to Ezra, who had stood by me despite everything. Despite the fact that we once hated each other. Despite the fact that our lives were tied to this guild forever. I knew I could count on him, and he could me. If I went behind his back like this, everything would be over.

He would never trust me again.

And if I was being honest with myself, Kaya could do so much better than me. She was a social butterfly, and I was a recluse. I could never make her happy. She was meant for much greater things than being tied to someone who was happy as a peon of the guild for the rest of his life.

She could rule this realm if she wanted to. She could replace Holden as commander when his time came to an end, and these people would follow her without fear. She was just that kind of person.

Perhaps that was part of the reason Ezra wanted to keep her safe. Because he knew, as well as I did, that someone would try to take advantage of her good nature and use her for their own gain. She was so trusting, and that was evident in her friendship with Asher. She chose to see the good in everyone, even when there was so much bad staring her right in the face. She never saw that part of people.

If I hadn't made her hate me already, the stunt I pulled at our last training definitely did, so much so that she stood me up this morning. I had waited an extra hour, just assuming she was making me sweat as punishment. But then one hour turned into two, and there was no sign of her. The young recruits started showing up with their leads, and I left quickly at that point.

I deserved the cold shoulder; I really did. But for some reason, I felt I had to give her an explanation.

Something.

It was midweek again, and Ezra sent word that he would be home for dinner this evening. If I wanted to talk to Kaya about what happened, I had to arrive before him. After stewing for most of the day on it, I finally decided to confront her.

Staring at their small cottage, I wondered what sort of shit I was getting myself into. The thought of facing her had my stomach knotting in a way it hadn't since I was a scared young child out in the training field for the first time. I closed my eyes and let out a breath before heading for the door.

I didn't knock, simply letting myself in. Kaya was standing before the stove, something sizzling in the pan before her. She didn't so much as glance behind her as I latched the door and kicked my shoes off. I hung my jacket on one of the hooks before pulling my mask down my chin.

"Hi."

Gingerly, I stepped deeper into the room, ignoring how tense my shoulders were. She didn't respond to me, but I saw her own shoulders go rigid.

She was mad.

"Ezra home yet?" I asked.

"No." Clipped as it might have been, it was still something.

"Can we talk, then?" I nearly whispered the question, my nerves getting the best of me. Smacking the spoon onto the counter, she whirled on me. I involuntarily relinquished a step when I saw the irritation burning in her eyes.

"What, Cillian?" she snapped.

"Kaya. I'm sorry about the other day. I really am," I began. My mind had turned near leaden, the words getting lost as I worked my jaw. "You just… You can't do that again."

"Excuse me?" she nearly shouted.

I blanched, my teeth grinding together. "The touching. You can't do that. It's not right." I was making a fool of myself, but I couldn't stop it. None of this was coming out like I meant it. "What I mean to say is—" What did I mean to say? I didn't know.

She shook her head and turned back to the counter. Her knuckles whitened around the spoon, and I wondered if it was about to snap in two under the pressure.

"You're young. Maybe when you're older, you'll understand."

"Understand *what*, Cillian? Understand that you are a complete asshole? You act like I'm just some simpering child." She was facing me once more, edging ever closer as her voice rose with each passing word. "I don't know what you and Ezra are on about, but I'm not a child. I haven't been a child for a very, *very* long time. I would say that innocence left me with the first life I took." She raised a finger as she closed in on me. I took a few steps away, but she met me step for step. "And don't you pretend that you tried to stop me. You let me grab your hand. *You* grabbed *my* hand."

"Kaya, it wasn't—"

"Wasn't what, Cillian? Wasn't approved by my *brother*? I'm so tired of him controlling me. Of you following his every wish like some lost—"

"He is my friend, and he deserves respect, not someone who's going to go behind his back and try to seduce his sister. I can't do that to him." I hadn't realized I moved closer to her. But there we were, nearly chest to chest, glaring at each other. Both stubborn. Both unrelenting.

"You said no matter how much *we* may want to." Her eyes still held that fire, but her voice was nearly a whisper. "This isn't one-sided, Cillian. Don't pretend that it is."

I looked away for a second, fighting with myself on what to say. My mouth dropped open, the words on the tip of my tongue—

A click from the turning doorknob had us both scattering—Kaya back to the stove and me toward one of the sitting areas. I was just about to drop into one of the chairs, defeated, when the front door swung open, and in came not only Ezra but Wren as well.

"It smells amazing in here," Ezra said as he pulled Wren into the sitting room. I caught the glance that he darted between me and Kaya, but he said nothing as he gathered me into a hug. Wren's arms wrapped around my neck as she joined in, and in spite of the fight with Kaya, I smiled at my friends.

This is what it was all for. This closeness that I never wanted to leave, even if it meant denying myself something I truly, painfully wanted.

"How was your assignment?" Kaya didn't cover up the annoyance in her voice.

"Uneventful, thankfully," Wren said. She shot me a questioning look. I shrugged my shoulder and shook my head. Wren rolled her eyes and tacked on a sideways grin. The gesture left a sour taste in my mouth.

"What's for dinner?" Ezra asked as he embraced his sister.

"Deer. With garlic and vegetables." She rested her spoon back onto the counter and turned toward the room proper. "But I have plans tonight, so you guys enjoy."

"What do you mean you have plans? It's family dinner." Ezra sounded as offended as I felt.

"I mean, I have plans. Don't wait up." Grabbing her jacket, she left the cottage, slamming the door behind her.

"What was that about?" Wren asked.

"No idea. She wasn't in the best mood when I got here." I tried not to let the guilt get the best of me. Guilt for hurting Kaya. Guilt for lying to Ezra and Wren.

Guilt for wanting to follow her out that door, drop to my knees, and beg for her forgiveness.

Chapter 13

Kaya—Six years ago

How's training with Cillian going?"

Shepard leaned against the wall next to me as we gazed out at the expanse of trees surrounding the city. He had gotten us guard duty, wanting to give us a break from the outer patrols we'd seemed to keep getting stuck with. It was a nice change, and the view from up here had always been one of my favorites.

"I quit going."

He turned to look at me, a bemused look on his face. "Why is that?"

"He pissed me off. And I think I've learned enough." I adjusted my stance, alleviating some of the tension that was building in my hip.

"I'm still learning, even in my old age."

"You're thirty-five. I'd hardly call that old."

"Compared to eighteen and all the problems that come with it."

"What problems?" Shepard really knew how to push my buttons.

"Overprotective brothers, unrequited love. The works." A rare, satisfied smile graced his lips as he watched for my reaction.

"I don't know what you're talking about."

"So, is that what happened? Cillian still hiding his feelings?" He gave me a sheepish grin. "It's pretty obvious."

"I don't think the man has a single feeling in his body," I grumbled. I heard him laugh but refused to acknowledge him further.

"You know, Kaya," he began. I dropped my head back with a sigh, bracing myself for the lecture I knew was about to come. "It's not as easy as you want to believe."

"What isn't?" Shepard only gave me a look. "Call my attention piqued, Shep. I'm all ears."

He chuckled softly before saying, "Life. All of it. It's not all black and white. Good and bad. Sometimes choosing love means giving up other things."

"I don't see what he'd be giving up. Ezra would understand."

"I don't think it's about Ezra at all. I think it's more about the path he thought his life would take. And then you came in and wrecked it all. Made him question everything." Shepard took on a far-off look, and I caught myself hanging on to his next words. "As someone who has experienced more of this life than you have, trust me when I tell you that it can be hard to give up on what you thought you'd made peace with. Uncertainty can cause people to make poor decisions, like deny themselves something that would be good for them."

"How does one make that person see they're being stubborn, then?" I quirked an eyebrow at him.

"You can't rush that sort of thing, kid."

I let the silence fall between us as I mulled over what he had said, and I could understand where he was coming from. I had always been open to change and to experiencing new things. When there was something I wanted, I went for it. No matter what.

But Cillian hadn't ever been that way. He was content to do what he was told and comfortable staying in one place for the rest of his life.

"Thanks," I murmured. A grunt was the only response I received, causing a half smile to tug at my lips. Pushing off the wall, I tucked my jacket around me against the wind. While it was warm at the height of the day, the evenings did get chilly. And with the sun completely behind the horizon, the wind was beginning to get brisk.

"Where you off to?" Shep asked, not bothering to turn around.

"To find the boys. Maybe I'll head to the south side of the wall for a change of scenery." My boots clicked against the stone walkway as I put distance between me and my mentor.

"Be careful with Asher, Ky."

I waved him off, not deigning to respond to the dig. I just wished people knew Asher the way I did. But deep down, I knew that was the point. Asher was not unlike Cillian in that regard.

Reserved. Private. Secretive.

Whatever. I wasn't even privy to all of his secrets, but I trusted him enough to be his friend and know that he was a true and kind person beneath all the rumors and speculation.

If Holden really had a problem with him, Asher would have been nothing more than bones beneath the dirt at this point. There was a reason that wasn't the case. That reason was why I could look beyond everything else—everyone else—that said Asher was bad news. Even if I would never know what that reason was.

Because really, he was the only person in this entire realm who knew me so wholly and completely. Who understood me without having to justify myself or even speak a word.

And there he was, secluded within the south tower. Just as I knew he would be. In the same way that Cillian knew what training grounds would be free, I knew where Asher would always be stationed. His schedule never deviated.

"Do you ever think of leaving this place?" Asher's eyes never left the treetops far below as he spoke.

"Not at all. I love it here." I came up behind him, locking my arm around his waist and pressing my face into his back. His hand found mine, pressing it into his abdomen as I embraced him with all my strength.

I could sense his smile as he said, "I get bored."

"Why don't you ask Holden to be dispatched to one of the other kingdoms?"

"I'm not sure if he would. And those sorts of missions aren't usually what people come back from." He wasn't wrong. It wasn't that those assassins and spies always died, but they were usually lifelong intelligence situations. Normally, they'd entice their way into one of the courts, feeding information back to our realm, just in case.

"I sure would miss you if you left me. But I'd understand." I dipped my head beneath his arm, coming up before him. His arms braced around me, and still, his eyes remained outside of the wall. "I do admire your dedication, though. It could be useful out there."

"Maybe one day I'll take the plunge." His lips brushed the top of my scalp. I leaned into his kiss, closing my eyes in the comfort of our familiarity. "I heard you stopped training with Cillian."

"Does anyone have anything better to do than discuss me and Cillian?" I snapped.

His arms tightened around me as he said, "What's going on?"

"Rejection hurts."

He snorted, and I actually laughed out loud. "He'll come around." His hand began stroking the hair that was draped down the front of my arm.

"How can you be so sure?" I asked.

"I've seen the way he looks at you."

"And how does he look at me?" I could feel my cheeks heating. I'd seen those looks and hoped I hadn't made it all up.

"Like he hates himself." His head came to rest atop mine as his fingers twined in the ends of my hair. I grabbed that hand, holding it in my own as I stared off at the night sky.

"I feel like he's supposed to be mine." I paused, digging deep for the right words. The right explanation. "Like he was made for me. I can't really explain it. But when I look at him, I feel as if he's a part of me. As if he's what I've been missing my entire life, and I've finally found it." I blinked back the tears forming in my lashes. I hated crying, hated the emotions Cillian seemed to dig up within me.

"I know what you mean, Kaya. And I think he's warring with that himself. Give him time to figure it out."

"To figure out his so-called honor?" I rolled my eyes even though he couldn't see it. "That's what he said. He can't betray Ezra's trust. He's too honorable."

"There's no such thing as honor. Not when it comes to this."

"I can't just pretend he doesn't exist while I wait for him to figure it out." I dropped my head back onto his chest and closed my eyes.

Asher planted a kiss on my forehead and said, "Don't. Go back to training. Make your presence known."

I let out a low laugh. I knew he was teasing, at least about making my presence known. Without a doubt, I knew he wanted me to continue training—with anyone. He was right about giving Cillian time as well, though I hated to admit it.

"I love you, Asher."

"I love you too, Kaya."

Someone was hurt.

It was an unconscious thought brought to me by the power writhing beneath my skin. It vibrated with an energy that urged me to heal. To find the wound that was marring someone in the crowded streets and take care of it.

But there were so many people. And it was so hot. The sun beat down on my head as I trailed after Finn and Nash. My eyes darted around me, looking for a patron with a bandage of some sort.

It was like I could smell the blood. There was a cut about two inches long and deep enough that they should have already sought out a healer.

Perhaps they were on their way to find one. One of these people could have been heading to the healer's quarters now.

But there was Cillian. My stomach bottomed out when I saw the wrap that was tightly wound around his palm.

Of course.

I stalked toward him, not bothering to tell either of my friends what I was doing. I'd catch up momentarily. Cillian stopped short when he saw me walking his way. The man almost looked frightened as I came to a halt and offered him my upraised palm.

He looked at me questioningly. I made a show of flexing my hand, gesturing to his wounded one. Understanding flashed in his eyes as I silently rolled mine.

He rested his palm atop mine without uttering a word. I unwrapped his bandage a bit more delicately than I would my average patient. I silently reprimanded myself. This man was a trained fighter. I didn't need to take it easy on him. The Wildewood knew he didn't take that sort of consideration when it came to me.

Just as I thought, it was two inches long and rather deep. Fresh blood began seeping from the wound as I pulled the rest of the bandage from it.

My power lunged from me, diving into Cillian without warning. I watched in horror as his wound knitted up instantly, leaving nothing but remnants of fresh and dried blood in its wake.

Too slowly, my power reeled back in. I had to coax it slightly as it tried to journey further beneath Cillian's surface. I looked at the ground, swallowing as I felt that power relinquish its hold on Cillian and slither its way back into me.

I felt empty.

"Thanks. You really didn't have to—"

"It wouldn't let me walk by without healing you. I could sense it from blocks away."

"I was heading to get it looked at just now."

"Well, now you don't need to bother. You're welcome." I made to shove past him, but his hand on my shoulder stopped me.

"Kaya, you should really come back to training." His eyes were soft on me, and I watched as the outline of his lips tightened beneath his mask.

"So I've been told." His brow furrowed, but he didn't ask by who. "If you'll have me, I'm sure everyone is right. What could it hurt, really?" Other than my heart.

"Tomorrow?" I was just imagining the spark of hope in his eyes—his voice.

"Sure. See you then." I waved him off, heading for where Finn and Nash waited by the fountain at the center of the city. They both wore amused looks, and I shot them my own cold one as a warning.

Thankfully, neither made a comment as I caught back up with them. Instead, they swapped knowing glances before turning from me and heading into the awaiting masses.

Chapter 14

Cillian—Six years ago

'm sending Olen to the North."

Holden leaned back in his chair, hands steepled before him. He kept glancing out his office window as he told us his plans. I stood silently back, knowing well enough that I would be staying within the city, as was always the case.

"The North is the most likely cause of this situation. That *king* of theirs always seemed like a rotten fruit." His fingers tapped together as he pursed his lips. "Olen, I want you to travel there under guise of an emissary. We'll talk specifics later, but you'll be acting as ambassador on our behalf, using the pretext of lucrative trade. Anything. Just make it believable. Find out anything you can about what his connections might be to these husks that keep landing here."

Olen was ten years my senior, around Shepard's age. He had white hair that rested about at his shoulders, and his features were hard, his temperament unmoving. He'd make the perfect, condescending lord. That, combined with his ability to manipulate wards and locks, made him a valuable asset to the mission.

He nodded to Holden, quickly accepting his newfound position. Though, Holden wouldn't accept anyone's refusal of a job. I crossed my arms, glancing around the room full of assassins, spies, and guards. Each one of us brought something different and unique to the guild. All of us were valuable in our own way, and Holden knew just where to put us when we were needed most. He'd never failed in extinguishing a threat to our way of life.

This was the closest he'd ever gotten to losing control of a situation. I wondered how he felt. Even his outward composure was beginning to crack if only just a fraction.

Asher's eyes caught mine, the other fire wielder assessing the gathering just as I was. We were the only two of our kind on this continent. Our powers were rare but not unheard of. Not like Lucy's. She was a special case.

My eyes landed on the little blonde, the only one of us sitting in Holden's small office. Being special did have its perks, but it had its downfalls as well. With the ability to control the free will of others, she was kept under Holden's close watch at all times.

Not that she would ever use that power for her own gain. She was far too pure and true for that sort of thing.

Lucy's eyes flicked to mine, and I turned my attention elsewhere. That elsewhere happened to unintentionally be Asher once more, who seemed to be watching me as well. I felt my jaw tighten as I thought of what Greyson said all those weeks ago about seeing Kaya with Asher and how close they were. I hardened my stare, but he didn't break his gaze from mine.

I'd be damned if I looked away first.

The corner of his mouth curved up into a grin, and it took everything in me not to walk over to his side of the room and knock my fist against that annoying smile. I clenched said fist, imagining what his flesh would feel like on my knuckles.

It was like he could sense my thoughts. His smile grew, and I could almost hear the silent chuff he let out.

"That's it for now. Go home, get some rest." Holden's dismissal snapped my attention back to the present. I rolled my neck, feeling a new sort of tension growing there. Deciding to wait until everyone else cleared out, I leaned against the back wall. I didn't take my eyes off Asher as he sauntered from the room, nearly laughing as he threw me a backward glance.

I was going to throttle him.

"Something up between you and Ash?" Lucy chimed from my right. I glanced down at her and noted how she watched Asher as well.

"Ezra asked me to keep an eye on Kaya while he's gone."

"Oh, and I bet he doesn't like that they're together, does he?" Her golden hair shimmered in the fading sunlight filtering through the open window.

"They aren't together," I grumbled.

"Are you sure about that? They looked pretty cozy in that tower." She said it like it was amusing.

"Greyson already told Ezra about that weeks ago. She said they're just friends."

"Oh. No, I saw them just the other night. She and her group had wall duty. Ky gave Shepard the slip and scurried her way into Asher's tower. They were snuggled up most of the night." Her smirk was just as agitating as Asher's. Her green eyes sparkled, undoubtedly enjoying the intel she got to relay.

I watched her expectantly, waiting for more.

"I mean, maybe they were so close since he's a fire boy like you. That makes you guys extra warm, right? It *was* a chilly night, after all." She flashed me a wicked grin, then skipped out the door.

"Are you staying focused, Cillian?" The question caught me off guard as I watched Lucy leave.

I turned to face Holden. He had been watching my conversation with Lucy with rapt attention, it seemed.

"Yes, sir."

"I need everyone focused on the task at hand. We can't afford for our minds to be on trivial things." He gave me a pointed look as if he knew exactly what it was my mind was focusing on.

"I understand, sir." I clasped my hands behind my back. Ever the faithful servant awaiting my next order.

"I hope you do. Bad things happen when our minds wander." He stood, rounding his desk. He stopped before it, then took a seat atop the surface as he said, "The last thing I want is for something to happen to you. To any of my people, but especially you. I feel responsible for you—"

"I know. Since you and Father were best friends, I get it. Don't worry about me." I swallowed past the lump in my throat.

"Alright. Take the night off. Read a book. Take a walk. Meditate. Do whatever you need to do." Another pointed look.

I nodded, then pushed off the wall and walked from the room. The door snicked shut behind me, leaving me alone in the dim corridor.

Take a walk, indeed.

I let out a sigh that had the guards eyeing me. I ignored them as I walked down the hall and out the front door. Beneath the night sky, I felt more grounded and open than I did within Holden's manor. Slipping my hands into my pockets, I raised my face to the stars above, inhaling deeply.

Meditate. That was exactly what I needed, though my body definitely did not want me to sit still. A night walk sounded much better at the moment, anyway. The air was warm against my exposed skin, and the night was still. No clouds littered the sky, and the city was settling in for the night. Still, heading outside the wall to do a long lap sounded better than chancing running into someone I would feel obligated to stop and talk to.

I passed through the south gate and started walking. As I walked, I cleared everything from my mind. Or I tried to.

Thoughts of Kaya kept swimming to the surface no matter how many times I tried to float them out and away from me. Images of her face from those weeks ago in the training yard were burned into the backs of my eyelids. Every time I tried to shake them free, they became more defined.

Hours passed, judging by my position to the north of the city. Still, I fought those images to no avail. She was with me in my every waking moment, and I couldn't seem to get peace even when I fought for it. Her voice fought its way into my mind—

"Even when we're training, I get a sense…" Kaya's voice wasn't just in my head; it was above me. I craned my neck upward, trying to make out the silhouettes atop the city wall. She wasn't supposed to be on post tonight, so why she was up there, I wasn't sure.

"What does he think about it?"

My blood chilled when the second silhouette's voice floated down to where I stood flush against the wall. Asher and Kaya were seemingly unwise to my intrusion, and my gut twisted knowing they were there together, alone within the tower. Part of me had hoped everyone had seen it incorrectly. Had hoped that it hadn't been Kaya up there with him at all.

I clamped down on my anger, trying to slow my racing heart as I strained to make out what they were saying. It was nearly impossible, given that they were so far above me, but the occasional snippets made their way down to me on a gust of wind.

"You're the only one I can talk to—" The wind chose the most inopportune time to pick up. Their voices kept getting cut off.

I caught only a piece of what was said next. Asher's voice cut in and out, but I made out something that sounded like *love* and *Ky*.

My stomach hollowed out. Swallowing, I rested my head against the stone and tried to ignore the putrid feeling in my gut. As silently as I could, I crept around the wall and scurried off toward the inside of the city. It would have taken another couple of hours to make it back to the gate I came from, but I needed to get home now.

I slipped through the north gate ten minutes later and wound my way through the depths of the city. It still took time, but eventually, I saw my tiny cottage on the outer edge of the neighborhood.

The key was in the door before I could think about it. I was through the doorway another breath after that, yanking the mask from my face and running my fingers through my hair. I pulled at the strand, giving my raging thoughts something else to focus on for a moment. The pain in my scalp didn't last though. The pain in my heart, however, was a different story altogether.

They were in love, and I was a fool.

When I awoke in the morning, the throbbing pain in my chest waned slightly. What little bit that had dissipated was replaced by anger. When she had laced her fingers through mine that day in the training grounds, I had thought she felt at least a little bit of what I felt for her. And with her anger afterward…

Today was another training day, and unfortunately, I would have to face her after last night. She didn't know what I had overheard, but I didn't think I could keep my temper in check. Almost in confirmation, the candle on my side table burst into flame.

Good. She needed to see this side of me. Not everyone she faced would be as nice as I had been these past months.

Ignoring the small flames now littering my cottage, I dressed quickly, lacing my boots with precision as the dread slowly wound its way around my stomach once more. Extinguishing the candle as I stood, I slinked through my doorway and into the early morning.

It was still dark out, only the whispering of light grazing the sky above as the sun slowly ascended. The city was silent still, just the way I liked to start my days. The fewer people I ran into right now, the better.

I slipped from the gates and into a tree, making my way to the farthest training ground from the city. When I arrived in the clearing, the sky had brightened just enough for me to make out the gray clouds swirling above.

It would rain soon. I could almost feel the shift in the air pressure from last night. It felt heavy—on edge—a great weight was about to be unleashed upon us.

Rustling sounded from behind me, and I waited for Kaya to break through the line of trees. I could feel her essence encroaching on me. She felt soft and light, almost like the first sprouts of spring breaking through the still-frozen dirt. Almost as if she were a part of the forest itself.

"You're late."

"You changed spots on me," she complained.

"I just figured you overslept." I couldn't keep the bite from my tone.

"Why would you say that?" she asked as she got closer. Her eyes were soft—expectant.

"I just assumed you were out too late with your boyfriend last night." My jaw was tight as I ground out the accusation.

Her brow furrowed, and I could see the obvious confusion on her beautiful face. "Boyfriend? Really? Who ratted me out this time?" She was defensive, and I didn't care that I was the cause.

"No one. I saw you two for myself. Didn't you tell Ezra that there wasn't anything between you and Asher?"

"Yes. Because there isn't. We're friends."

"Right," I said, nearly rolling my eyes. Or perhaps I *had* rolled my eyes because the look she gave was enough for me to change the subject. "Enough talking. Get to warming up." I turned from her and leapt into a jog, setting the pace for our warmups. I couldn't even look at her, too agitated by her denial. As if I hadn't seen them—heard them—last night.

After a moment of hesitation, I heard Kaya take up a pace behind me. She made no protests as I pushed her to her limits, not holding back like I normally did. But she surprised me and didn't falter one bit, not even when I started on the lunges or the arm work.

And especially not when I threw a dagger in her direction and took up a fighting stance without saying another word to her. I waited, not tearing my eyes from her as she calculated her first move. Even I could feel the hardness of my features. Her face began to mirror that stoniness as she finally lunged to my right.

I deflected her without thought, pivoting and letting her stumble a few steps before she righted herself. She whirled, coming back at me almost instantly. I shot out of her way once more, but not before she landed a kick to my shin.

Grunting, I moved to the offensive. I leapt forward, bringing my dagger crashing into hers. I could feel her muscles straining beneath the force of me, trying as she might to push me off.

She couldn't. Instead, I found myself flat on my back, her foot having swiped my legs out from under me. Normally, I would have seen it coming, but I had been too distracted by the wicked gleam in her copper eyes.

She was atop me in a flash, dagger pressed to my throat. Her elbow came down painfully upon my hand, breaking the grip I had on my own blade. I dropped it into the dirt, and she knocked it out of my reach.

The blade still stinging against my skin, she loomed over me with a murderous look. But all I could see were those copper eyes, bright with pride from overpowering me. And those rosy cheeks, flushed from our spar.

Her full lips were curved up ever so slightly on each side.

And then, a drop of rain landed on her cheek and trailed its way down the curve of her warm skin. It disappeared between her thick, parted lips, and my complete focus narrowed in on that one spot. On her mouth, so deep and naturally maroon.

Her tongue darted out briefly, collecting that little drop of rain and tasting it. Her eyes stayed transfixed on my face like she, too, couldn't look away. And then I felt that tugging once more behind my ribs as my power stirred—as it reached for *her*.

Before I knew it, her wrist was in my hand as I tore the blade from my throat. Flipping her beneath me, I registered a moment of shock flit across her features a fraction of a breath before she was flush with the ground and my lips were covering hers.

I swallowed her gasp, plunging my tongue between her parted lips before my mind caught up with my body. My lips moved, devouring hers greedily. Her body was pressed between mine and the dirt, her lips soft beneath my own; every curve of hers felt better than I had ever dreamed it would.

And I had dreamed about this a lot, but now, reality was hitting. It crashed into me like a wave as the rain began falling harder onto our entwined bodies.

What was I doing?

Before I could break from her mouth, her arms gripped around my neck and pulled me closer to her. Having sensed my moment of hesitation, she refused to let me act on it. Her mouth began moving in tandem with my own, almost furiously. Dancing her tongue with mine—biting and nipping her fill. I savored the taste of her. Her arms around my neck weren't enough, her legs wrapped around my hips, drawing me ever closer into her warm embrace.

That force within me kept reaching out toward Kaya as if it was trying to touch her. I tried to reel it back in, and it thrashed against my command.

The rain came beating down harder, finally breaking apart our kiss. I hopped to my feet, pulling Kaya up with me and dragging her toward shelter. There was a cave not far from here that would keep us safe from the cold, wet weather until the storm passed. She didn't fight me as I pulled her along at a run without saying a word about where we were going. She simply gripped my hand firmly in her own and trustfully raced close behind me.

Ducking into the cave, I paused for only a moment to turn my body into hers and pull her close to me. The warmth of our flesh kept the chill from the rain at bay. As she looked up into my eyes, I could feel the irregular palpitations thrumming in my chest.

She was just so damn beautiful.

My hands were wrapped around her waist, but I didn't remember putting them there. I didn't dare move them either, especially not when she was allowing me to touch her. Not when she was looking at me under hooded lids, her thick lashes fluttering as her eyes narrowed back onto my mouth.

I was a fool, but for once in my life, I didn't care. Not about the repercussions. Not when we were alone, secluded in this cave. No one would see us.

No one would know.

Slowly, so slowly, as if I were moving through water, I inched myself back toward the stone wall of the cave. Kaya's steps didn't falter as she moved with me; our skin seemed somehow melted together like molten wax dripping from a candle. The puffs of air cresting from her lips brushed against me, causing my mouth to go dry. I licked my lips as my back finally impacted with the wall.

Her hands were on my chest, pressing firmly, and her fingers were gripping at my dampened shirt. Crushing me into the wall with her own body, I could feel that tug in my stomach once more.

Tugging me toward her.

Inclining my head slightly, I gave her a moment to back away. To stop this if it wasn't what she wanted. Instead of stepping back, her eyes fluttered closed, and her chin tilted ever so slightly higher as if she was reaching for me.

And I reached back.

My mouth crushed against hers, months of hunger bursting from the dam I kept it locked behind. I parted my lips, brushing my tongue across her mouth. She opened for me instantly, and my body turned molten as our tongues danced together once more.

Suddenly, her fingers were twining in my hair, and I wasn't sure how they ended up there. I felt my knees give way, my back sliding down the wall. Kaya followed me as my body collapsed under my need—her need—*our* need. When I hit the stone floor, she was instantly there, straddling me and devouring each kiss I gave her.

A small, almost foreign part of me screamed that this wasn't right. But this *was* right. The feeling of her atop me, her tongue in my mouth, tasting me—it was a heaven I had never known, and I never wanted it to end. And then that power inside me reached for her. No. It spiraled toward her; everything else fell away, and I knew this was the most right thing that had ever happened to me. Nothing else mattered but she and I.

"Ky." Her name dripped from my tongue, and I wondered if she could taste the desperation dripping from me as well.

Her hips shifted forward in response, pressing down firmly against me. The movement sent a surge of pleasure from where we touched, and I couldn't stop myself from groaning against her lips. Our kiss deepened as she ripped at my hair, rolling her hips forward again and savoring the response it elicited.

But then the rain outside the cave stopped its pounding against the mud and stone. With the abrupt end to that rhythmic noise, my sense of reason came crashing back into my body.

"We need to head back," I gasped against her lips reluctantly, nudging her back by the shoulders. I could see her weighing each of my words as they filled the silence around us, judging my tone and the cadence of my voice. I tried to keep my face neutral, not wanting to see the hurt flit across her face as it had when I refused her every time before. I didn't know how much more I could push her away. I didn't know how much more she could take before she moved on.

I wasn't sure if I wanted her to move on from me or not, but I did know that I wouldn't be able to take losing her.

That's what this all came down to, I realized. I couldn't bear losing her, nor did I want her to have to go through the pain of losing me. And ultimately, that's what would happen with the life we lived. My parents never expected the ends they eventually met, both so young. First, my mother, then my father not long after—leaving me alone in the world. How could I bring that upon Kaya? Upon myself? Or any children we might have if it ever came to that?

And there it was. The truth I had been avoiding. The reason I pushed Kaya away. Yes, I didn't want to defy her brother in that way, going behind his back when he was the only true friend I had ever had.

But wasn't Kaya my friend as well?

I couldn't lose her, couldn't have her feel that pain of losing me. So, it was easier to keep her at arm's length before things went too far.

I hoped I hadn't taken it too far today. The way she was looking at me with such hunger in her eyes had my stomach dropping with unease and desire, a most frightful mixture.

She leaned forward and brushed her mouth against mine once more before dismounting and pulling herself to her feet. Reaching an arm down, she grabbed my hand and helped me up as well. My fingers slipped from hers the second I was righted, and I forced my feet to shuffle toward the mouth of the cave and onto the drenched ground.

Birds were chirping, their trills growing louder as they swooped low to catch their breakfast now that the storm had passed. Drops fell from the trees around us as we headed back toward the city. I heard Kaya trailing behind me, though I couldn't make myself look back at her.

Neither of us spoke the entire way, and I could feel a tension building between us.

She knew.

Perhaps I was that obvious in my behavior, but she knew what I was about to do. I could feel it in my gut. My power flipped and thrashed as if in response to the feeling I carried with me.

As if *it* knew, too.

I could feel the eyes of the guards on us as we walked through the gate and into the city. It was like they could see the shame written on my face.

Or perhaps it was the fact that we were coming in from a rainstorm with barely a drop on us. What they thought happened was beyond me, though I wasn't sure if they'd be that far off from the truth of it. But I would never give them more reason than this to suspect anything happened between us for fear of word getting back to Ezra. I wondered if he would suspect what had occurred between us or just assume I had led her to the safety of shelter and nothing more.

Still, Kaya was silent behind me. As her cottage came ever closer, that silence felt heavier and heavier. An agonizing weight upon my shoulders. My heart.

I could see Ezra bobbing around in the kitchen through the window, even from this distance. I hadn't known he would be back today, and my throat tightened for an instant. I slowed my pace, stopping just before the gate that surrounded their little garden.

"I'll leave you here."

"Cillian, you can come in." She eyed me warily.

"No, I think I should go." I refused to meet her eyes, instead watching as my feet toyed with a pebble. "I'll see you in a couple of days," I said, then stepped around her and down the street.

I didn't look back.

Chapter 15

Kaya—Six years ago

I couldn't decide if I liked torturing myself or if I was that naïve.

Cillian didn't know what he wanted; that much was abundantly clear at this point. Yet every time he showed me a hint of something more than friendship or obligation, I fell right back into that spiral.

The sad thing was that I would keep doing it. I would fall over and over again just for one moment of his time.

And I hated myself just a little bit for it.

He had kissed me so fully and thoroughly that I thought he had finally given up on his idea of honor and how that meant he couldn't be with me. Yet, with how quickly he left me at my front gate—Ezra staring at us through the front window—every bit of hope I had evaporated in the hot sun like the water pooled on the ground at our feet.

I could feel my lack of attention but couldn't pull myself out of the pit I had landed in. Ezra watched me as I moved like a wraith through our cottage. I could feel the weight of his gaze on me but couldn't bring myself to care. I was too stuck in my own mind, beating myself up about what had transpired with Cillian.

I couldn't make him come around, no matter how much I wanted to.

"What's wrong?"

A jolt ran through my body; Ezra was finally fed up enough to break the silence. My head snapped in his direction. He was folding laundry that had been abandoned in the basket since the last time he was home. I should have folded it for him, but I hadn't had any extra time with the patrols and shifts our unit had been on so often lately.

"Why do you think something's wrong?" I asked, not even convincing myself.

"You haven't said a word other than *hi* since you walked through that door. And that was nearly three hours ago." He raised an eyebrow, and I rolled my eyes.

"I'm just tired from training."

"Is that why Cillian looked like he'd burned someone's house down?" His arms crossed over his chest, his weight settling against the table.

My eyes narrowed on him, astounded by what he was implying. "Doesn't he always look like that?"

"Quit teasing, Kaya."

"There's nothing wrong, Ezra." I leaned my head back against the chair, shutting my eyes. If he kept looking at me like that, I was going to spill my guts.

He snorted.

"I can't speak for Cillian. I don't know what his problem is. But there's nothing wrong with me. I'm just fine," I lied as I double-checked my mental shields. The last thing I wanted was for him to see what had happened this morning. I unfolded myself from the chair, making my way into my bedroom for some peace. "Quit hovering," I added over my shoulder before shutting him out.

"Do you think I'm absolutely insane?"

It'd been three days since my tryst with Cillian in that cave. I still couldn't wash the taste of him from my mouth.

Since then, Ezra had returned to the docks. But this time, Holden sent my cadre out there as well. He'd wanted fresh eyes on the lookout, and I wasn't upset about it at all.

He'd sent Cillian with his unit this time, to the chagrin of my brother and Wren.

And Asher, who sat beside me. Our feet dangled into the sea below the wooden dock. No ships were set to arrive today, so it was a pretty easy evening for us. Asher and I had been lounging for almost an hour by this time, the sun heading into its descent below the horizon.

"I think you're not fully in control," Asher answered. He inclined his head toward my torso, and I looked down, almost expecting to see something obvious there—a wound, a growth, something.

"Perhaps," I said dismissively though that force inside me twisted slightly in answer. "Maybe he's just a good kisser." The smile that graced my lips mirrored Asher's. He huffed a laugh.

"He can't be that good."

"Why's that?" I asked, my interest genuinely piqued.

"Well." He cocked his head toward me, quirking an eyebrow. "I'm pretty sure you're the only person he's ever kissed."

"No way."

"Is it that hard to believe? Have you ever witnessed him even *look* at another woman?" His shoulder playfully bumped into mine. That easiness between us had always been there. It was almost as if Asher was just a different version of myself, one that was all-knowing and wise. One that never judged, only helped.

"That definitely did not feel like a first kiss," I confided. He'd heard me go over the details of that day at least three times by this point, probably more. And as someone who had kissed many people before, I knew a first kiss when I felt one.

"Maybe you just haven't kissed anyone worth kissing before him. So, you wouldn't know the difference between an experienced kisser and someone who has no idea what they're doing." He gave me a playfully condescending look.

"Fine, I'll bite," I said, turning so that my body faced his.

His arm shot out, his hand gripping my throat firmly. My lips parted as a small cry escaped from between them. His eyes darkened, his head tilting toward mine as he narrowed in on my lips. Almost like he was putting on a show...

I let my eyes flutter closed just before his lips pressed into mine. He moved against me, coaxing my mouth open and then slipping his tongue inside. He tasted almost sweet, his tongue warm and languid against my own. My hand slid around his neck, and I deepened our kiss slightly, allowing the full force of him to consume me.

We kissed for a few minutes before Asher finally pulled back, smirking at me. His eyebrows rose in question.

"Nope. There's no way that was the first time," I breathed.

"Okay, so maybe it's just his natural skill that's making you feel all of this." The way he stroked a finger down my cheek didn't match the playful way he spoke. Yes. He was definitely putting on a show.

I smirked at him. "If that were the case, I would have fallen into your bed long ago rather than dreaming of falling into his."

His teeth gleamed in the sunlight. Then he laughed. "I do love you, Kaya. I really do. But I don't think Cillian would allow that."

I dropped backward onto the dock in defeat, my back absorbing the warmth from the wood beneath me. Cillian wouldn't be with me, nor let anyone else. Stretching my hands above my head, I said, "I love you too, Ash. I always will."

"He loves you too." Asher lay beside me, rubbing a hand along my thigh before crossing his arms over his eyes. "He's *in* love with you. He'll come around."

"I hope you're right," I whispered. And it was then that I noticed it. A prickling feeling scathing across my skin. I glanced at Asher, wondering if he felt it, too.

When I noticed the smirk slipping along his lips, I had my answer.

Someone was watching us, and I had a feeling I knew just who it was. I waited for the sound of boots against the dock from my brother angrily marching toward us, but they never came. Instead, the feeling dissipated after a moment, and we were left in silence.

Asher and I eventually parted ways and headed to our separate bunkhouses tucked just inside the forest, not far off the beach. When I ducked inside the small building, I spotted Shepard stuffing items into his pack.

"We need to leave now." He offered no other explanation as he pushed past me and into the night. I looked toward Finn for an answer.

"Two husks were found inside the city wall." He looked on the verge of tears. An icy chill settled over me, and I wasn't sure if it was dread or Finn's power lashing out.

"What aren't you telling me?" I demanded. I noticed then that Nash was nowhere in sight. Panic consumed me, but before I could ask again, Finn finally responded.

"One of them was Nash's sister." I could see a single tear escape from Finn's lashes as he continued, "Nash disappeared as soon as we got word. Holden wants us all to go back and be with Nash when they put her down."

My gut lurched as I pictured it. "Why haven't they done so already?" I was going to be sick.

"Nash wanted to say goodbye." Finn handed me my pack, the contents already placed back inside. I took it, unable to meet his eyes, as we left the bunk and headed to find Shepard. It felt like forever before we arrived back at the city. I thought perhaps the trees were prolonging our journey. Like they were trying to protect us from what we were about to see.

Images flooded me for the entire journey. I couldn't stop seeing that shrunken mess of a body we had witnessed in that cave. The memory haunted me, but what haunted me more was that Nash's sister had become just that. Yet, her soul remained trapped in that husk. I wondered idly if she knew what was happening to her or if some part of her still remained within that shell.

I hoped she wasn't conscious. I prayed that any bit of her life had long since washed away.

Finn and Shepard were silent as we made our way back through the city gates. Were they having the same thoughts—the same memories—flash through their minds?

Slowly, we trudged to Holden's manor, a giant monstrosity on the edge of the city, nestled closely to the city wall. Shepard had mumbled something about the husks being kept in the cellar.

No one questioned us as we passed through the door and headed to the left. We weaved through the corridors, the halls eerily silent in our wake. Guards eyed us as we went, with knowing, sad looks on their faces. I tried to keep my head high, to keep up a brave façade for Nash.

He needed to be strong. But if he couldn't, we would have to be strong for him.

As we came to the stairs leading into the cellar, cold dread washed over me. It was from more than just the damp stone walls leading down into the abyss. Something within me could sense the disturbance in the air—the wrongness of what was waiting for us below.

That power in me recoiled with each step down we took. I wondered if Finn's and Shepard's powers were doing just the same within them.

Finn shuddered in front of me.

The hair along my arms stood on end as my feet finally hit the cellar floor. There was a faint moaning echoing off the walls. I couldn't tell where the sound originated from, but it grew louder as we made our way deeper into the cold room. Shadows swayed along the far wall; two looked as though they were sitting upon chairs, and the rest stood before them. A few had bowed heads, and I could identify one as Nash without needing to make out any of his features.

My eyes pricked with tears, and I tried to blink away the burning sensation. It was no use. Hot, salty tracks began trailing down my cheeks as my throat tightened. I pushed in front of Finn and Shepard, quickening my pace to go and stand next to Nash. To do what, I didn't know yet.

His head rose as he heard me approach, and I could see the reflections of tears trailing down his cheeks. They shimmered in the moonlight that filtered in through the tiny windows carved into the walls near the ceiling of the cellar.

A sob broke through his lips, and it was echoed by a moan coming from one of the seated figures. I collected Nash in my arms, his head resting on my shoulder as his body shuddered. Stroking his back, I nestled my face into his neck as we embraced; another set of arms locked around Nash.

Finn.

And then the three of us were encased in another set of arms, strong and defined.

Shepard had never been affectionate. He had only offered minimal snippets of praise but never so much as a touch on the shoulder. But now, he held the three of us with such ferocity that a sob of my own burst from between my clenched teeth. He held us tightly, the only thing keeping us together.

And perhaps he was.

Eventually, Holden's whisper broke the spell we were under.

"We need to proceed," he coaxed gently. A chill shivered down my spine as we all broke apart from each other. Nash wiped his eyes and nose with the back of his hand, nodding his head in answer.

He cleared his throat, turning from us and reaching toward Holden.

I almost thought he was going to embrace the man. But then, out of nowhere, Nash whirled, the glint of metal slashing through the air. I could hear the song of the blade as it cut through empty air, then an audible thwack as it made contact.

One silent moment later, the head of one of the shadowing figures thumped to the ground. I was thankful it was too dark to make out her features—so like Nash's. No one said a word as one of the other men collected his own blade, then sliced it through the neck of the second husk. I couldn't make out its features, either. Who that second figure might have been, was unknown to me. And now was not the right time to be asking questions.

Not as Nash crumpled to his knees and began sobbing.

The sound was so guttural that I felt a piece of my own heart had broken off. This time, though, it was Finn who collected him in his arms. Hauling him up, I ducked beneath his other shoulder, and the two of us carried him from the cellar. Shepard followed closely behind, the near silence of his footfalls almost thunderous in the stagnant chamber. As we walked, though, I got the eerie feeling that I was being watched. Why, I wasn't sure. But I didn't dare look back to see who it was.

We pulled Nash along, wedged between us. We didn't let go of him or even loosen our hold. Not as we weaved through the empty, dark streets of the city. Not as we made our way into his dark cottage. Not as Shepard opened the door for us to get him inside.

Not even as we laid him down on his bed. Finn and I climbed in with him, tucking him between us as he wept. And we wept with him like we were all children once more.

Though older than he, his sister was still young. She was beautiful and strong.

Yet even she had succumbed to whatever was plaguing our island.

Chapter 16

Cillian—Six years ago

"W here's Kaya?"

Even though I tried everything within my power to keep my voice level and uninterested, I could still taste a hint of jealousy within the words. Ezra and I had been walking along the beach when we saw Kaya and Asher kissing on the dock.

She had been so adamant that he wasn't her lover, yet what we saw today said otherwise. Ezra hadn't been happy either but remained silent about it. I could barely hold my tongue, but I did so for fear of drawing unwanted attention from him.

"Her unit had to go back to the city." The sorrow in his voice had me meeting his eyes even though I was still plagued by guilt over what Kaya and I had done—the shame over my feelings for her.

"What happened?"

"Two husks were found within the city. One was Nash's sister." He swallowed as he tried to school his features.

I stood swiftly, panicked. "So, whoever is doing this breached the city?"

Ezra leveled a look at me before saying, "I think whoever is doing this has always been in the city. I don't think this is some outsider. Nor another realm dumping their garbage on our lands like Holden seems to think."

I sat back down, considering. What Ezra was implying could get him in a lot of trouble. I lowered my voice as I continued, "You really think one of our own is doing this?"

"There is no doubt in my mind."

"Who?"

He leaned back in his wooden chair. His fingers scratched against his jaw, his face contemplative. "I have theories, but nothing I want to voice until I have concrete evidence."

I nodded, understanding why he wanted to wait until he could prove it. With his ability, he would be the best person to figure out who was behind it, if this was, in fact, someone within our ranks. How someone within our midst could betray our way of life in such a catastrophic sense, I couldn't fathom. The draining and siphoning of another's power was not only forbidden but punishable by death. It was a disgrace to the Wildewood and its willingness to bless us in the way that it did.

Or so the fairy tales said. I, myself, wasn't sure how much truth there was to the tales. We had our sacred tree, yes. But was it actually *the* tree? The one that bestowed these powers on us? That allowed those with powers unending passage through the forest? It was hard to say. No one was allowed close enough to touch it.

Because if they did—

"I hope Nash will be alright," Ezra whispered into the blackness, pulling me from my internal spiral.

"It's not easy losing family. I couldn't image losing anyone like this, either. It's inhumane."

We settled back into a tense silence. My thoughts whirred in circles, wondering who might be causing this plague. The only light in our bunk was a few flickering candles, kept strong by my ability. The flames danced off Ezra's features. I tried not to notice all the times his gaze flicked in my direction, like he was assessing me.

As if he could see into my very soul and not just my mind. He'd promised me long ago he'd never invade my privacy. Never delve into my mind without consent. I was sure to keep my mental walls up and sealed tight, just in case.

I was in turmoil and didn't know how to fix it. Every time I closed my eyes, all I saw was Asher—his hand around Kaya's neck, his tongue in her mouth.

And Kaya. Wrapping her toned arms around his shoulders. Pulling him in closer. I could see the hint of a smile on her lips as they moved with Asher's.

Even after I dozed off, they were still all I could see. The dream warped slightly, and their kiss turned angry. Asher's hand began clenching Kaya instead of caressing her. Her lips stopped moving, her arms dropping from around his neck as she grappled at the tense fingers squeezing her jugular. She was choking and sputtering, her eyes wide with fear. As if she couldn't believe he would ever harm her.

I bolted upright, a cold sweat dripping from my chest, heart pounding. The early morning rays pierced through the window. My bunk faced the sea, and I could hear the crashing of waves upon the shore. I looked over toward Ezra's cot.

It was empty.

My body was tense. That dream felt like… more. Like some outside force was trying to tell me something. Was Kaya hurt? Was Asher truly going to harm her? I had heard the rumors about him, just as everyone else had, that he had done away with his own cadre some years ago. That he had snapped or something like that. I wasn't sure if I believed them. I wanted to think that Kaya was right about him; I wanted to trust she was a good judge of character.

And he did seem to genuinely care about her, even though it got under my skin that he did so.

Scrubbing my palms across my eyes, I shook the thoughts from my head. I was overthinking this. Kaya was well-trained. Lethal, if I had to accurately describe her. She had killed those intruders in the forest without a second's hesitation, and I had thoroughly trained her since then.

The girl could take care of herself.

And frankly, she hated the way Ezra and I worried about her. The last thing I wanted to do was piss her off again. I'd done enough of that already.

I pushed back the light cover, my feet connecting with the cold floor. The chill against my soles brought back the image of Asher's fist closing around Kaya's throat. I shivered.

I changed quickly, lacing up my boots tightly before I burst through the door and into the early morning air. The breeze blowing in from the sea was refreshing in the summer heat. The scent of salt tickled my nose, the sand grinding beneath my feet. I could see the guards at their stations.

I could also see the many watchers stationed just within the trees and out of sight of the oncoming ship.

More goods were to be unloaded today, courtesy of the South. We'd send them a minuscule amount of crops as payment. They didn't expect much in return, thinking we were just a charity case they felt obligated to help.

I headed toward the dock to help when the ship arrived, mentally classifying this as my workout since I had overslept. Asher stood by one of the pillars, staring off into the horizon.

Anger flooded me, catching me off guard. My jaw clenched, and I ground my teeth together. I couldn't stand this guy; I couldn't stand the images that kept coming back to the surface.

His hands on Kaya, his mouth over hers.

I really needed to sort through my issues.

A hand on my shoulder had my body tensing. I whirled, instinctively reaching for the dagger at my side. My power surged, but Ezra stood just behind me, a look of shock on his face.

"Easy, killer. Just here to tell you that Holden sent word. You're to return to the city." His hands were raised in front of his body, a look of amusement etched into his features—no more of that worried, morose look from the previous night.

"Seriously?" I asked as I rolled the tension from my shoulders. I couldn't hinder my annoyance.

"Yes. He's calling a few back. Since…" Ezra didn't finish, but he didn't have to. Holden wanted more people he trusted within the city after that blatant attack on our people.

"Just when I finally got a little bit of freedom from him," I mused.

"Sorry, man." Ezra shrugged. He understood how I hated being couped up within the city He and Wren felt bad when they left me behind. But duty was duty, and they had to abide by it. "At least you'll be there to watch out for Kaya. Can't say I'm mad about that."

"Right," I said. I looked away from him, checking those mental walls once more. They were up. "Is Asher staying out here?" I couldn't help but ask. Ezra had seen them, too. He was angry about it as well. Though, perhaps not as angry as I was, and definitely not for the same reasons.

"He's staying here." His jaw clenched. Ezra watched Asher with caution.

I furrowed my brow in question, not wanting to ask it aloud with so many wandering ears within range. Ezra met my eyes and gave a slight dip of his chin.

Perhaps that dream was trying to tell me something after all.

Chapter 17

Kaya—Six years ago

The tragedy of last night stuck with me for the entire day. My body was weighed down with sorrow for my friend and his only living family.

Now, it was just him.

I couldn't imagine losing my brother. Idly, I wondered if that pain would be less just because Ezra and I had no blood ties. But no. I knew that pain would be just as great. The idea of losing my brother brought tears to my eyes; the thought alone was enough to break my heart. I prayed to the Wildewood that the figurative pain was something I would never feel.

Finn and I did what we could for Nash. We helped him lay his sister to rest beyond the city wall and said a prayer over her grave once she was buried. Afterward, Nash sent down a piece of his power into the dirt that covered her. Shepard stood watch behind us, silently monitoring the forest around us, just in case.

The two of us held Nash as wildflowers sprung up. More would grow consistently over her grave from now until the end of days. Her body rested beneath one plot within an entire field of flowers. Loved ones that were long gone but never forgotten. Our people buried all our dead here, and I knew that Cillian's parents were somewhere out there as well.

I glanced ahead, barely making out the silhouette of our sacred tree. It was the tree that bestowed us with power—the one that would forever watch over our dead. I could almost feel it thrumming in time with my soul.

We left Nash at his cottage, worn out and weary. The sun was sinking behind the city wall, casting an ominous glow against the stone surrounding us. The storefronts loomed high above, their shadows darkening patches of the road as Finn and I parted ways, only a low grunt in farewell passing between us.

The city was silent, which in and of itself was eerie. Our island was always bustling, but with the assailant infringing on our safety, many people seemed frightened of leaving their homes at this late hour.

I felt unsure about staying in my own cottage alone as well. I didn't blame the people for their unease since I felt that same sensation clutching at my chest. Scanning the shadows, sure that someone was watching me, I darted my gaze back and forth. There was a prickling along my neck, chills eliciting bumps from my skin.

I was being dramatic. The streets were empty. Everyone was holed up in their homes, exactly where I should have been.

I unlatched my front gate, making sure to snick it shut behind me. If someone tried to come up to my house, I'd hear the latch coming apart and would be ready before they hit the front door.

My key slid into the lock, turning with ease. Slipping inside, I latched that lock back into place as quickly as I could. I hung my keys on the hook by the door and bent to unlace my boots. Kicking them off, I grabbed the flint from the entry table. Sparks flew when I struck it against my dagger, igniting the small candle Ezra and I kept at the ready just inside the door.

A soft glow emanated from the wax, illuminating the small cottage. Everything was still and silent, just as it was supposed to be.

My footfalls were nearly silent against the wooden floor as I padded into my bedroom. Setting the candle on the side table, I pulled my shirt off and tossed it onto the heap of clothes in the corner. My pants and undergarments followed, and I headed back into the main area, making my way into the bathing room to wash up. Unfortunately, the water in the tub was cold, and I didn't have the time or energy to light a fire and warm it.

Instead, I sank into the chilled water and scrubbed my skin clean as quickly as I could. I began shivering as I dunked my head beneath the surface and scrubbed soap through my hair. The sound of the water echoed through my mind, dulling my senses and sending my body into a state of calm despite the clutching cold of its depths.

When my lungs felt as if they would burst from holding my breath for so long, I rose to the surface. The chilled water plashed from my hair, dripping a steady stream down my back. Overly cold now, I pulled myself from the tub as quickly as I could, water splashing onto the floor. I wrung my hair out before wrapping it and myself in towels. Even with the towel covering me, I was still shivering.

My body shook the entire way back into my bedroom, the candle balanced precariously in front of me. The shaking flame danced ominous shadows across the wall; the light outside was completely nonexistent.

Pressing the bedroom door closed behind me, I plunked the candle onto my table and the towels onto the floor. I kicked them from my path, aiming for the heap of laundry that I needed to tend to at some point. I ignored it, though, heading straight toward my chest of drawers. My nightclothes rested in the top drawer and after pulling them on, I dragged a brush through my unruly dark waves. Water still dripped from the ends, and I tried to squeeze as much liquid from them as I could. I debated opening a window to let in some of the warm night air but rethought that decision as images of Nash's sister plagued me again.

It was dry enough.

Moonlight filtered in through the window, enough for me to make out the outlines of my furniture so I didn't trip over anything in the dark. Not that I didn't already have every inch of my room's layout memorized. Blowing out the candle, I pulled back the blankets and nestled into my soft bed. The head of which faced the window, a precaution that had been ingrained into me. It was the closest access point from the outside to my sleeping form. I would be ready if someone tried to breach my domain.

Unease roiled through me. How someone had gotten into the city unnoticed was beyond me. But I vowed not to be the next victim if I could help it. Even though I felt a nervous tension in my entire body, my eyes began to droop with exhaustion—both from the physical strain of the day as well as the mental and emotional. It was almost like a weight was strapped to my lashes, and no matter how hard I fought it, my eyes soon closed completely.

A soft tapping caught my attention, but I couldn't seem to will my eyes back open. My body was heavy, my eyes stuck shut with sleep. Perhaps I was simply dreaming things. Perhaps it was the wind causing a stray branch to tap against the cottage.

I rolled to my side, dismissing the noise entirely and nestling further into the blankets. Their warmth caressed me, coaxing me further into unconsciousness.

Scratch, scratch, snick.

I bolted upright, dagger in hand, then scanned my room. Not an ounce of sleep remained in my body as terror cascaded through my veins.

That had been my window unlatching; I was sure of it.

Dread washed over me as I registered a dark figure crouched just outside my open window. The pane began swinging further inward, a shadowy hand grasping my window frame.

I flung my blade at the figure, missing the mark in my fear. Wood splintered as it burrowed deep into the frame just beside the assailant's hand. Whoever it was beyond the window snatched their hand back, hissing in displeasure.

I jumped from the bed as fast as I could, intent on prying the dagger free and sinking it into their heart. Before I could get two steps toward the dagger, however, the silhouette flung itself into the room, landing with a soft thud.

"Kaya, it's me."

The melody within those words drifted into my soul, my power dancing with their notes. Every surging fear clinging to my skin and gut evaporated as the angles and planes of Cillian's face came into focus. Though there was barely any light left, the familiarity in his face was evident. And he wasn't wearing his mask.

"Why are you here, Cillian?" I breathed. My heart was still racing, though it was no longer from fear.

"I knew your brother wasn't here, and I needed to talk to you." He crept closer. I relinquished a step. His hand came up and rested on my biceps. A shiver skittered down my arm from the warmth radiating from where our skin met, and that fire within his blood sank into my flesh.

"What is it?" I whispered.

That damned hand. Cillian extended a finger, trailing it from my arm up to my neck, leaving a line of heat in its wake. It skated along my jaw before coming to a stop just below my chin. He tilted my head, forcing my eyes to meet his.

"I'll do anything. *Anything* for you to choose me." His face was inches from mine, his breath coming out in hot puffs against my lips as he spoke. "I will, Kaya. Please. I can't—"

"I'm already yours, Cillian," I interrupted. My lips remained parted even after the words floated from them. I watched as his eyes danced across my face, checking the sincerity of my words. Hot tears pricked at the corner of my eyes, exhaustion overpowering my ability to keep my emotions in check. Too long had we been dancing around this.

But finally, *finally*, he was here. He was facing it head-on.

His lips crashed into mine with a fervor that rivaled our previous encounter. My arms wrapped around his neck just as his body slammed against mine. I could feel his fingers digging into my back as he deepened the kiss. I could feel his desperation, his plea for more within his movements. I gave him everything his demanding touch asked for.

Kissing him back as forcefully as I could, I tasted him. The claiming did not quell my desires but sent my body craving *more*. My tongue dipped between his lips and was met with eagerness from his own. A guttural moan rumbled in the back of his throat, the reverberations radiating into me, traveling down my body and in between my thighs.

Beneath me became only empty air as I was lifted from the floor. I wrapped my legs around his hips, and his hand dug into the backs of my thighs. Slowly, he moved us toward the bed, my heart skipping a beat with every step. He lowered me onto the bed, gently pushing me so that I was lying back against the soft blankets. He remained hovering above me, but our kissing didn't falter as he braced his hands on either side of my head. I grappled at his shirt, pulling it free from his pants.

My hands snaked beneath the fabric, tracing up his skin, feeling the light speckling of hair along his torso. A groan of my own broke free as his muscles contracted beneath my fingers. A small part of me thought that I was still dreaming, that I was making this up.

Then Cillian lowered himself onto me, the weight of him so magnificent and comforting. It was as if a piece of myself was finally settling into place, and I had finally found my home.

That force inside of me started swirling, ever captivated by Cillian's mere presence. I could feel it reaching out toward him, brushing against the underside of my ribs.

Was he hurt? Was my power trying to break free in order to heal him? Or was it something else altogether?

I broke our kiss long enough to settle myself further onto the bed. My hands grabbed at his bunched-up shirt, pulling him with me. He crawled above me, and his mouth found mine again. His taste was hot and familiar—familiar in a way I couldn't explain. My power reached out again, spiraling toward him as he wrapped me in his arms.

My breathing quickened as I pressed my body harder into his, my hands finally pulling the shirt from his body. Cillian half sat up as I ripped the fabric above his head, my hands grappling for his hot skin once more. His mouth found mine instantly, just as hungry as mine was.

"Kaya," he breathed into my mouth. I drank the words down, not stopping myself as my hands roamed over his skin. He pulled his mouth from mine, so I moved onto his collarbone instead, sucking his flesh into my mouth, tasting the saltiness there. "I've never done this before," he whispered, his voice wobbling over a groan.

My head fell back onto the bed, my eyes finding his in the moonlight. "Neither have I," I confided. His eyes sparked in surprise. But then a smile cut across his mouth for a second before it connected with my neck. His kisses were gentler now. Slower. I felt like he was savoring every second. As if he, too, wanted this moment in time to stand still. My fingers wound through his hair, tugging as his languid kissing and sucking sent pleasure all the way to my toes.

I clenched my thighs around him, a need building between them. I rolled my head to one side, lifting my chest up to press myself further into his mouth. His tongue licked a trail down my skin as he pulled the shoulder of my nightshirt down my arm, freeing my breast. He caught my nipple between his lips, licking the tip and sucking it further into his mouth. I hissed, the sensitive flesh tingling from the softness of his tongue.

I ripped my arm from the constraints of the fabric, the shirt coming to rest along my abdomen as I held Cillian's head to my chest. My fingers stroked through his soft hair, and a guttural noise rumbled from his throat as he licked along my breasts and back up to my neck. I couldn't breathe, couldn't choke down enough air as he explored my body. I could feel myself tightening, arousal pooling as his touches became more assured.

When his lips found mine again, I was more sure than ever before. I wanted Cillian, needed him. Our skin pressed together, molded to one another like we were two halves of the same coin, finally come back as one. Briefly, I released him to tend to my clothes, slipping them further down my body. I didn't even care that my favorite nightshirt would be stretched beyond repair as I worked it past my hips. Cillian lifted himself, allowing me to remove the items and kick them away.

He paused his kissing to let his eyes rove over the skin that was displayed for him. I felt his attention snag between my parted legs, and the warmth building there intensified. A blush erupted along my cheeks, my already hot skin near scalding as his eyes trailed back up to meet mine. His open expression turned dark, and I felt rather than saw his hands move to the waistband of his own pants. The knuckles of his hands brushed against my abdomen as he fumbled with the buttons there. When they came loose, he slid the fabric down, and I couldn't stop my eyes from landing right on the length of him.

I didn't think my want could get any greater.

We watched each other for a moment, committing this instance to memory. This was something I would treasure forever—of that, I was sure. He was everything to me. Everything I had ever wanted. Everything that I didn't know I needed.

And the look on his face told me the same thing: that it was us. It had always been us, would always be us.

Still holding my gaze, his hand began trailing down my arm. It danced over the skin on my stomach, and I held my breath as it continued its descent. I tried and failed not to tremble as his fingers slowed just above my pelvis. My mouth was nearly watering as I nodded my head once, assuring him that this was what I wanted.

Upon receiving my confirmation, his fingers dipped between my legs, feeling the wetness there. I moaned at the light contact, tilting my hips forward in encouragement. His body lowered closer to my own, his mouth finding mine once more as his fingers explored my most sensitive area.

I whimpered with want, with need, as he pressed further against me, then dipped inside. I could feel his hardness pulse against my hip in response. I spread my legs further, trying as I might to wrap them around him. I wanted to feel him against me, his heat radiating into me. But then he slipped a second finger inside of me, and I cried out, head dropping onto the bed and eyes rolling back.

I had never been touched like this before, and the feathery strokes of his fingers sent my mind into a frenzy of lust.

"Cillian," I panted. His mouth was on my neck in an instant.

"What?" he breathed into my skin.

His fingers moved in and out of me slowly, savoring the feel of me the way I was savoring him. "I want all of you," I barely managed to say between whimpers.

The immediate emptiness I felt when he removed his fingers drew a cry from my lips. But then he caught that cry between his teeth and nestled between my thighs. "Are you sure?" he asked, giving me another chance to back out. To call it off.

But I had been chasing this for months already. My power was still swarming behind my ribs, reaching out to him. I tried to keep it at bay, to keep it locked up, but it was getting too hard to contain.

"I'm sure. I want you. Always."

His gray-blue eyes pierced into mine, a world of emotions swimming in them. A flash of his teeth gleamed in the moonlight as he smiled slightly, timidly. I tilted my head up just enough so that I could run my tongue along his lips. His body loosened atop me and his hips ground between my legs. I could feel his soft skin as the length of him pressed against my flesh.

Reaching a hand between us, I curled my fingers around him. He moaned against me, pushing his hips up further, driving himself deeper into my grasp. I angled him toward my entrance, spreading my legs to accommodate his hips. His forearms steadied on either side of my shoulders, balancing his weight. My free arm wrapped around his torso and pulled him against me, needing that weight to be pressed into me as *he* pressed inside of me.

Then, my power finally broke free and dove into him. As that power met with his, hot and singeing, I could feel it sear into his flames, dancing between us in a joining all their own. I gasped, and I felt Cillian do the same. His forehead came to rest against mine as he finally started to press inside me.

I could feel my body adjusting to him, his length slowly burrowing deeper into me. It felt foreign but right. It was a pressure sliding into me and I gasped as he surged deeper.

And deeper.

When he was seated completely, a surge of pleasure shot through me. The smallest amount of pain laced that feeling, but it was minimal and something I clasped onto. I wanted to remember everything about this moment.

"Is this okay?" Cillian asked me.

I huffed a laugh into his ear. "Yes," I whispered, moving my hips, willing him to keep moving within me. He obliged, kissing and nipping at my jaw as he did. Our powers still danced between us, relishing in the fact that we were now one. That they, too, could now be one.

Cillian moved slowly at first, gently as we kissed and tasted one another. As that pain lessened, it turned into something else entirely. The pressure built between us, and his movements became hurried along with our panting breaths.

I couldn't get enough of him. My teeth bit into his shoulder as he quickened his pace even more, some feral need overtaking him. That pressure kept building and building, and I was almost hysterical with the feeling, the gasps coming louder as the feeling rose ever higher.

And then I peaked, Cillian and I crumbling together with it. My body tightened around him, and I felt his do the same as he groaned my name. My hips ground against him, drawing out that feeling as long as I could as he slowly stilled inside of me.

When the pulsing between my thighs finally ebbed, as did our power. It retreated back into us, just as sated as we were. When I took inventory of it, though, it felt like it was less than before. Yet it was more. Different. Changed.

Just like me.

Cillian's fingers stroked over my shoulder and tangled in my hair as he nestled against my body. I breathed in his earthy scent, memorizing the feel of him as he softened inside me. He dragged a blanket over our bodies as he rolled off me and tucked me beneath his arm. I curled around him, hooking a leg over his and laying my head against his chest.

We didn't speak, content with listening to the other breathe. I focused on the beating of his heart beneath my ear, its thumping slowly returning to normal. My power settled back beneath the surface, resting.

My body hummed, each of my nerves ever aware that a part of me rested outside of my body—beside me. Our closeness was almost not enough. I wanted more of him, wanted to be entwined with him forever.

But then my limbs became heavy once more, my mind becoming fuzzy with them. Eyelids drooping, I let the darkness consume my mind. I was no longer afraid to fall asleep after the horrors of the day.

Now safe within Cillian's arms.

Chapter 18

Cillian—Six years ago

I could hear birds chirping outside of the window, but I was unwilling to open my eyes just yet. My dream was slipping from me slowly, and it had been the most wonderful one I'd ever experienced. I felt more rested than I had in a long time.

Groaning, I went to stretch my arms above my head. But something was across my right arm, weighing it down. I was pinned beneath something, and it took a moment for last night to come crashing back down on me.

After a jolt of realization, my eyes flew open and landed directly on Kaya.

Her lashes nearly brushed her cheeks, her eyes softly fluttering as she still dreamed beside me. Her hair was a tangled mess of dark waves splayed across the pillow beneath her. The heat from her skin warmed my side, causing me to start sweating.

But she was just so beautiful. I didn't have the heart to wake her just yet.

Instead, I memorized her face—the curves of her body that were uncovered, the curves I could still make out below the blanket that clung to them. Her dark skin was nearly unblemished—no sunspots to be seen.

No scars save for the one marring her forearm. The one left behind from when she saved me by using her flesh to guard me from attack.

I should have known then.

A piece of her rested inside of me now. I was sure of it. It was twined with my own power, so small it was almost unnoticeable. But it was there. A part of her would be with me wherever we went from this moment on.

We were forever linked in that way. In many ways it now seemed. She was my everything and I refused to let her go. How I would break the news to Ezra, I wasn't sure just yet. But that was something we needed to do at some point.

Just not yet. I wanted to live in this secret for a little while before everything went to hell. Before we felt the wrath of her brother raining down upon us. Because there would be wrath. I just hoped it would be short-lived. Perhaps Ezra could see past my betrayal and be happy for us.

I nearly snorted. Ezra was not usually a forgiving person, especially when it came to his sister.

Kaya began stirring next to me and I gently slipped my arm from beneath her. Rolling onto my side, I propped my head on my hand. She stretched out with her arms above her head, her legs going straight as a board. The motion pulled the blankets down her body, unveiling her beautiful breasts. My eyes hungrily devoured them. I couldn't keep the smile from spreading across my lips as she finally opened her eyes.

Her answering smile sent my heart skittering.

"Good morning," she said, her voice husky with sleep. I touched the exposed skin of her stomach with my free hand, skating my touch up her body, then cupping her breast. My own body pulsed and hardened in response, and I could feel my cheeks reddening slightly as she watched my every move.

"How are you feeling?" I asked as I pried my eyes from her peaked nipple.

"Never felt better, actually. I slept very well." She smirked at me, then turned on her side. Her breasts bounced with the motion, her arm coming to rest just beneath them as she reached to kiss me. She tasted like nothing I'd ever experienced before—sweet and divine. I would never be able to shake the essence from my memory. Not that I would want to.

She pulled back before I was finished tasting her. "Are you okay with… everything?" she asked almost hesitantly.

Guilt clutched at my gut. I had been horrible to her. I knew that. But now, after everything, I realized just how foolish it had been. I had risked everything for this idea of honor, for the terror losing her caused me.

My fingers trailed along her reddened cheek as I said, "I was a fool. This is what I've always wanted, Kaya. I'm sorry I fought it for so long." Our lips met again, and we kissed slowly, deeply. My power danced beneath my skin at the feel of her next to me, her power inside of me.

The snick of a latch had us jumping apart midkiss. My body iced over as we both silently listened for more sounds.

Steps on the front path tapped an even rhythm, nearly inaudible from her bedroom. A key being inserted into the lock of the front door followed, and Kaya's expression mirrored my own.

Absolute terror cascaded into me as we heard the undeniable sounds of Ezra coming home from the docks.

The blanket flew off of us, and I wasn't sure who it was that had flung it away. I didn't care. I rolled to my feet, keeping my movements as quiet as possible while Kaya threw articles of clothing at my face, one after the other. I snatched them from the air, stuffing my limbs inside the pants and shirt, grabbing my boots from the floor. We were a flurry of hurried movements as we heard the knob to the front door begin to turn.

Kaya flung herself at me, drinking in a final kiss before shoving me out her window. I nearly fell backward on my ass, thankful for my fast reflexes keeping me from whacking my head on the rocks strewn about. My hands weren't as lucky, abrasions marring my skin from catching myself in the dirt.

Kaya latched her window without a glance down at me. She knew well enough that I'd rather be bleeding outside her window than caught by her brother, naked in her bed.

I heard the front door shut behind him, and I kept my head below the window. Crouching, I hauled myself and my boots from their tiny garden and over the back fence, landing with a soft thud on the road. Luckily, no one seemed to be out just yet; it was still so early in the day. My eyes darted around the surrounding area regardless, scanning for anyone who might have seen me sneaking out of Kaya's room.

Like some sort of thief.

I swore I heard a soft snicker but didn't see anyone around. My mind was playing tricks on me, it seemed, my anxiety skyrocketing with the near discovery. Ezra would find out about us eventually, but not like that.

I preferred to live.

I had been floating along for the entire day until I received word from Holden as evening closed in. He was calling another meeting since more husks had been found outside the wall during the night I had spent with Kaya.

Outside the wall, inside the wall, along the shores, it seemed they were popping up everywhere. Yet, we were no closer to finding out who was behind it, who was siphoning these powers. No one showed signs of an uptick in ability. So, either it was one of us, as Ezra suspected, or they were very, *very* good at hiding.

"I still haven't received word from the North since sending Olen into their midst." Holden paced his office as I stood uncomfortably next to Ezra.

He kept glancing my way, almost sensing something was different about me. I kept checking and double-checking that my walls were up so that he didn't accidentally get a glimpse of something he didn't want to see. Something I didn't want to show him.

Kaya had been on my mind all day.

"I expect it will take time for him to gain their trust and learn anything. Until then, we need to keep up our defenses. I know I've asked a lot from you all—too much at times—but I need to ask more." Holden leveled a glance my way. Lucy nudged my side, and I glared down at her. "The east has seen the most influx of husks. I think that's where whoever is behind this is lurking. I'm sending you all that way to keep watch. Indefinitely."

I glanced around at those of us in attendance. There was me, Ezra, Wren, Lucy, a couple newer members of the guild, and Asher. It seemed to me like a pretty big team to go unnoticed in the eastern forest, but who were we to question command.

Perhaps that's just what he wanted: for our presence to be noticed. To deter whatever threat was wreaking havoc on our land.

I didn't think it would work.

We nodded, none of us daring to voice any concerns we might have had. He dismissed us with a wave of his hand before turning back to his desk. Filing out one at a time, none of us spoke as we weave through the city and out into the forest beyond. Slipping into a tree, our cadre regrouped out in the abyss. The trees loomed above as always, the forest deep and dark around us.

It wasn't until then that one of us decided to speak.

"I don't know what he thinks we're going to accomplish out here," Lucy huffed as she kicked at the dirt. "I'd bet my life the person behind this is in the city." She scowled ahead, though I could barely see it.

"Perhaps. Or perhaps he's here with us." Ezra mumbled the accusation under his breath.

"How do we know it's a he?" Wren asked without pause. Disdain dripped through her words as she rounded on Ezra. "It could be anyone. We shouldn't make any assumptions before we have cold, hard proof."

"Let's just make camp. Come up with a rotation plan. Some sort of strategy for keeping watch. For hunting this person down." Asher's command was heavy—reasonable even to me.

Ezra gave me a look that had me dropping my wall just a fraction. *One of us needs to be sure we're on rotation with him. To keep an eye on him.* His voice reverberated in my mind with a fervor I almost didn't recognize.

Understood. I slammed my wall back up before he could dig any deeper than surface level. If he thought it was odd, he didn't show it. We dispersed, canvasing the area for a stronghold, eventually selecting one of the many caves that littered the island.

The plan we enacted was simple—we stood watch in groups of two as the others slept. During the days, we would pair off as well, rotating partners to provide everyone with different advantages while someone stayed stationed at our stronghold. We didn't want anyone to get too comfortable. When someone got comfortable, they got careless.

Lurking in the shadows—in the unseen realm—was something that each of us knew how to do adeptly. But sitting atop trees in a silent forest was not helpful in the slightest. We had been out here for days, and nothing had happened other than the scampering of forest creatures and the pestering of insects.

I wanted to be back in the city with Kaya, not melting in the hot sun and making no headway on this mission. Ezra was near, subtly eyeing me as my legs swung from the tree branch. My walls had been up this entire time, yet I could feel his suspicions grating against my nerves.

"What?" I finally hissed toward him. Maybe I was reading into this. Maybe my guilt was getting the best of me. Either way, I needed to know what he knew.

"Everything alright with you?"

My head snapped to him, my brow furrowing. "Why wouldn't it be?"

"You're acting strange." His mouth tugged up on one side. "You're always strange. But it's been more pronounced lately." He laughed lightly at his own joke.

I chose to remain quiet while I organized my thoughts. "I think it's just the attack in the city."

"Yeah. It terrifies me. Especially since Kaya is there." He looked up toward the sky for a moment. "Alone."

"I'm sure she'll be alright," I tried to assure him, though my plummeting gut said otherwise. In that unease, Kaya's bit of power reached out, caressing my ribs in a sort of embrace. I found myself clutching at my chest as if I could reach inside myself and hold that piece of her.

"Cillian, you know you're my truest friend." He paused, thinking about what he was going to say next. I noted how his eyes landed on my hand, the one I stroked across that small ache in my heart. His eyes met mine once more, resolved. "Nothing will change th—"

A flash of red beneath the tree had us dropping to the ground, our conversation unfinished. We sprung into a sprint after whatever was running through the trees. Ezra raced in front of me, cutting me off as he pursued the target.

Perhaps it was nothing. But we couldn't take that chance.

I could hear the snapping of twigs and the rustling of underbrush as whoever we chased kept just out of our reach, out of our sight. But then the noise settled into silence, and I watched as Ezra pummeled through a tree, careening himself onward in hopes of capturing them. I followed a step behind. But when I emerged on the other side, my body was struck still by cold, icy fear.

Husks. So many of them I couldn't count. Ezra drew his blade beside me as the mindless corpses registered our arrival. Their groaning radiated in the open air around us, coaxing more fear to coat my tongue like acid. With seemingly unseeing eyes, they tracked us, thrashing their jerking limbs in our direction. Their fingers were jagged, clawing through the air as if it were flesh—as if it were *our* flesh—scratching with some undefinable need that stirred them.

And they were fast. One moment, we had a sizable distance between us; the next, they were grasping at my and Ezra's clothes. I broke through my fear, my blade falling into my hand in a heartbeat, tearing through dried skin and bone like it was underbrush. Ezra was at my back. Doing the same as we were surrounded.

The assailant was nowhere in sight. Not that we could do anything to detain them with husks enveloping us.

I could smell rot as what was left of their bodies fell to the ground. How long had they been out here? How had they gone unnoticed for so long? They were near decayed, though some sort of life still remained trapped within.

I hoped whatever consciousness they had once held was long gone. I prayed to the Wildewood that these poor souls were not suffering within their withering bodies.

Ezra was shouting something from behind me, but I couldn't make it out over the groans. I couldn't focus on anything but keeping my limbs attached to my body as I swung and swung my sword, hacking away, trying to break free from this mess. Hopefully, one of the others had seen us take off. Hopefully, someone would come searching for us.

We couldn't take them all down alone. It was as if they were multiplying. The more that fell, the more that seemed to surge for us.

Fingers ripped at my arms and my hair. I pulled my dagger from my belt, sinking it into the head of a husk next to me. Ezra's back was pressed hard against mine, and I could feel him working just as vigorously as me to fend them off.

We weren't going to make it out of this mess on our own.

Chapter 19

Kaya—Six years ago

Since the incident, people remained hesitant about staying in the city for longer than necessary. Though I was also uneasy about it, I took comfort in knowing that Ezra and Cillian were together, even though they'd been gone for a week. They would have each other's backs as they always had. I was sure of it.

The reassuring thought didn't keep dread from pooling in my gut, though. I was uneasy, every cell in my body on edge. My tongue felt sour, my stomach queasy. Something in the air was off; I just couldn't quite put my finger on it.

I was sitting on the edge of the fountain, finally having a day off from guard duty. The extended shifts and nonstop workdays were beginning to drain me, even though I knew it was for good reason. We couldn't allow more of our people to suffer, to wither and die at the hands of a tyrant who was hell-bent on gaining power. For what reason, though?

Tossing coins into the watery depths, I thought of the mess our realm was in. It reminded me of the fairytales of our land. Of our original queen who had been tricked from her throne. But just as she had fought back, so would we. We couldn't allow someone else to come in and steal away what was rightfully ours.

I was so preoccupied with my thoughts that I almost didn't recognize the shadowy figure weaving through the buildings and heading directly toward me. If it weren't for the fact that I had his mannerisms committed to memory, I might not have known who it was. Patches and bandages covered half his face, nearly obscuring his features. Only the right side was visible beneath the dirty, blood-soaked cloth. But the wounds weren't what halted my breathing and sent my mind spiraling with dread. The wounds would heal. I could heal them.

No. It was the look creasing the only visible part of Cillian's face that had my gut clenching and dropping further with fear. I wasn't breathing— couldn't suck down breaths—as he fell to his knees before me and clutched my hand within his.

He didn't speak, didn't move. My body began shaking uncontrollably. My hand went limp in his.

"Ezra." His voice was a raspy sob. I felt like I was going to be sick, but I forced myself to listen as he continued. "We were surrounded. There were so many of them." Tears streamed from his one uncovered eye as he choked on the words. My ears began to buzz as his words struck deep. I didn't want to hear more. "Too many of them. And only us. By the time anyone got there to help—" A sob racked from his throat, the sound guttural and haunting. It contorted his next words into something incoherent.

But I didn't need to hear them.

The ringing in my ears loudened as the void within me plummeted into black nothingness. I couldn't feel anything but a crushing weight on my chest, as a hole was ripped through my heart and my body was caving in on itself. I couldn't breathe.

I don't know how long I sat there unmoving with Cillian sobbing into my lap, his apologies piercing through the void one after the other. I felt none of them.

I felt nothing.

I blinked and noticed the city was black. It was nighttime. Hadn't it just been daylight?

Without saying a word, I stood, knocking Cillian from my lap, and walked away from the man who was supposed to protect my brother. My heart had shattered into a thousand pieces. It splintered even more as I walked away from Cillian's crumpled form, but I refused to look back, refused to see Cillian still crouched before the fountain, sobbing into his hands.

I wanted to vomit.

Instead, I walked. I walked without knowing where I was heading as my head pounded in my ears—floating through the city like a phantom as the night darkened further.

I didn't know how long had passed before I realized I was standing before Holden's manor. How long had I been standing here, staring without seeing? The guards eyed me warily. Ignoring the looks of pity they tried to hide, I pushed past them without stating my business. This was not something they would normally allow, but they said nothing to me as I strode through the doorway and up the stairwell. How my body knew where Holden would be was beyond me.

I felt my power seemingly lead me where I needed to go; it knew what I needed more than I did.

I didn't care.

I drifted through the manor like a ghost, idly aware that I was heading toward the old library. The door creaked open before me on a phantom wind. My hand drifted forward and pushed the wood inward, gingerly stepping onto the plush, ornate carpet inside.

Stacks of books lined the walls. The ceiling towered high above, so high that ladders were attached to the shelves to assist with reaching those books at the top. Many different wingback chairs and tables littered the room, a hearth stationed on one side.

Ezra would have loved this place. I could almost see him sitting in one of those chairs, a book in his lap. Just like he did at home.

He never would again.

His face swam in my vision, those features forever frozen in time. I would never see his eyes crinkle with age or tell him about my love for Cillian. Never thank him for bringing Cillian into our lives. My life.

He would never be a father.

How was Wren? Did she know? Could she feel that loss?

Blinking away my sorrow before it could spill over, I took note of all the pieces artfully displayed in the ancient library. But it wasn't any of these things that really caught my attention.

No. It was the statue placed in the center of the room. The one mentioned in all the tales of this land, and I was seeing it for the first time in my life.

If I hadn't been so numb, so heartbroken and defeated, I would have fallen to my knees in awe before our ancient queen's likeness. The white marble looked seconds from coming back to life. Every detail was near perfection, from the etching around her eyes to the waves of her hair. The curve of her lips. The veins in her hand.

A hand that reached out toward her traitorous lover.

I stepped closer, studying the statue. Studying the history it showed. The queen had been beautiful, as had her lover. It was no wonder the two women were compelled toward each other. I wondered if they had also felt that pulling, that yearning, from their powers. Just like the connection I had with Cillian. Like the one Ezra had with Wren years ago.

"Kaya."

Holden's voice was softer than I had ever heard it before. I dropped my hand before it connected, closing my eyes. I felt rather than saw him walk to my side, his essence encroaching on my own. It grated against me in my agitated state.

His fingers brushed my arms as my tears finally began flowing freely. "I am so sorry, my girl." He whispered the sentiment. Holden was never one for emotions, and his pity had my knees weakening. I opened my eyes, searching for a seat to place my heavy weight upon. Holden clutched my form and guided me across the room.

As we sat, the door creaked open once more, and Shepard stepped into the library. His face was impassive but the sorrow in his eyes as they found me was unmistakable. He crossed the room without saying a word.

"Cillian told you, I presume?" I almost couldn't stand the softness of Holden's tone. It was so unlike him that it grated roughly against my nerves.

I swallowed the lump in my throat and nodded.

"If there's anything we can do during this time—"

"I want to leave." The words startled even me, but as they settled between us, I knew I had meant them.

"Leave?" Holden asked, his face furrowing. I looked at Shepard, praying he would have my back as he always did. No matter what. I watched as he set his jaw but settled in to defend my request.

"Yes. I can't stay here. Not now. Send me somewhere. Give me somewhere to go—something to do—far away from here." I sucked in a deep breath, trying to steady my wobbling voice.

"I don't know if there's anything out there for you," Holden said, still using that too-soft tone with me, as if I were about to break.

"Find something. *Anything.* Send me on duty, or I'll leave on my own." My fist clenched and unclenched before I dropped my head into my palms. "I need to leave this place." That ache in my heart pulsed as Ezra swam in my vision once more, and my mind wandered to that field of wildflowers in the forest. Was he there already? Was his body lost?

I didn't dare look up as Holden remained quiet for a long time. Shepard stood stoically before us, waiting for Holden's decision.

The thought of going home to that empty cottage made me want to die. The thought of Ezra never returning home left a sickening feeling in my heart. The idea of never seeing him again...

"The South." I looked up, hope sparking within me, but not enough to stifle the pain. Holden wasn't looking at me, his eyes distant as a hand rubbed across his jaw. "We've gotten word of a husk found a few years back. Abandoned on the beach. Perhaps whoever made that one knows more about what's going on here." His eyes found mine, a new determination resting in his gaze. "You'll travel there, plant yourself in their midst. Find out anything you can about it. It seemed like an isolated incident, but perhaps we brushed it off too easily. Perhaps they stopped shitting where they ate and chose to dispose of a weaker realm instead. Act as an assassin if you must, but gather what information you can."

My eyes blazed at the prospect. Perhaps he was right. Perhaps Olen would find the North was innocent, and it was, in fact, from the South instead. Or perhaps it was a dead end. Either way, it got me out. It got me away from the pain.

The emptiness.

"You leave tonight."

A finality rested within me now that I had a purpose. Something to do for the greater good as I worked through the shattering ache within me. But still, I watched Shepard stiffen out of my periphery. He made no objections, though, as I nodded my agreement to Holden and walked from the room. It was abrupt, but I needed the distance. If I had the distance, perhaps I could pretend this was all a nightmare.

I felt Shepard following me as I descended the stairs and walked from the front door. But I didn't stop walking until I made it back to my empty cottage.

It was dark inside, and I paused before the gate. Unwilling to go inside just yet.

"You're sure?" Shepard finally asked.

"I have to do something," I breathed.

"But leaving? This is really what you want?" His hand landed on my shoulder, and I turned to face him. "You're making a rash decision."

"I need to find out why, Shep. Why this person is doing this." I tried to swallow, but my throat was too constricted. "If I can find out why—who—maybe Ezra's death won't be in vain." I inhaled before continuing. "I can't do that here. Not when everywhere I look I see his face and feel that crushing loss. He was all I had."

Shepard gave me a look that said I was full of shit. I ignored him and stormed through the gate. I didn't focus on anything within the cottage as I walked to my room. Because Ezra's presence was everywhere here. I could even smell him. It was like he was just in the other room.

Grabbing the first bag I saw, I stuffed in a few changes of clothes—a few personal items. A silhouette leaned against my doorway, but Shepard said nothing as I passed with my back to the window, chewing my bottom lip.

I turned back to my desk, ripping parchment, a quill, and ink from one of the drawers as an afterthought. I scribbled some incoherent words atop the page before tossing the quill onto the wood and turning away.

I refused to read through it, refused to think about it as I walked past Shepard and out the door. Out of the house we went, neither of us speaking as we proceeded to leave the city altogether.

The guards watched us as we left, disappearing into a tree and emerging deep within the forest. Tree by tree, we traveled to the docks. There would be a ship waiting to leave, I was sure. Holden wouldn't have insisted I leave tonight if there wasn't one ready to disembark. It had almost been too easy to persuade him, but I didn't dwell on that, didn't care. It had been his order that had killed my brother. This was the least he could do for me.

I could hear the crashing waves before we even broke through the tree line. My senses picked up on tens of people keeping watch as the ship was finished being loaded. The sand shifted beneath my boots as I set my path on the dock.

The last time I'd spent a considerable amount of time with Ezra was out here, right before Nash lost his sister. Now, I could feel the depth of the pain my friend held.

Holden had robbed me of so much time with my brother over these past few months.

Wood creaked as my heart pounded, my feet beating against the dock. The sound echoed through my skull, drowning out thoughts of Ezra. I was almost there. I was doing this. I would not fail in my mission. Shouts erupted from those aboard the craft, calls that it was almost time to set sail. The salty air stung my nose, pricking my eyes and setting tears running down my face.

"We'll be here waiting, Kaya." Shepard sounded sad, and my throat tightened further as I faced him for the last time. "Come back to us."

It was no longer the salty water making the tears roll from my eyes. I flung my arms around my mentor, nestling my face into his chest. He met my hug in ferocity as I whispered back, "I promise." I didn't acknowledge who that *us* was. I wouldn't think about what I was leaving behind. I couldn't.

We parted, and I didn't look back as I climbed the ramp and boarded the southern trading ship.

I wasn't sure if I had lied to Shepard or not. I wasn't sure if I was simply running away from everything. All I knew was that the moment my feet dropped onto the ship deck, the force inside me settled and calmed.

Even if I would one day regret this decision, I knew it was the right one to make. It was the path I was meant to go on, though I only wished my journey to this moment had been slightly different.

But that urge to venture from this land was strong. Stronger than my contrition over leaving.

A piece of me would stay on this land in my absence, though.

After

Chapter 20

Kaya

The water was unsettled beneath the ship, causing it to sway haphazardly. My stomach lurched. I had never been one for sea travel, and that, combined with the idea of arriving home after so many years, made me uneasy. I had this foreboding sense of doom as the trees on the shoreline slowly crept into view.

Farehail.

I had missed my home; that much was true. I did not, however, want to face everything I had left behind. Everything that I knew was no longer there, waiting for me. I wasn't ready. I wouldn't have come back here if I had any other choice. I would have never come home if it weren't for that force urging me to. I would rather have stayed lost for the rest of my life. I would have rather they ended my life, actually.

Yet, as the ship floated ever closer to the shoreline, my heart began to pound, nearly breaking free from my chest. It wasn't only for fear of what lay ahead but also anticipation.

Six years. I had been gone such a long time. Would things be different? Would I be expected back at my post like nothing had ever happened? Would my cottage still be there, waiting for me? Perhaps someone else had come along and made it their own in the time I'd been gone.

There were so many questions running through my mind. I tried not to dwell on any of them for too long. I tried not to let the guilt plague me. There were so many loose ends I had run away from. I was terrified of seeing those ends once more.

Those domineering trees crept ever closer.

I shut my eyes against the blinding sun, blocking out how it reflected off the glittering sea. The wind whipped my dark hair around my face. The tendrils tickled my skin as I tried to calm my breathing—my racing heart. My grip tightened on the railing as I heard the call, alerting the crew of the oncoming shore. We were about to dock.

This ship would head back to the Southern Kingdom. I would deboard and make my way through the minuscule trading port and into the forest. It would leave me here, alone on this forsaken island.

I wasn't ready.

But I had to. I couldn't be selfish. This wasn't about me. This was for the greater good. Something was coming. I could feel it deep within my bones. I could feel it in the pulsing of the power beneath my flesh. I felt it in the wind that whipped through my hair, the wind that pushed the sails closer and closer to shore.

If I chose to stay on this ship and sail off, everyone I had ever loved would be destroyed.

He would be destroyed.

And for him, I would do just about anything. To keep him safe.

When my boot hit the ramp leading down from the trading ship, a hideous creak sounded and proceeded to follow me as I made my way down and onto the awaiting dock. Goods were already being unloaded courtesy of the Southern Kingdom, which still thought Farehail to be the depleted realm of over a hundred years ago, even after all this time.

Guards littered the dock, inspecting the goods and thanking the merchants from the South. They kept a close eye on those unloading the goods, not allowing anyone to wander off into our territory without notice. I kept my head low, not wanting any of them to recognize me and report my arrival before I could do so myself. I had changed immensely over the years, but not so much on the outside as in.

My stomach was in knots as I passed them by and headed straight toward the forest. I had no doubt that they marked my departure and were following somewhere close behind. The shouts and commands from the ship slowly faded away as the chirping of the birds swept in beneath the canopy.

This forest was home.

A sort of settling washed over me as I breathed in the fresh scent of earth and dirt. The dim light and cool air beneath the trees calmed my senses and eased my aching heart as I crept closer to the pine before me. This was where I was supposed to be. I was sure of it. Though...

A thrum, thrum, thrumming emanated from somewhere deep in the forest. I couldn't necessarily hear the noise. Rather, I could feel it radiating beneath my chest, almost like the forest itself was pulsing. Something about it felt oddly familiar as well. I couldn't quite place it, and the incessant tug that accompanied that feeling made me uneasy.

A twig snapped behind me, but I didn't turn to see who was following. I knew it was someone from the guild tailing me to ensure I wasn't up to anything nefarious in their realm. Eventually, they would realize who I was and dismiss me altogether. Right now, however, they didn't stop me as I slipped inside the tree and disappeared into the awaiting void.

Sunlight pierced my eyes as I came out the other side, miles away from the docks. I was in one of the training yards; that was all I could decipher from where I stood at its edge. I trudged across the expansive opening. It was about noon, so no one was out training. Most of the guild trained in the mornings and finished well before lunch. Everyone was surely at their posts or completing other various jobs.

As I walked the rest of the way to the city, my stomach twisted into knots. Everything I had left behind came crashing down with each step closer to the stone wall I took. My mouth was dry as the towering archway of the west gate came fully into view. I could see the faces of the guards high above me—some familiar, some not. Undoubtedly, they had spotted me the second I emerged from the tree in the training yard and had marked my every move since.

Feeling as though I was weighed down by lead, I had to force my feet to keep their unfaltering pace as I approached the two guards stationed at ground level. One was tall and lanky, the other standing shorter than me. Their faces were bland and impassive, showing no indication that they knew who I was. Or what I was here for.

"Can we assist you with something, miss?" the shorter guard asked. He looked vaguely familiar, though I couldn't place him. Someone must have recognized me, or else none of them would have allowed me to get this close to the city.

"I'm here to see Holden."

Both guards continued to stare at me, no emotions passing over their faces as they assessed me. Their hands were within easy reach of their weapons, always ready for anything. Always.

"Is he expecting you?" The lankier one spoke this time, just as impassively as the first.

"No. I have an open invitation."

"I'm sorry, but we can't just let anyone in."

I ground my teeth before answering, anger and impatience welling up inside me. "Obviously, someone here knows who I am, or I would have been dead long before I reached this gate. So, either let me in *now* or go find Holden so *he* can. And you know as well as I do that if he has to take time out of his busy schedule to deal with something like *this*, he won't be happy in the slightest." I crossed my arms over my chest and tapped my toe against the dirt. I'd stand here all day if I had to, and I would make sure these two idiots knew how much of a mistake it would be for me to do so.

The shorter guard glanced skyward, and I tracked his gaze toward the tower wall. The sun was blinding, so I couldn't make out who stood atop it. Whoever it was must have been the one who recognized me because the guard relinquished a step and motioned for me to enter the city.

I gave him a smug look as I pushed past him and into the mass of people beyond.

Home.

I was home.

My gut wrenched, those feelings of turmoil and desperation I had shoved down all those years ago suddenly resurfacing. I felt like I couldn't do this. I couldn't return to this life like nothing had happened before. I couldn't make everything go back to how it was before Ezra died.

I kept my head high, eyes forward as I wended through the city and toward Holden's manor. He would be my first stop, probably my only stop of the day. I needed to relay the past six years to him. What had happened.

What people were capable of.

I needed to know if they had stopped what was happening here.

Everything seemed fine as I closed in on Holden's place. People were about the city. Guards watched relentlessly. But that's how it had always been here. We were always disciplined with the safety of the island and everything it held.

Luckily, those secrets were still safe with me.

How I had the will and ability to keep those secrets locked away for so long was beyond me. But sometimes, the will of that power within was a force to be reckoned with. Over six years, it fought to keep this land safe.

And for just a moment longer, it would be. But the dangers of this world were still evident and inadmissible.

The large double doors towered in front of me, and the guards at either side seemed wary, but they let me through without an interrogation. Someone from the wall must have sent word of my arrival. Holden would be waiting.

Creaking inward, the doors opened to a dark foyer. It was silent, though I knew more eyes lurked within the shadows. My own eyes darted around me as I made the short trip to Holden's office. An edge settled along my shoulders and down my spine, my body waiting for an attack.

I had to keep telling myself that I was safe here. It would take some getting used to. I hadn't been safe for a long, long time.

I rapped my knuckles on the ornate wood that housed Holden's private study. Shuffling sounded for a moment before the door was flung open, revealing a much older, much grayer Holden.

His eyes landed on me, assessing me. They scanned me from head to toe, and I watched his brow furrow before disbelief replaced the confusion.

"Kaya," he breathed as if he were seeing a ghost. "Kaya." He said my name again, trying to convince himself I was truly before him. Letting out a small breath, he broke into a smile. "I can't lie. I wasn't sure I'd ever see you again."

He took a step back and motioned with one hand for me to enter his office. I could feel his eyes on me as I passed him and sat in the lone chair before the large desk. He took his place behind it, leaning forward and steepling his hands on the desk.

"How are you?" he asked, almost hesitantly.

I licked my lips, then pressed them together as I decided how I wanted to start. My heart began hammering in my chest as the memories rushed forth, each stumbling over the last as they tumbled from the walls I had so carefully crafted around them. To hold them in so that I didn't sink beneath their weight.

"There's so much to say."

I snuck myself back through the city, nothing more than a silhouette in the alleys, a new weight lifted from my shoulders. I wasn't ready for any heartfelt run-ins with long-lost friends, though.

Or worse.

Holden had assured me that my cottage remained my own. Normally, when someone passed away, their lodgings were given to new recruits. But since I was still technically living, he thought it best to keep it available on the off chance I returned home.

Home.

It didn't feel quite as whole as before. But that probably had a lot to do with the fact that there was no more Ezra. My heart ached worse than it had in years. I was too close to my past for comfort right now, and it was about to get worse. Honestly, I wished Holden had given the cottage to someone else. I would have rather stayed elsewhere than in an empty home no longer occupied by my brother.

I slinked around a few people out on a stroll. They didn't even register my presence. I smirked to myself, delighted at my refined skills.

I had brought home so many new tricks.

My breath hitched when the cottage came into view. Unchanged. That was the only thing that came to mind. Time hadn't touched it in my absence.

My eyes darted around as I scurried through the front gate and drew out my key. Holden had given me a spare since mine was long gone. Lost on my journey, never to be returned.

I didn't like the idea of there being a way to access my house out there, but there was nothing I could do about it. Not that anyone who would come across it would know what it went to. But the thought still made me uneasy.

I slipped through the front door, bracing myself for an onslaught of feelings.

Time had, indeed, been kind to this place. There wasn't a thing out of order. There wasn't even a speck of dust. I thought I would be overcome with emotion when I got here, but I didn't feel anything.

Other than relief.

Ezra had existed. It was evident in every inch of the main room. His books stood on shelves, looking as if they had all just been read. His spare boots sat on the floor just beneath where his coat hung on the wall. His favorite chair was still here—empty but welcoming.

He had lived; he had been real. His things still sitting about the cottage gave me a comfort I hadn't felt in so long. Ezra would not be forgotten. Not by me. Not by—

My thoughts stopped as I walked closer to the bookshelf and I swiped my finger across the wood before the row of books. Holding it up to my face for inspection I realized there wasn't a single speck of dirt on it.

I glanced about the room, reassessing.

There wasn't dust anywhere, actually, not on any surface. Not a single spiderweb rested in any of the corners or across the doorframes.

Nothing about this space said that it had been unoccupied for as long as it was. Maybe Holden had it cleaned regularly.

I shrugged it off, heading to my room to take inventory of my things. My brother's door remained closed, but mine was swung in on itself.

Everything within looked just the same as I had left it. Except…

The scribbled note I had left on the desk was now gone like it had never been there to begin with. I almost wondered if that part of my leaving had been nothing but a dream. Those moments after I learned of Ezra's death were dark and foggy—half memories. It was as if I had unwittingly tried to block them out with the pain.

I rifled through my drawers in search of a change of clothes. I hoped to find something that would still fit. Years had passed, and in those years, my body had changed drastically. While I was gone, I wasn't able to train like before. Most of my muscles were gone, withered from lack of use. In their place were softer curves that I wasn't sure would fit in my previous attire.

I grabbed what was once my loosest articles and headed to the bathing room for a long soak. This room, like the others, was immaculately clean. Soaps still lined the tub, which I was grateful for. I wasn't ready to head out into the city to shop for supplies.

I willed a kernel of power forth, coaxing water out of nowhere and filling the tub to the brim. New tricks, indeed. Fire flowed after, heating the water as I chose not to think where these abilities had come from. Who they had come from.

I swallowed hard, then undressed, blinking back the stinging in my eyes. That special piece of power fluttered behind my ribs, suddenly more alive than it had been in years. Perhaps being close to its source gave it a renewed sense of life.

Lowering myself into the bath felt like a blessing. I felt like I had been on that ship for months. In reality, it had been about two weeks, but the lack of proper amenities weighed on me after living in the Southern Kingdom for so long. I had been no better than a prisoner, but at least it had its perks.

I groaned, sinking my head beneath the surface, allowing my body to float. Hair swayed out around me, tickling my skin as the water settled. When my lungs felt like they'd burst from the lack of air, I sat back up. Leaning back, I rested my head on the rim and let my worries leave my body for just a moment.

I headed toward the rise in the middle of the city, Holden's weekly briefing set to take place shortly. He'd expect me there now that I was back on the island. He had already implied that I would take my place back in his ranks.

I was happy to have something to do—happy to be serving someone good and working toward the betterment of our realm.

Our meeting earlier had been hard. Holden was horror-struck when I told him of my time away. And when he told me that nothing had been resolved here...

I almost didn't believe him. Everything in the city seemed like it was back to normal, back to the way it was before the husks started showing up. The fact that no one had been caught was unbelievable. Though, apparently, the husks stopped appearing shortly after I left. There were no more instances, no more deaths.

The person who was inflicting the horrors could have left along with me.

That was unfortunate timing and caused many rumors about who was truly behind it all. One person of interest was me. Another was Ezra. That one hurt.

And another yet was Asher. But I refused to believe it was him. And I knew it hadn't been Ezra just as well as I knew it wasn't myself.

I took the steps two at a time, climbing higher atop the rise. Holden stood at the front, the expanse before me already filled with bodies awaiting information—schedules, duties, whatever else he felt he needed to assign for the week. Sloan stood at his side, her face hard and unmoving as always.

Sweeping my gaze left and right, I noted who still stood before me that I knew, who I hadn't yet met since I had left. My heart stuttered as my eyes landed on Shepard standing off to the side, arms crossed in the back row with a scowl on his face.

Gray had begun to speckle his hair, but other than that, he looked completely unchanged. I sidled up to him as quietly as I could, crossing my arms across my own chest in a mirror image of him.

I didn't speak, simply drank in the feeling of his presence next to me. He had been the closest thing to a father I had ever known. I hadn't realized it at the time, but I knew it in my heart now.

I felt rather than saw when he realized it was me who stood beside him. He jumped, and I almost laughed at the usually unfazed man.

"Ky," he breathed. His hands fell, but then swept me up in a half hug. His head dropped atop mine as he crushed me closer. "When did you get back?"

"Earlier today." I hugged him back, but it didn't last nearly long enough. Shepard gave me a half grin, then resumed his post. But the grin stayed spread across his lips, a new twinkle in his eyes.

"I'm glad you're okay, kid." He glanced around as more people made their way atop the rise. "Have you seen him yet?"

"I met with Holden as soon as I arrived," I answered.

Shep smirked and shot me a sideways glance. "Not who I meant, and you know it."

"Not yet." I felt more unease stir in my gut at the thought of facing Cillian.

As if summoned by my thought, Cillian made his way atop the platform and filed through the rows of people already present. He didn't so much as glance behind him to where Shepard and I were standing as he made his way to the front—a small mercy. If I had to face him at some point, I'd prefer it not to be in front of everyone within the city. But that piece of power that once belonged to him reached out, trying to grasp for him. I reeled it back in, though it writhed against me in protest. Longing pulsed in my soul as well, and I knew that force wanted me to go to him.

"How bad was it?" I asked, not needing to elaborate.

"Bad."

I glanced over at Shepard, but his gaze was on the back of Cillian's head. His face was guarded, so I couldn't read into it any more than he was willing to give.

"But he'll come around with time, I'd say," Shepard added with a glance down at me.

I sighed, unable to say more before Holden started speaking. I checked out, too lost in my own dreadful thoughts to really pay attention to what was being said. Not that Holden hadn't already discussed what was next for me when we met earlier. I was simply there to show face, to be a good, faithful peon.

Go back to how things used to be. That's what he wanted. Just in case old problems should ever arise, he'd kept the alternating schedules for those on the wall, on the docks, and scouts out in the forest. He was taking no chances when it came to the possibility of whoever it was coming back and starting up again.

Holden didn't believe any of us were behind it. He believed that the culprit became uneasy after the incident with Cillian and Ezra, thus fleeing. Coming that close to being caught wasn't worth the risk anymore. I wasn't sure I held the same sentiment.

"How do we know this informant wasn't compromised?" My attention snapped back into the present as Cillian's voice speared through me, a knife to the heart. My jaw tightened at the familiar notes of his voice. It had been so long since I had heard his alluring tone. Emotions and memories began flooding me.

Informant? Were they talking about me? Judging by Shepard's body language, they must have been.

"This member is well-trusted and strong. What they endured proved as much."

"The possibility is there whether you trust them or not," Cillian snapped. Bumps erupted along my skin at the challenge in his voice. I had never known him to speak to Holden in such a manner. What had changed in my absence?

"Do you question my loyalties, Cillian?"

Everyone slowly turned in my direction before I realized it was me who had spoken, my tongue loosened by that power beneath my ribs.

I watched as Cillian's body went tense and still. His head remained forward for a moment while his fists clenched. I could see the tension still knotting in his shoulders as he slowly turned to where I stood rows behind him. The crowd parted slightly as their eyes darted between us.

He faced me halfway, his one good eye swimming with shock and remorse, and... that was hatred in there, too. I couldn't see the set of his mouth beneath the black fabric, and his other eye remained closed, a jagged scar running from above his brow and disappearing beneath his mask. The eye must have been too damaged for use.

I probably could have saved it if I had stayed all those years ago.

I swallowed the guilt, keeping my head high even though I wanted to slither behind Shepard and use him as a shield. I vaguely became aware of people murmuring my name, but I paid them no heed. I couldn't pull my eyes from Cillian even though my heart was cracking in two all over again.

Just to contradict me, my power danced beneath my skin in his presence. I dared not move under his heavy gaze as he stared at me— stared into me—from across the rise, his attention locked on me amidst the crowd of people.

I wondered if he was feeling that turmoil of emotions just as I was. Holden must have dismissed everyone because suddenly, I felt a hand grabbing my shoulder, pulling my focus from Cillian. I was lifted into a hug, and I realized it was Nash excitedly talking in my ear.

"I've missed you so much!" he exclaimed, almost too loudly for how close we were. I wrapped him in my arms and gave him a squeeze before he dropped me and allowed Finn to take his place.

When we parted, the first thing I noticed was how much taller they both had gotten. How much their features had hardened over the years. They looked so much older than before, but it was still them. I could see it in the playfulness that lit Nash's eyes, the softness in Finn's.

I made a quick glance over Finn's shoulder, scanning quickly for Cillian. He was gone.

"Give him time," Shepard whispered into my ear as his hand gave my shoulder a tight squeeze. His body went rigid for a second, his fingers digging into my flesh as he added, "Also, he didn't just lose you and Ezra. Wren's gone too."

I didn't even get a chance to process the new information or the heartache that followed. Shepard stepped from the rise and disappeared, and I was left with my old friends, who were looking at me expectantly.

"What?" I asked, my guard shooting up, my body reeling from the new, sharp pain in my chest.

"We want to hear what happened," Finn surprised me by saying. It had always been Nash without the filter.

"I promise I'll fill you in. What I'm allowed to fill you in with," I said.

"Allowed?" Nash questioned.

"Holden doesn't want me talking about everything. He said it could cause hysteria amongst the people. You know how guards can't keep secrets." I gave them a half smile.

"Do you want to get together for breakfast? Our usual spot," Nash offered, a hint of sadness etched into his features. It was then I noticed the change there. Not within Nash alone but within Finn as well. They seemed closer than before, but not just because of my lack of presence over the years. Closer in a more intimate way. I smiled to myself, knowing they'd finally found something in one another that I'd seen all along.

I blinked back tears of happiness before responding. "I'd like that very much."

Sleeping was going to be easier said than done.

I hadn't slept well for the past six years, but being back in my old home which was empty, would be another trial altogether. It felt so different in here. Vacant. A shell of what it used to be. My power could tell that these walls hadn't occupied life in years, and it unsettled me.

That, and the fact that my nightclothes were too tight; I was forced to sleep in one of my too-big shirts that wasn't actually too big anymore. Even though I was beneath the blankets, I felt exposed.

I really needed to get new clothes tomorrow. Mentally making a list of everything I needed, I stared up at the ceiling in my room. My eyelids wouldn't lower, and my body was on alert, telling me that I was in danger. Though my mind knew I was safe here, I couldn't shake this unsettled feeling in my bones.

I rolled to my side, thinking over my plans for the morning. I'd take my old clothes from the house first thing. That way, when I got back home, I'd have a place to put what would actually fit me. I'd have to get some food as well.

The lock on my window snicked, the sound distinctive and sharp in the otherwise quiet cottage. My heart hammered in my chest, but I ignored the sound of my window almost silently opening. A muffled thud followed, nearly too quiet to hear. But I had gotten quite good at detecting such things.

I waited a few heartbeats before I rolled over and propped myself up on an elbow. "If I'd been asleep, you might have actually snuck up on me."

Cillian's eye didn't sparkle with amusement as I hoped it would. No. He remained with his hands in his pockets, leaning against my chest of drawers. His eye wasn't even on me, but instead gazing at the floor in front of my bed.

My gut wrenched, over six years of regret forcefully crashing into me. "Cillian."

"You left."

Two words had never hurt me so harshly. I didn't answer. Instead, I pushed myself into a sitting position. The movement finally drew his eye to me, and the look he held caused my own eyes to start burning and my throat to tighten.

"I lost him too. And you left." The words dripped like acid from his tongue.

I couldn't speak past the constriction in my throat. Didn't know what to say even if I could. I chewed my bottom lip, biting harder than necessary as I tried to stave off the tears threatening to overflow.

Cillian looked away from me and out the window. His hands left his pockets and clenched into fists. He tucked them under his arms, trying to keep his anger at bay. "I don't even know why I came here," he began, still not looking at me. I was thankful his attention was elsewhere, though, because a tear had slipped from my lashes at this point. "I guess I want answers."

"Holden asked me not to say anything to anyone. At least, not everything," I whispered.

"Where did you go?" His attention was back on me, hard and unflinching.

"South," I bit out, hating how the memory tasted on my tongue.

"You were there the entire time?" he asked, raising that one good eyebrow. The muscles in his face must have been compromised during the attack because his other brow remained unmoving. More guilt lashed its way inside me at the realization.

"Yes." The word was barely audible.

He turned his head away again, crushing his eyelid closed as he did. He was so quiet for so long. I was afraid to move, afraid to breathe for fear of scaring him away. My heart felt like it was about to snap into a million pieces.

"Why didn't you stay away?"

The question did what it was intended to do. My chest ached beyond measure, and I couldn't stop the tears as they cascaded down my cheeks. Cillian pushed off from the chest and stepped back toward the still-open window.

But I couldn't let him leave. Not like this. Not when every fiber of my being screamed at me to touch him—to feel his skin beneath mine, to kiss away the last six years of pain and longing.

I leapt from the bed, my body slamming into his back. My arms clawed their way around his torso, my fingers digging into the muscles on his chest. I buried my face between his shoulder blades, the scent of him stabbing into my senses. I began sobbing, and I hated myself for how weak I sounded.

"Cillian," I pleaded, my voice cracking over his name. I clung harder to him, noting how he had stopped in his tracks to allow me this moment. His heat melted into me, and for the first time since I left this place all those years ago, I felt like I was truly home. I felt it in the curve of his shoulder blades, the texture of his shirt beneath my fingers. I felt it in my very bones and in the way he hesitated. The way I could feel him using every ounce of willpower not to touch me back. I whispered, so softly that if I hadn't been pressed against him, he might not have heard it, "Is it still there?"

His heart pounded beneath his flesh, the thundering escalating and reaching something deep inside of me. I listened intently to the way it quickened as his hand finally covered mine, my fingers still digging into his front. His skin seared mine, and I choked on a sob. The power deep within me fluttered with hope. Cillian's fingers trembled slightly as he whispered, "I've thought about you every day for the last six years."

The words sounded regretful. I sobbed against him, that ache in my chest growing with every breath I sucked in. I had done this to him. I had put him through hell, and here I was, breaking apart over it, as if I had the right.

His hand gripped mine. The pain that lashed through me as he pried my hand from his chest was worse than anything I had endured in my entire life. He said nothing as he stepped away from me and climbed through the open window without a backward glance.

He disappeared into the dark night, and I was left alone.

Hollow.

Chapter 21

Cillian

The pain when she left was one thing. But the pain of her returning home was another thing altogether.

I couldn't breathe.

I should never have gone to see her, either. That accomplished nothing and only reignited the anger I thought I had gotten over. Apparently, I had just buried it deep down inside myself because the second I saw her, I hated her again.

Except, that was far from the truth.

For over six years, I had been living a half life. Part of myself was no longer with me. Both figuratively and literally. She carried a piece of my power with her, and I had her inside me. But her absence was ever present in my soul. No kernel of power could fill the void she had left.

However, it did give me comfort on the hardest of days to know that I had something that belonged to her, and she of me. Some sort of line connecting the two of us. Even though she didn't cherish it as much as I did, apparently.

How she could have left me, I didn't know. After what we had shared, what we had done. We were as good as bound together for the rest of our lives, and that meant something. Or at least, it was supposed to mean something.

Losing Ezra hadn't been easy for anyone. She would have seen that if she had stayed. She might have been a wreck and unable to face it, but so were Wren and me. We could have helped each other through it. Instead, she abandoned me. And then, so did Wren.

I hated myself for the way my heart betrayed the rest of me. I wanted to stay away from her, to punish her for what she had done. But I couldn't.

Even now, she was within my sights, flitting from store to store as she shopped for goods, and, apparently, a new wardrobe, which I understood her reasoning for. She had changed immensely over the past six years. Where before lean muscle covered her body, but now, she was now all curves and valleys.

Get it together, Cillian, I scolded myself. Casually sidestepping someone inspecting fruit from a stand, I kept as far back as possible without losing sight of her. I probably shouldn't have been following her, but I refused to let her disappear again. Yes, she was back, but who knew how long she'd be able to stand living here and facing everything she'd run from before.

Another shop caught her eye, and she was inside before I could blink. I paused, pretending to inspect some baskets an artisan was selling. They were beautiful, actually.

"Are you done following me?"

The hairs on the back of my neck stood on end. I turned to see Kaya standing directly behind me. She must have rushed straight to the back exit of the shop to have snuck up behind me so fast. Her eyes held a bemused glint, but her body was tense. Power surged beneath my flesh, though I wasn't sure if it was hers or mine as I pushed it back down. I looked her up and down just to watch her squirm under my gaze.

She shuffled her weight from foot to foot.

Good.

"Just making sure we have nothing to worry about," I said, if only to make her mad.

"You're kidding me, right?" She raised an eyebrow at me.

I gave her a look that told her I was completely serious, even if I was lying. Her brow furrowed, and I smiled beneath my mask. "One can never be too cautious, Kaya. You have been gone for quite some time. Anything could happen."

"If Holden isn't worried, you shouldn't be either," she huffed indignantly.

"Was Asher with you?" My heart skipped a beat as I asked, not sure if I truly wanted the answer.

Kaya scoffed before rolling her eyes and turning on her heel. I watched her stomp down the road and back toward the direction of her home. Part of me was glad she hadn't answered. Though, another part of me knew it was because he had been.

Asher had left the island a year after Kaya. I had hoped it didn't mean he'd gone in search of her. I couldn't stomach the thought of them being out there together. But in my gut, I knew that was why he had left.

To be with her.

I couldn't even blame him. When Kaya got into someone's head, it was nearly impossible to get the idea of her back out. She had been in my mind every second of every day for the entire time she was gone. And long before that, if I was being truthful with myself. She was still there, ever present in the confines of my most secure thoughts. I couldn't shake her, no matter how hard I tried.

And I had tried so hard.

That force inside of me swirled beneath my ribs as I watched her disappear around a corner. My palm rested along my stomach like I could reach in and crush that power between my fingers.

I wanted to forget her. But I also wanted to run my fingers along every inch of her skin. Down each of those valleys and over those curves, learning the new planes of her body. I wanted her scent on me, to taste her, to wrap myself around her and lose myself completely.

I wasn't following her.

Well, I *was*, but only to be sure she was still herself. Just as I had told her, we couldn't be too careful. A lot could happen in six years. Anything could happen, really. She might not even be Kaya, but someone else's will hidden beneath her beautiful face.

It had been a few days since she had confronted me in the streets, and she knew I watched from the shadows as she went about her days. The irony of it wasn't lost on me. Something Ezra had asked me to do before, I was now doing willingly and for a completely different reason. Mostly.

Currently, she was out to dinner with Nash. I had never seen him as a threat before, but now I wasn't so sure. The way she was glowing beneath his attention had my blood boiling. The ringing of her laugh grated against my ears. She had never laughed around me.

She knew I was here. She had to. That's why she was putting on such a show.

My hand slid across my jaw. I ground my teeth, working the tense muscles free. I hadn't realized I had gone so rigid. I sat in the back of the small shop, my bowl of untouched food before me.

My stomach churned. Unease knotted my gut as my power tried reaching out for Kaya. Again. I couldn't even count how many times I'd had to shove it back down this past week. It wanted me to go to her, but I wasn't ready. I wondered if she had the same thing happening within her. Or if she could compartmentalize that better than I could.

My attention snagged once more on my quarry as they got to their feet. Nash thanked the cook before grabbing Kaya by the hand and walking out into the night. I didn't miss the way his fingers threaded through hers or the way she nudged her shoulder against his. I gave them a few moments of space before doing the same, causally strolling from the shop with my eye scanning for the couple.

I spotted Nash almost immediately, leaning against a wall and smiling at me.

Kaya was nowhere to be seen.

I cursed inwardly. She was avoiding me, but I couldn't blame her. I had offended her when I accused her of being up to no good. In all honestly, I didn't believe that for a second. But I would use any excuse I could get to follow her.

Nash shook his head and walked off, and I swore I could hear him laughing.

"Just talk to her."

I nearly jumped out of my skin. Shepard watched me with an amused expression. I was letting Kaya cloud my focus a little too much if I had let him sneak up on me so easily.

"Mind your own business," I responded.

He huffed an annoyed laugh before continuing, "I remember how out of your mind you were when she left. That doesn't just go away."

"A lot has happened since then."

"Yet nothing has changed. You're still watching her longingly from the shadows while she practically begs for your attention." He took a step down the alley before adding, "And you're still too stubborn for your own good."

I clenched my retort between my teeth before stomping in the opposite direction. My sights were set on Kaya's cottage, and my plan was to check on her before I headed to my own house.

But she wasn't there.

"Shepard, I'm going to have you check the west perimeter. It'll be something easy to get Kaya back into the routine," Holden said. I stood at the back of his office, unsure why I was even there. I was supposed to be on wall duty.

"Do you want us to start on the south side or north?" Shepard asked, his gaze ever steady on Holden. Sloan talked with Lucy and another recruit to the side of the office. Lucy kept sending uneasy glances my way, and I cocked my head to the side in question.

Holden went on, but I was too focused on the silent exchange to hear any of it.

"Cillian will go with you since Nash is on the docks." I started, jumping at the sound of my name. I looked over to where Kaya stood, her back was rigid, shoulders tense. The exact opposite reaction to the last time Holden ordered me to be a part of their cadre all those years ago.

Shepard nodded once and I scowled at them both. Knowing I didn't have a choice once Holden willed something, I internally acquiesced to being stuck with Kaya for days.

We were dismissed and each of us was given an hour to go home and pack for our scouting mission. Nothing would come of it. The island had been silent since Ezra died and Kaya left. But Holden was right; it would be good to get Kaya back into the habit of everything. She really needed to get back into training as well.

Perhaps I would bring up that issue soon. It would be a good excuse to talk to her rather than skulking after her in the shadows. Though, I wasn't sure I was ready to give in to that temptation.

We met outside the city gates, and one by one, we slinked into a tree, disappearing into the void. We were spit out miles from home, surrounded by trees and not much else. The birds swooped high, and critters skittered from the branches at our intrusion.

"Finn and I will go north—you two, head south. When you hit the docks, meet back there," Shepard said, gesturing to a cave cut into the side of a steep slope.

I didn't even try to protest, knowing it would do me no good. Shepard shot me a sheepish grin when Kaya turned to scan the forest behind us. I raised my middle finger to him in response. Finn's teeth gleamed, his eyes crinkling as he smiled and thumped Shepard on the chest before the two headed north.

Kaya whirled on me. "Well, I guess you don't have to follow me now since we're stuck together." I wasn't imagining the acid in her tone.

"Have I done something wrong?" I asked innocently.

"Other than your obvious distrust of me?" She quirked an eyebrow. "Maybe it's the fact that you'll follow me and keep tabs on me, but you won't actually talk to me."

I pressed my lips together, fighting the retort that wanted to rip from my throat. How could she be so mad at me when *she* was the one who left?

She hissed at my lack of response, throwing me the most hateful look she could manage before turning on her heel and marching into the trees. For a second, I felt a little bit bad about everything. About not talking to her. About keeping my distance. But then I thought back to that night—the one where she left. I remembered finding her note and the utter shattering heartbreak that crippled me, even when I didn't think I could feel any more pain after watching my best friend be torn apart in front of me.

I swallowed any bit of remorse I had from the last couple of weeks and followed Kaya deeper into the forest. No. It was her who would have to make amends for her wrongdoings.

She headed in the direction of the shore. It was about half a day's walk from where we currently were, but it would give us both time to cool down.

I wasn't really sure how much longer I could keep this up. Even with my anger still present, I still wanted her. Every fiber of my being was screaming at me to touch her, and I fought that urge as hard as I could. But it was constant, and it was wearing me thin.

I turned thoughts of her over and over in my mind as I watched the sway of her hips in front of me. Her dark hair cascaded down her back just as she had always kept it years ago, though it was much longer now. The sun glinted off each strand, causing them to shine softly. I could almost feel it gliding through my fingers as it had during that night we shared before everything went to shit.

My power danced with that memory. I squeezed my eye shut against the need building beneath the surface. I was weak. When it came to Kaya, I would always be weak.

We walked in silence for hours before I couldn't stand it anymore. Scrounging up every bit of courage I had, I began, "Kaya—"

Her gasp cut me off. A second later, my train of thought shriveled as I watched her dart between two trees and rush toward the shore. Curious about what caught her attention, I jogged forward a few steps.

I halted abruptly when I saw what had her rushing into the water.

A husk lay in the shallows. Terror coursed through me and froze me in place as memories came rushing back. I couldn't move, couldn't breathe as I peered at the figure swaying in the water. I hadn't seen them once since they had torn Ezra to pieces beside me, as I was unable to help him. Save him. That terror seized my heart again as Kaya approached the figure.

It wasn't until she had nearly dragged the body from the water that I realized it was only a man. His body wasn't shriveled and gray, though it was quite ashen. His eyes were closed, his lips nearly blue as Kaya pulled him onto the sand.

Immense strength still lurked beneath her skin, hidden beneath that softness.

Sensing there was no danger, my body unlocked, and I hurried to her side. Kaya's hands danced over the man's skin, searching for wounds she could heal with that beautiful power of hers. Palms landed over his chest, and she squeezed her eyes shut to focus. After too many heartbeats, her stare found mine.

"We need to get him to shelter. He needs heat. *Now.*" The command should have startled me, but the urgency in her eyes was all I could focus on. I leaned forward, scooping the man's soaking body over my shoulder and standing under his weight. My legs protested, but I pushed through the pain as Kaya led me to a tree and into the blackness within.

Chapter 22

Tynan

When I awoke, I knew I was dead.

I had to be. Because the woman hovering above me was too beautiful—too flawless—to be of this world. Her dark skin glowed radiantly in the light of a crackling fire. Black hair dropped over one shoulder, the tresses long and lustrous. If I were to touch them, I knew they would feel softer than the finest silk.

Her copper eyes looked like molten honey. There wasn't a doubt in my mind that her red lips would taste just as sweet as the ripest berry.

All of this told me that I was dead. Well, combined with the fact that I had been near death already when I blacked out due to dehydration, being lost at sea for who knew how long, then drowned in those salty depths during a storm.

I was beginning to regain sensation in my body, though I could feel something hard beneath my back. The heat of some fire was warming my skin. I shivered still, the memory of the cold water lingering.

There was a sharp ringing in my ears as well. So even though I could see the woman's exquisite mouth moving, I couldn't make out just what she was saying. I stared, not comprehending what was happening around me, not really caring, either. I could have spent the rest of eternity staring at this woman's lush lips.

She shook me violently by the shoulders, but still, my ears wouldn't stop ringing. The only thing it accomplished was making my teeth knock together, the feeling singing into something I could only describe as pain.

Pain. Huh. Maybe I wasn't dead after all. Surely, if I were dead, there would be no more pain.

I listened once more to my body, picking out the different sensations skating across my skin. I could still feel the pain from my teeth being knocked together. I could also feel a slight prickling from the heat of the fire. My legs were getting a bit too warm from where they rested next to the flames. I felt how pebbles dug into my back, biting into the hurt there, and I realized I was lying on the hard ground of what appeared to be a cave.

Alive.

The thought had a smile spreading across my lips, and I watched the woman's face turn from shock to concern in a blink. I had made it, though. Against all odds, I was here.

She probably thought that I was mad, insane, that my mind had slipped into something not quite there from the ordeal I had undoubtedly been through.

If only she knew the half of it.

The woman put her hands on my arms. She held me in place as her bright eyes turned a bit hazy. I was confused for a moment, but then I felt it. A rushing sensation that slithered within me. It filled me, and I felt my power purr in its presence.

She was a healer. How fortunate.

She was searching for something else to heal within me. The fact that I was alive right now must have been thanks to her. The concern on her face said it all; my state must have been bad. I wondered just how close to death I had actually come this time.

I opened my mouth to speak, but all that came out was a dusty cough. The woman removed her hands, that power leaching from me with the absence of her touch. She began searching frantically for something behind her. It wasn't until I saw a hand extending an item toward her that I realized the two of us weren't alone.

I dropped my head sideways, taking in the other person within the cave. His back rested against the stone wall, but I couldn't make out much of his face. Half was covered by a black cloth, while the other was scarred immensely.

Not unlike my own, though my scar cut across my face at a different angle than his. The bridge of my nose took the brunt of the impact, whereas his eye seemed to have taken the worst of it.

The woman snagged my attention with a skin of water, and my body surged forward to meet her offering. I gulped greedily when the liquid met with my tongue, unable to stop myself from draining the contents.

Gasping for breath as she pulled the empty skin away, I wiped my mouth with the back of my shaky hand, and her dainty ones dove beneath my back to help me as I tried to sit upright.

I worked my jaw again, praying the dryness was cleared enough for me to speak. "Where?" The question was a gnarled rasp, but the pair understood all the same.

"We found you in the water on our shore." Her voice was a melody that rang inside my chest, the notes clear and precise. Her hand steadied my shoulder as I moved to a sitting position. She sent more waves of the healing calm through our connection as I groaned.

"Where?" I rasped again, this time more forcefully.

I caught the glance she sent her companion but was unable to decipher it. Caution? Uncertainty?

"We might as well tell him. Holden won't be sending him away once he sees." The man regarded me coolly, assessing my intent. What he thought I could do in this state was beyond me. I could barely keep my head level due to exhaustion.

"Farehail." Her response was clipped, hating to give the information away.

I blinked a few times, processing. Farehail. The desolate island to the west of my home. The place was in ruins, though still inhabited. I nodded, the movement sending a bout of dizziness through me. I felt queasy, undoubtedly from all the water I had just consumed.

"We're going to have to take you with us," the man said. It wasn't a suggestion by any means, and I mashed my teeth together at his command. I swallowed my retort and chose to remain silent. I had no other option, and honestly, a tiny, forgotten island was the best place for me to be.

The woman glared at the man before turning back to me. "Can you tell us your name? Where you hail from?" she asked, with more politeness and concern than the one-eyed man used.

I met her copper eyes, my body stilling as I stared into her swimming irises. My throat nearly dried up again as I further assessed her beauty. Her cheeks warmed slightly under my gaze, and I wondered if I was making her uneasy.

"Tynan," I whispered. Tynan. The name that had kept me sane during my journey on the treacherous sea. "North."

Those copper eyes sparked as I stated the latter, and she shot another look over her shoulder at the man. His one eye darkened as they seemed to exchange some silent conversation. For all I knew, they could be doing just that.

"We need to find Shep," she said to him. There must have been more of them elsewhere. I wondered who these people were to her. This man. Holden. Shep. Was she involved with any of them?

What was I thinking? They were probably about to kill me, yet I was worrying about the love life of some woman I didn't even know. She was rather breathtaking, though, so it was hard to help myself. I did love to collect pretty things.

"I'm not leaving you alone with him." There was a finality to the statement, and the one-eyed man scrutinized me further.

"Kill, he can't even sit upright without my help. Do you honestly think he could pull anything while you're gone?" I watched her roll her eyes and tried to stifle a snicker. My amusement must have shown because she offered me a small smile in return. "Besides, if he does, I'll just slit his throat. Problem solved." She tossed a dagger I hadn't know she held into the air, catching it easily a second later.

My smile melted away, but hers grew. There was a feral glint in her eye. One that I recognized. She delighted in scaring me, I realized—that power giving her a thrill. Perhaps she was like me and had once been powerless…

"Ky," the one-eyed man said. It sounded like a plea, but it died on his tongue as she glared at him. Ky. *Ky.* What a beautiful name befitting a remarkable woman.

"Find Shep. We'll need help taking him to Holden."

Who was actually in charge here? The man—Kill? That was ominous— shook his head in reluctant agreement and stomped off in the direction of the exit. Or I assumed it was the exit because his footsteps grew silent, and I could tell that the woman and I were alone.

"Tynan." The sound of my name coming from her lips sent a thrill through me. "How did you end up on our shores?" One eyebrow rose as she studied my face. Her features remained calm—soothing—as she rested a hand across the back of my own, and she watched me as I racked my brain for an answer. She was waiting for me to lie, I realized.

So, I chose to tell her the truth.

"Olen." Her eyes widened with recognition at his name. "You sent him north."

Her dagger was pressing against the skin of my neck before I could say anything more. I hadn't even seen her move before she was nearly atop me, blazing rage consuming her. The blade stung my flesh uncomfortably. I froze, the power inside me going just as still at the threat.

"I mean no harm," I continued, even though I should have known better. My throat was still raw from days without water and nearly drowning. Speaking hurt, and the sound grated on my ears, so I tried to be as direct as possible. And this woman didn't seem to want to listen to any fluff. "He told me everything. Husks."

She pressed harder into me, the searing pain deepening as blood trickled down my neck.

"Want to help," I croaked, splaying my hands wide in surrender and trying as I might to lean away from her blade. She matched my movements inch for inch.

"They've been gone for years," she gritted out. Her eyes remained hard, though I didn't miss the agony that flashed through them.

"Caught?" I asked, knowing she'd understand. This woman was not dim.

Her jaw hardened. She didn't answer.

"It'll happen again. Matter of time. Once they get a taste…" I trailed off as I heard footsteps begin to echo off the stone around us. More than just one set. Three, if I heard correctly. I watched as shadows stopped just out of my sight.

Indeed. Three men, it would seem, judging by their builds. Their features were obscured by the flames of the fire.

"Kaya," one said. His voice was different than the one-eyed man's. Gruffer.

"It appears Tynan here knows our secrets already," she hissed, not daring to take her eyes off me.

Chapter 23

Kaya

We should have killed him.

Why we were bothering to take him to Holden was beyond me. He knew too much, and if, by chance, he got away from us, there was no doubt he would spread the word about our weaknesses to others. We couldn't risk it. Not after the hell I had been through to keep everything as it was.

The only thing that kept my temper in check was the fact that I knew Holden would share my outlook. He knew what had happened while I was gone. He would see the importance of eliminating whoever this man was.

Currently, he had Cillian's mask wrapped around his eyes, so he couldn't see where we escorted him to. With his face covering off, I could see the extent of Cillian's scar for the first time since my return. Not only had the wound taken his eye, but it had marred his mouth as well. The ridge extended to the side of his mouth, pulling his lips down into a constant half frown.

Though it didn't look much different than the Cillian I knew before.

I let out a snort, and all eyes turned to me. I stifled my smile, cheeks going red. "Sorry," I muttered, unable to stop the grin from growing as I looked full-on at Cillian. His brow furrowed, but he didn't ask any questions.

It was wrong to laugh, but if I didn't, I just wanted to sob. The guilt was all-consuming every time I looked at him. I could have saved his eye. I could have saved his mouth. I wondered if he'd let me close enough to see if I could still do anything for him. I could still maybe smooth some of the angry, red ridge from his features and repair the muscles in his lips. I could possibly even be able to assist with his eye because, surely, he was in pain. Even after all this time, there was no way a wound like that would have healed correctly and without problems.

Tynan's steps and breathing were labored as we corralled him through the forest. We could have just taken the nearest tree, but we needed him good and turned around before we got back to the city. We'd done circles already, stepping through trees sporadically so that he didn't know which way was up. But he was laboring hard, so I signaled for Shep to lead us home.

He directed our cadre toward a pine, and I grabbed Tynan by the forearm. His muscles gave within my hold, soft beneath my touch. He was no fighter; that was certain. Now that he was standing, I could see that throughout every inch of his body. He was soft, not hard and defined like the men of Farehail. He'd lived a cozy life in the North, it seemed.

"Kaya." Cillian's voice caught my attention. He glared down at me, eye on where I was connected with the stranger.

"I'll be fine," I stated, though my heart constricted at his obvious concern for my well-being. Perhaps there was still hope, as Shepard said.

He nodded once, then slipped into the tree before me. He was willing to let me have my way but unwilling to give me space.

I could deal with that.

I wasn't sure if this man had any power or not, so I checked my grip on him as I walked into the tree. The last thing I needed was for him to smack his head on the bark if he wasn't gifted. His body had endured enough. I had healed so much after pulling him from the water—his dehydration, fractured bones, a concussion, and the fact that there was enough salt water in his lungs to brine a meal.

Regardless, he'd be let through the tree as long as I held firm.

He followed my lead willingly, though he had no choice when he was blindfolded and surrounded by so many people with blades. As we sank into the bark of the tree, I felt his muscles tighten. We were out the other side before I could give it a second thought. Cillian waited, the wall of the city within view behind him.

"I'm utterly exhausted," Tynan breathed, so only I could hear.

"Almost there, though I don't think you'll be getting much rest with Holden."

I watched his throat bob as he swallowed.

Cillian led the way back to the city. My hand stayed firm on Tynan as I felt Finn and Shepard fall into step behind us. Guiding the stranger through the forest, I wondered who he truly was. He said he wanted to help and that Olen had told him everything. But why would Olen risk it all like that? Either he had been compromised, or he had truly trusted this man.

And what had become of Olen? Holden had told me he'd never returned from the North. There were so many questions simmering within me, but I knew I had to wait for Holden to ask. It wasn't my place.

As we approached, I could see the guards stiffen at what they beheld. We had gone out on a routine scouting mission and had come back with a strange man, blindfolded and guarded. Orders were shouted, and a unit came out to meet us. Cillian talked with them as they each marked our newcomer. After words were exchanged, an escort was formed around us so that we could make it safely through the city and to the manor.

There would be no risk taken in case Tynan was faking, biding his time for a chance to escape. If he made a run for it in the city, he would be swallowed up instantly.

He could commit countless atrocities before we found him.

I was startled by a hand closing around mine. Tynan had clutched onto me, his fingers trembling slightly atop my own.

"I think I'm going to be sick," he whispered almost silently. I knew what he was asking. I should have just ignored him, but the wobble in his voice plucked at a soft spot I still held within me.

I sent my power diving into him, sending cooling waves of calm throughout his body. I could feel his fatigue as my power traveled its course. I could feel utter terror writhing in his gut.

He was afraid to die. Afraid we were taking him to our executioner.

I sent my healing power into the knotted mess, pulling apart threads of dread and knitting them back together with tranquility. My steps didn't falter as I worked, and I could feel Tynan's body relaxing beside me— beneath my touch.

I felt something else as I finished my work inside him. A featherlight touch swirled around my power.

His power.

And just like that, my wariness of him lightened. He had power but had chosen not to try to use it against us. He had caressed my own rather than try to harm it. Or worse. If he had any malintent, this would have been the best opportunity to act on it, as I had learned during my six years away.

We arrived at Holden's and were carted straight to the cellar. My stomach lurched with the memories of the last time I had been down here. I tried not to dwell on the sound of swords tearing through flesh or the otherworldly moans I could still hear in memory.

Guards pulled Tynan from my grasp, shoving him into a lone chair in the middle of the floor. Holden appeared from the shadows, having been waiting for our arrival. A guard must have sent word of our return and the company we brought.

Holden wasted no time; he yanked the fabric from Tynan's eyes. Blinking, those eyes found mine almost immediately.

He regarded me with hesitation, his eyes dancing over my face. They were sage green, light and crisp under the bright rays piercing through the tiny cellar windows. He was scarred, too, though not as maliciously as Cillian. Tynan's scar stretched across the bridge of his nose, cutting his face in half horizontally. The scar was pale, a stark contrast to his umber, healthy skin. It had healed well, though, cared for by someone after whatever had caused it. His black hair was unruly and tousled across his forehead, hungrily consuming the shadows around it.

Though his features were striking, he had a softness to him in more than just his body. He seemed kind. And as we looked at each other, I wondered what the fuss was about.

He was just a man who had been through a distressing misadventure of sorts.

"Talk," Holden commanded. He loomed over Tynan, a hard expression disguising any unease he might have felt. I silently pleaded for Tynan to speak, not wanting Holden to have to pry the information from him forcefully.

"As I told," he began, his gaze clashing with mine again, "Kaya." A slight nod of his head as if he were asking my permission to speak my name. I stared at him, unwavering. "Olen told me about what was happening here. I want to help."

"Where is Olen now?" The question was icy, and I could have sworn the temperature in the cellar lowered. Maybe Finn's power was spiking.

Tynan glanced down, his head hanging slightly. "A lot has happened in my kingdom lately. He didn't make it. I came here to tell you of this and to offer any assistance I could."

Holden swiveled his head in my direction, casting a look over his shoulder. I couldn't be sure, but I guessed he was comparing this story of the North to one I'd told him. I nodded.

"Leave us." I didn't hesitate after Holden's order; I simply turned on my heel to head back up the stairs.

Cillian, on the other hand, voiced his irritation. "You're telling us to leave you alone with this man?" he asked, bewildered. Those around us dared not stay to witness Cillian's further defiance. They scattered, no one lingering more than was necessary. I shuffled my foot impatiently, hoping to catch Cillian's attention before he made matters worse.

"No, Cillian. I'm ordering you out while I finish interrogating him. He may have information that is not yet fit to be released to the public." Though it was dark, I could still see the way a vein pulsed in Cillian's forehead. He didn't like being excluded from something this important. It was out of character for Holden, so I understood Cillian's frustration.

"You know nothing about him. He could be lying." Cillian looked offended, but Holden only looked at me.

A slight shake of my head was all Holden needed for confirmation.

Cillian looked affronted, his eyes darting between us. He knew we were keeping secrets from him as well. He clamped down on his retort and trudged from the cellar, not sparing me a glance as he pushed past me.

Pulling in a breath, I steadied myself for the onslaught that was to come. Holden waited patiently for me to depart before beginning. Sloan took Cillian's place along the wall as I exited the cellar. I didn't miss the way Tynan's eyes found mine before I turned to leave.

The light within the manor was striking compared to the darkness of the cellar. My stomach bottomed out at the idea of what Holden could do in order to get the information he so desired. But if Tynan had been telling the truth, there was nothing to worry about. And Holden and Sloan could take care of themselves.

Cillian stood before the manor doors, a scowl across his face. Hands in his pockets, he waited impatiently for me. Or I assumed he had been waiting for me, as everyone else was long gone save for the guards stationed before the doors.

"What don't I know?"

I closed the few remaining steps between us, coming to a stop a little closer than necessary. The heat of his body sank into me at this distance, and I saw him notice it too. I stared up into his gray eye—swirled with blues near the iris—and watched as it softened slightly. "Believe me, Kill. If I could tell you, I would. But he ordered me—"

"I shouldn't have even asked you again." I could almost feel his resolve as he blinked and looked away, his hard expression diminishing instantly. He knew as well as I did that Holden's orders were law. If he wished it, we were to abide by it.

So, I changed the subject. Bringing up something I'd been so curious about since Shepard had told me. "Cillian, what happened to Wren?" I softened my voice immensely, knowing that I wasn't going to like the answer just as much as he wasn't going to like saying it.

He swallowed and looked away, but I didn't miss the way his eye started to redden, blinking rapidly. His jaw was working over the right words to say. My gut plummeted.

"She, um." His voice had gone raspy. Pausing, he cleared his throat to no avail. "She hanged herself. Not long after."

I slammed my eyes shut as I tried to block out the pain. When they opened again, I noticed how Cillian's hand reached out toward me. My body went weak with the need for him, the need for him to comfort me, but I didn't reach back. It was he who should fully extend that bridge, that forgiveness after what I had done to him. I waited, my heart in a choke hold as his fingers paused midair.

Then they clenched into a fist before dropping back to his side. My heart dropped along with it; the moment was gone.

And so was he.

"He stays," Holden announced the next morning. I sat in his office, Tynan and Sloan both at his side.

"And then there were four," I said, eyeing Tynan warily. I didn't think he was dangerous, but he seemed too at ease at Holden's side. Too... comfortable. Too soon. "I assume he's convinced you of his innocence? His willingness to help?"

"It's true, Olen told him everything. But Tynan here seems to have further insights into the matter." Tynan smiled as Holden spoke his praises.

"Yes. That whoever it was will start up again. Tell me, Tynan. Do you speak from experience?" I didn't hide my undertone of accusation. The night had been long and fretful. I'd tossed and turned and had plenty of time to think about everything I knew of the strange man. Something wasn't quite adding up. He seemed harmless, and I wanted to believe that, but I had met people like him before. I would be more wary this time.

"I've witnessed people who've been... hungry. That hunger doesn't seem to fade. Rather, it grows." His speech was eloquent. It looked like he'd had a much-needed full night's rest as well as a bath. Now that he was dressed in fresh clothes and groomed, I could see just how striking he truly was. Regal, almost.

"Until then, what is he supposed to do?" I asked. "Why am I here?"

"Until then, he'll be learning the land from you." Holden held my gaze. "The two of you are alike. Your stories are similar. So, I think it's best that he learns our ways from you."

I settled back into my chair, crossing my arms over my chest. I couldn't refuse, though everything inside me told me that I should at least try. "Do

I at least get to know the story he told you?" Holden glared down at me. It was worth a shot. "I'm to be his chaperone?"

"You're to be his mentor."

I looked up, expecting to see Holden smiling at me. Instead, his face was serious. "Mentor? To *him*? He must be at least ten years my senior."

Tynan smirked.

"It's not up for debate, Kaya." I took that as my dismissal and sighed. Standing, I lowered my head in a stiff bow before leaving the room. I could feel Tynan as he followed me out. But I wouldn't speak to him. Not where Holden or Sloan could overhear. So, I kept my eyes forward as I left the manor. Wending through the city and out the gates, I kept walking until I hit the closest training yard.

"What's first on the agenda?" Tynan's teeth gleamed as he looked down at me. He looked absolutely wicked. I felt like nothing more than a mouse caught within his den. A viper ready to coil around his prey.

I shook the thought away.

"Training. Because I'm out of shape due to my absence from the island, and you're just out of shape to begin with." I gave him a once-over for emphasis. "Have you ever worked a day in your life?"

A sort of darkness dropped over his features for a second. When I blinked, it was gone. I almost thought I had imagined it. Almost. "I had a different sort of upbringing than you, it would seem."

"Privileged? We have those sorts here as well. Those with money who are exempt from this life." I gestured wildly around me.

"I didn't even realize this place had such amenities. Imagine my surprise when Holden explained Farehail's ruse. And what a perfect ruse it is."

"You realize you'll never be leaving this place, correct? We can't risk our way of life, so you're stuck here." I stepped closer to him.

"It's a good thing I have nowhere else to go," he said. That was sorrow in his voice. I almost felt sorry for him. What had this man been through? How had he gotten that scar?

"Then you understand," I said.

He nodded, and I could see his comprehension clearly. He knew he'd be killed before he left this island.

Without another word, I led Tynan through a light warmup. One of the many warmups Cillian had tortured me with all those years ago. Cillian's eyes were on us as we moved, hidden somewhere in the trees surrounding us. I could feel their weight on me but didn't let on to Tynan that we had an audience.

The less he knew, the better.

Sitting on my bed, I leaned against the wall as I read a book by candlelight. It was late, but my mind wouldn't stop working. Tynan convinced Holden of his need to help far easier than was normal. It made me wonder if Holden didn't already know more than what he would let on. Something was happening again; I just knew it. And apparently, he valued whatever Tynan had told him.

There was a creak, a gust of a breeze, and in popped Cillian through my window.

I flipped the page in my book, not looking up to greet him. The window clicked closed, and the air in my room stilled once more. He was so silent I almost didn't hear him as he crept closer to the bed. But then the mattress dipped beneath his weight, and my book dropped from my grasp.

His back was to me, broad shoulders hunched forward slightly. I knocked my book away and rose onto my knees. I became immensely aware of the fact that my new nightdress fell to midthigh. I tugged on it slightly, trying to hide some of my skin, as I walked on my knees toward him. From behind, I could smell his scent, and the memory of it sent me back to different times in this bed. He made no sound, no movement, as I approached.

Timidly, I touched my fingers to his shoulders. He didn't pull away, so I pressed in slightly, kneading the muscles into submission. He was tense, so I leaned more of my weight into my hands. After a moment, his head lolled back slightly, coming to rest against my collarbone. My heart skipped a beat. Without thinking, I pressed my face into his hair and inhaled deeply, his smell easing a bit of that constant ache in my chest. Our bodies were flush, and I could feel where every inch of us touched. I clenched my thighs together to stifle the tightening I felt between them. His hand reached up and wrapped around my own, stopping the work my fingers were so artfully doing.

Cillian turned slightly while still gripping my hand, dragging me around himself. I half fell onto his lap, his arm cradling my back to keep me from sliding to the floor. His hand clasped around my wrist as he lowered his forehead to press against mine. His one good eye closed, and I raised my free hand to drift my finger across the scar marring his eyelid. He twitched beneath my touch but didn't pull away.

No. He held me tighter, his breath deepening, grounding himself. My power swirled inside me, tickling the inside of my ribs as it reached for him. Coaxing me forward. But still, he didn't close that little bit of distance between us. And I wouldn't—couldn't—until I knew he was ready.

His arms folded around me as he pushed himself further onto the bed. My body followed him where he went, and as he leaned back to rest his head on my pillow, I rested myself right beside him. I heard his shoes as they thumped to the floor. He nestled into the blankets as I pulled one over us. I stroked my fingers across his face, along his scar, from his brow down to his lips as I watched his muscles relax, and he fell into a deep sleep beside me.

I was still stroking his skin when the darkness consumed me soon after.

Chapter 24

Cillian

There was something wrong about this stranger. First of all, how had he managed to wash ashore, and from *where*? Yes, the North. But how did he get here? I hated that Kaya and Holden wouldn't tell me anything. Holden had never kept things from me before. And Kaya...

She was only doing as ordered. But still. There was something important I didn't know, and for some reason, it meant that this *Tynan* was welcome on our island.

Holden only had the best interest of the people in mind, so I knew I should trust him. But something about this man was off.

It might have just been the way he'd been eyeing Kaya that I had a problem with.

Ever since he'd come to, he'd only had eyes for her. It was as if he'd been starving, and she was his last meal. Though, that wasn't far off from the truth. She had basically brought him back from the brink of death.

She should have let him die. He was about to bring a whole list of problems our way; I could just feel it. No, it wasn't just because he looked at her like he wanted to take a bite. It was something deeper. Something I couldn't quite put my finger on. But it was there.

Maybe that's what sent me to Kaya's after his arrival. Fear that something was wrong. That something bad was about to happen to her.

I wasn't sure just what it was, either. What kept pushing me back to her even though I was so angry. So hurt. I wasn't going to be able to stay away. And the way she had caressed me—held me—told me that she wasn't going anywhere either. I could feel it in her touches that she would be patient, that she would give me all the time I needed to work through this. She would be waiting for me on the other side.

And that made me love her all the more.

I left before she awoke, still too cowardly to face her in the light of day. I was half sure she was actually awake when I snuck out her window, but she made no objections. I knew if I stayed, I would never leave her side again, and I wasn't ready to forgive her just yet.

My heart still ached with the memory of her leaving.

Currently, I could see Tynan from where I stood atop the tower. My rotation for guard duty was here, and I wasn't as annoyed by it as I normally was. It gave me a better view of our newfound *friend*.

He stood beside the fountain, watching passersby as they went about their day. I assumed he was waiting for someone because he kept checking over his shoulder and down the busy streets. Perhaps Holden was meeting him, or someone else was coming to keep an eye on him.

Good. It was for the best that someone stayed by his side. Holden might have trusted him enough to let him live here, but we didn't know who this man truly was. Or what he could be up to.

And why had Holden been looking to Kaya when asking Tynan questions? As if Kaya would know if he was telling the truth or not. It didn't make sense, though Kaya told me there were things she wasn't allowed to say.

It made me wonder just what she had lived through while she was away.

Tynan perked up, and so did I. I guessed he saw who he was waiting for, and I leaned casually over the edge to get a better look. There were so many people out that it took me a moment to see who he was looking at.

My anger flared as Kaya closed in on him, a polite smile on her face. His returning smile sent my blood boiling. I could nearly see his teeth gleaming from up here, those fangs ready to sink into her flesh. They exchanged a few words, and she began leading him away.

Holden tasked Kaya with chaperoning him. Yesterday's training session wasn't to be an isolated incident like I'd hoped. I added that to the list of issues I'd be taking up with Holden.

As they walked, so did I. I made my way along the small path, following them as best I could. Others stationed atop the wall looked at me in question, but none commented as I stared angrily down upon the city.

Tynan closed as much space between himself and Kaya as he could without actually touching her. I could still see that stupid grin plastered on his face. If only I could hear what they were saying to each other. Luckily, I could tell just where they were going.

When they were out of sight, I climbed down the ladder. I'd surely get a tongue-lashing for leaving my post, but Holden would get much of the same in return for sticking Kaya with someone who could be a murderer.

The past had proven he didn't care much for her well-being. Allowing her to leave the island on her own was not a smart move. She could have died; our secrets could have been forced from her with no one to help protect her. And his refusal to let me go after her...

I'd never wanted to strike someone so badly as I did at that moment. They were dark days, and I wasn't proud of everything I did during that time in my life.

Mine and Holden's relationship hadn't been the same since.

It was easy to stay hidden behind them since they were too deep in conversation to notice me. They wandered through the city, two people out for a morning stroll. It was nearly impossible to keep my anger at bay. How could she be so trusting of this strange man?

For all we knew, he was the one behind the attacks to begin with. He could have been hiding out this entire time somewhere on the island and feigned his near-death experience just to intrude upon our community.

Whatever he was here for, I was going to figure it out. And I wasn't going to let Kaya get caught up in the process.

I really hated the way he was looking at her.

I followed as closely as I dared as Kaya showed him around the city. It took the entirety of the day with having to stop for a meal at one of the taverns. I watched from outside as Tynan leaned eagerly closer to her as they spoke. When they were finished, I was sure to be nowhere in the vicinity. They continued their exploration until the sun started sinking below the wall.

The wall I was supposed to be atop and was definitely going to get in trouble for abandoning.

They parted ways back at the fountain, and I chose to follow Tynan to see where Holden had him staying. To my surprise, Tynan made his way back to Holden's manor. Maybe Holden wasn't being daft. With them staying at the same place under heavy guard at all hours of the day and night, Tynan couldn't get away with anything.

I left when he was securely inside, not bothering to return to my post. It was a lost cause at this point. I took a step back, turning and—

"You really love watching me, don't you?" Kaya asked, a shadow half hiding her face where she leaned against a building. I detected a hint of amusement in her question, though.

I swallowed my growing yell, but I could see in the way she smiled that she saw how she had startled me. "How have you gotten so sneaky?" I asked, nearly breathless. My heart was pounding in my chest, and I ran a hand over myself to try to steady it.

"New tricks," she teased. Her eyelids dropped slightly as she pushed from the building and sauntered closer. "Making sure I stay safe?" she asked in a sultry tone, batting those lashes at me.

"It's what I've always done best, isn't it?" I mused back with a small smile.

"That is true," she relented. She walked past me, and I fell into step beside her. I had to tuck my hands in my pockets to keep from grabbing hers. Her arm bumped me slightly, and I relished in the feel of her. The impact of her being against me.

"So, he's your problem, is he?"

"It would seem so," she answered. She didn't seem so happy about it. If anything, she seemed conflicted. "I can't tell if he's actually wanting to help or if he's got some secret agenda."

I shot her a glance, glad that she felt uneasy about him as well. And I told myself it wasn't just because of how he looked at her.

"Holden won't tell me what Tynan told him, so I don't know the whole story. But I'm gathering he left the North and was going somewhere for some reason and ended up here. Whether or not this was his intended destination is beyond me."

"But he mentioned Olen," I supplied.

"Yeah, but that doesn't mean they were friends. There's more than one way to get someone to tell you everything." She had a point.

"Well, all we can do is keep an eye on the situation, I guess." I hated that it was our only option, but without Holden on our side, there wasn't anything we could really do. We walked in silence for a while longer before we made it to her cottage. My thoughts swirled, conflicted, as she reached for her gate. I wanted to stop her or to follow her. I wanted to fall to my knees and beg to have her back. And I knew if I did, I would have her.

But at the same time, I couldn't seem to force myself to do it. My stomach was in knots, my power writhing within me and making me feel sick. And my heart... The constriction there was almost unbearable. I had only wanted her for years. I thought of nothing, dreamed of nothing but her since she had left. But now that she was back...

Copper irises gleamed as they scanned over my face. Her mouth settled into a slight frown, but she paused before stepping through that gate. She was waiting for me to say something, to do something.

But I couldn't.

It was like I was frozen in time, frozen in a spiral of self-punishment that I couldn't break out of.

She had left.

Because I had let her brother die.

Swallowing, I took a backward step away from her. Pain shot through me as her expression fell further. Another step away, and her fingers trembled slightly where they rested along the wooden post. Her lip wobbled, but she forced her face into a charade of a smile.

"Good night, Cillian," she managed, though I heard the constriction of her throat as the words were spoken.

"Good night, Kaya," I breathed back before turning away.

Apparently, it took Tynan a week to get the lay of the city. Kaya took him around with her everywhere she went. She showed him each of the training yards, the most popular shops, the meeting places for the guild, as well as every inch of the wall.

Anywhere she went, he followed closely behind. After each day, they would end with a couple of hours of training. They would run, practice their skills—or lack thereof—with swords and daggers, and work on strengthening their muscles. I watched them every step of the way. Each evening, I would be summoned to Holden's office for reprimand, though it was ineffective, to say the least. Holden knew as much but had to at least try to dissuade me.

He wouldn't do much else to me when it came to punishment. I knew it. He knew it. Everyone knew it.

A part of me also thought that he appreciated the second set of eyes on our newcomer as well. No matter how many times he told me that we had nothing to worry about when it came to him, I caught the glint of uncertainty in his eyes as he said it. Maybe I was simply making it up, but it was enough to reassure me.

Kaya was out of shape, I thought as I watched her for the eighth day in a row. Her workouts seemed to be getting easier for her, but she still wasn't as strong as she had been when she'd left. She was weak, yes. But Tynan was something else altogether.

He had absolutely no skill with a blade. And he tired very easily.

Wherever he came from, his life must have been cushy and lavish. To not have to fight for what he wanted, or do anything manual at all, spoke immensely of his entitlement. So even if he did have some ulterior plan, he would be easily overpowered by any of us.

Except maybe Kaya.

They were working on their cooldown, so I felt justified in my leaving. They would be coming back into the city soon, and thus far, I had no cause for alarm. That, combined with the fact that it was midweek, and something in me hedged me to present Kaya with our weekly family dinner.

The idea of it filled me with sorrow, and at the same time, it filled me with jitters. I would miss Ezra for the rest of my life, but I couldn't change the past. And honestly, something in me told me that he would be happy to know that we continued with his little tradition.

I slipped back into the city, heading straight to the market for my supplies. They were easily found, and I even splurged on a loaf of bread that smelled absolutely mouthwatering. Ingredients in hand, I made my way to Kaya's cottage and let myself in with the spare key Ezra had given me all those years before.

I set to work, not wanting to spare a second. I wanted the meal to be ready, the smells wafting into the streets when she arrived.

I made my way around the kitchen with ease, having cooked meals here frequently enough. This place would never become foreign to me. It was more inviting and felt more like home than my own cottage did.

Maybe that was why I couldn't let it sit empty, collecting dust while Kaya was gone. I had come by weekly to wipe down surfaces and keep everything in order. The thought of someone else moving in nearly killed me, and I fought tooth and nail to keep Holden from giving the place away.

I held on to hope that Kaya would return to me one day, though Holden didn't share my feelings. Oftentimes, I found myself wondering if he even wanted her to return or if he was glad she was gone. The idea never made much sense to me, so I chalked it up to my anger with him at the time.

I plunked the chopped vegetables and meat into a pot, lighting the stove with half a thought. My power purred, pleased at being used for such a task.

Another thought, and the candles along the table were lit as well.

The sun was setting quicker these days, the air holding the chill of early autumn. Stew with warm bread would be just the thing for this evening. I smiled, the savory scent just beginning to waft from the pot as it began to boil. While it simmered, I set about tidying the room, wiping down the table, and arranging the candles just so.

Kaya should be home in a matter of minutes, judging by her and Tynan's schedules from the previous days. I removed my mask, folding it neatly and setting it on the entry table.

I knew she liked seeing my entire face, even if the idea of my hideous scar being on display unnerved me. I wondered what she thought when she saw it. Did it remind her of my outright failure? Did it remind her of the fact that Ezra would never come back to her? All because of me.

I suppressed that thought. I didn't want to fall down that hole again, especially not when Kaya would be here—

Now. The gate out front unlatched. I grabbed a spoon from the jar and began ladling the scalding stew into bowls. The steam swirled up, bringing the decadent scent into my nose. My stomach grumbled even as it dipped when the doorknob turned.

I heard her step into the cottage, heard as she halted upon seeing my turned back. I smiled to myself as I grabbed each steaming bowl and turned to face her.

Seeing her was like falling in love with her all over again. Her eyes danced in the candlelight, the copper nearly glowing as a smile graced her lips. She was surprised, I could tell, but also so very happy. I smiled back at her as best I could, feeling that downward tug on the left side of my mouth where the muscles didn't work quite right.

She didn't seem to notice.

"What's all this?" she asked, finally stepping into the room and latching the door behind her. She turned the lock and kicked her shoes off.

"Family dinner," I said quietly as I brought the bowls to the table. The sound of the porcelain connecting with the wood cracked through the silence of the room. I dared another glance at her and caught the way her eyes swam with tears.

But still, she smiled.

"Cillian." I looked up at her again, not daring to breathe. Her lips parted, but she just stared at me for a long time before continuing. "Thank you."

I smiled, then went to collect the bread. She settled herself into one of the chairs and smiled up at me when I returned. I was captivated by her gratitude—her affection. I couldn't seem to look away as I took my own place next to her.

"It smells divine. And I'm starving."

"You've been working hard to build your strength back up. You need a good meal." I sliced off some bread and handed it to her. Her fingers brushed against mine, pausing slightly as she accepted it from me.

She snickered.

"What?" I asked, another smile playing on my lips.

"Do you ever get bored?" I could see nearly all her teeth as her smile widened.

"Bored?"

"With stalking me." She raised an eyebrow. I tried to smother my laugh, pulling my gaze from hers as my cheeks heated. She laughed heartily at my reaction.

"You know me." I smiled, happy about how easy we seemed to fall back into our old routine.

"Do I?"

Her question confused me. When I didn't answer, she elaborated. "You seem different than before. You used to just follow orders without question. That's changed."

I pressed my lips into a thin line, thinking about how to answer. Nothing came to mind that wouldn't make her feel more guilty than I was sure she already felt.

"It isn't necessarily a bad thing," she continued. "It's just different than the Cillian I knew."

"Good, different?" I asked.

She smiled, her eyelashes fluttering lightly as she said, "Yes. Sometimes, following orders without question isn't inherently good. Taking away someone's free will..." She donned a far-off look as her words trailed away.

I nearly fell from my chair when a familiar sensation began tickling against the inside of my mind. Kaya didn't laugh at my reaction; she only became extremely serious as she stared into my soul. That's when I realized what was happening.

Kaya was trying to slide into my mind—the way Ezra used to do.

I opened, albeit cautiously. Uncertain of how she could be doing what she was and unsure of what she wanted to tell me that she couldn't voice aloud.

Her eyes never left mine as information flowed from her and into me. It cascaded around me, tumbling on a current that I couldn't seem to slow. My mind devoured it eagerly. The past six years surged around me in horrifying detail, but I welcomed the tide.

When she finally slowed, I felt like I was going to be sick. She pulled from my mind and just looked at me, waiting for my reaction. My hands rested flat on the table, my body quaking slightly.

"That..." I couldn't form a response. My mind was still processing. Unable to absorb everything fast enough. "Holden knows everything?"

She nodded but then hesitated. "Mostly everything," she whispered.

I nodded, still reeling from the onslaught of horrors I had beheld. I watched Kaya with new perspective, and she watched as I took everything in. She was nervous; I could tell.

"Just give me a minute," I said as gently as I could.

She hesitated briefly, finding the right words. "Forgive me for what I did when I didn't think I'd ever make it back home." I watched as a single tear slipped from her lashes and landed on the table. She wouldn't look at me.

I was shaken, and I could tell that it showed even as my body felt completely numb. I couldn't calm myself, though, and I was trying as hard as I could to control those emotions. Her apology was baffling as well.

"Forgive you for what?" I asked, severely confused. What she had shown me wasn't in any way her fault. She had been confined and at the whim of a madman.

"Asher."

I blinked, then startled myself by laughing hysterically. "You really think I'm going to care about that after everything you just showed me?" My voice was almost shrill.

"Considering what we are, I figured you'd react differently." She sank lower in her chair, wrapping her arms around herself.

"Ky." I paused, waiting for her to look at me. When she did, I said, "We're tethered together. What happened when you thought you were caged there indefinitely is irrelevant. It means nothing." I spoke the words from my heart, willing that saddened look to vanish from her face.

She looked unconvinced, so I reached a hand for her, prying her arm free. I laced our fingers together and gave them a squeeze. "I love you, Kaya."

A dam had broken, and tears streamed from the corners of her eyes. She rose from her chair so that she could wrap herself around me. I pulled her onto my lap and kissed the tears away, the saltiness coating my taste buds. She nestled as close as she could, and I held on for dear life.

"I love you too, Cillian," she said before slamming her lips against my own.

The kiss was brief. The moment I opened my mouth to deepen, gut-wrenching screams rang out from the street. The two of us jumped apart, each landing on our feet in a swift movement. In a blur, we had our shoes on and were racing outside. The night was almost completely upon us, but a faint glow still emanated in the sky. The air had gone chill, though. I grew colder still at what we beheld.

Husks.

At least five of them with sunken eyes and sallow, gray skin walked through the street—if one could call it walking. Each movement was forced and strained, their limbs jerking as they made their way to... where? Everyone had vacated the area, but I could still hear their terrified screams, mixed with the ominous moans of what had once been people.

Kaya snatched her dagger from her waist, breaking into a run straight toward the bodies. I did the same, following her every movement as we closed in on them. Their eyes didn't track us as we began to put them down, though they tried to fight back like they were still sentient. As if they knew they were about to die and were not quite ready yet.

But they shouldn't have had any bit of soul left in them. No. That would have left them once their power had been removed. What was left was just a body, nothing more. There was no explanation for the way they seemed to move with a purpose.

Kaya moved through them, hacking away one after another as if she was used to doing such things. This was a big difference from the girl who couldn't sleep after seeing what remained of one in that cave long ago. She was skilled, her eye and aim never wavering as she sliced into them. Even for being out of shape, she knew just how to take them down.

I guarded her blind spots as she did mine, and together we dealt with the matter effectively. Bodies littered the ground before anyone else arrived. It could have been minutes or hours before guards finally showed up. My breathing was heavy, and I could hear Kaya struggling as well. She looked at me, eyes roving over every inch. Checking for wounds, I realized. I did the same, noting the gore splattered along her arms and even her neck. But none of it was from her.

Holden pushed through the surrounding guards and halted when he saw the mess. Cursing, he began barking orders. Guards collected the husks and all their pieces as quickly as they could, carting them off to wherever Holden wanted them.

He marched over to us, face full of icy rage. "What the hell happened here?" he demanded.

"We heard screams and ran out to find husks walking through the city," Kaya stated, her tone implying that it should have been obvious.

"Both of you?" he asked.

"We were eating dinner," I supplied. He regarded me before turning back to Kaya.

"Were there more?"

"Not that we saw, but that doesn't mean there aren't elsewhere." Kaya scanned the buildings but came up blank. I watched Holden as he assessed the situation.

"We need to comb every inch of the city," he said, more to himself than anything. He turned abruptly, barking out more orders as he marched back the way he came.

It was a long night after that. Kaya and I were recruited to help with the search. We checked the northern section of the city as well as the surrounding land outside of the wall. There was no sign of any more husks. There was no sign of how they got into the city as well. Holden had confirmed they were not any of our own people, at least not those who dwelled within the city limits. They could have come from one of the surrounding villages, though.

Exhausted, I walked Kaya home and bid her a good night. I waited until the lock turned behind her to leave for my own residence. It wasn't a far walk, but it did give me time to reflect on the night's events. What Kaya had told me.

And the convenience of husks showing up right after Tynan arrived.

Chapter 25

Tynan

I heard the screams just as everyone else had but didn't run to help. I knew the limitations of my abilities and knew I would be of no use with whatever it was.

I wasn't at all surprised when word reached me that it had been some of those *creatures* roaming about the city. When Holden found me after the entire debacle, I think it was that lack of surprise that raised his *suspicions*. I couldn't even blame him for his reaction one bit. I was new here, unknown in almost every way to them. I arrived spouting stories that this would happen again, and just over a week after is when the culprit chose to start once more.

It was convenient, especially if this person intended to try to pin these incidents on me. I didn't plan to let that happen, though.

Luckily, I had been sitting quietly in my room after I had finished my training with Kaya. If I wasn't with her, I was holed up in here. I would have been witless to venture off on my own at any point, knowing full well that if something was to arise, it would be pinned on me.

I had never lived anywhere as comfortable as this place, and I wasn't about to risk that stability. I was safe here, at least for the most part. I could earn my living honestly and without fear of being subjected to the whims of others and what was befitting of their desires.

Once Holden confirmed with my watchdog that I hadn't been anywhere other than with Kaya or in the manor under heavy guard, he left me to my devices, which consisted of me reading by firelight.

If I were a nicer person, I would have just told them who was causing all their problems. But it was much more fun to watch them agonize over it. I knew almost instantly who the culprit was. The fact that they couldn't see what was right under their own noses wasn't my fault.

They wouldn't have believed me anyway. What did I know of their land? Their people?

I did, however, know a thing or two about a thing or two.

When Holden finally closed the door to my chambers, I huffed out a small snicker as I turned the page in my tome. This one was on the histories of Farehail. It was quite interesting how far back their lies went. They had rebuilt nearly right after their old queen's demise. I did rather enjoy their fairy tale of that event as well.

Turned to stone—they weren't far off from the truth. Yes, they had been turned to stone, but it was by someone within their own realm. Not the will of the Wildewood, but a power that was no longer prevalent in this day. Or at least not that I had seen in a long, long time.

I'd visited their queen up in the library earlier in the week. It was definitely her, and not just a carved rendering. The statue was far too lifelike. I had studied her features for hours as I combed through the books within the library. It took me far too long to realize why she'd looked so familiar to me.

But then I saw it in the curve of her lips.

I smiled to myself, remembering the way Kaya held her mouth while she was lost in thought. What I wouldn't do to taste her, just once, if it weren't for the shadow that followed her everywhere we went. I had never known someone so codependent as him in my life.

There was definitely a history there. Give it time, though. She would come for me. Just thinking about it brought a smile to my lips.

My finger swirled along the rim of the chalice seated on the side table. I sent my power surging into the liquid, solidifying it into a freezing brick almost instantly. Pulling my finger back, I released my power, watching as the surface became fluid once more.

I was still weak from my stint on the sea, so flexing my abilities like this was tiresome at best. It would take me a while to return them to full strength. Admittedly, my full strength had never been that strong to begin with.

The powerhouse that was this island amazed me. More of its people had power than not. And their abilities were stronger than anything I had seen back home. Something was different about this place. About the strength those who lived here wielded.

I wanted to know more. The more I read, the more enlightened I was. However, it didn't explain anything fully. There was something different, and I vowed to uncover just what it was.

This place had its secrets, and I was beginning to think they ran much deeper than what I'd been told.

Kaya sent word for me to meet her in the training yard at first light. I wasn't sure what she thought she would get out of me at that hour because I was nearly useless even after I'd awakened properly. I hadn't slept well, as I'd stayed up quite late reading about the island.

There she waited between the trees, just a few steps from the cleared space she'd been torturing me in these past few days. She looked rather tired herself. Her purple undereyes reflected a restless night.

"You walk like a prince," Kaya stated when I came closer.

"Do you know a lot of princes, darling?" I gave her my most appealing smile.

She smirked back, skeptical of my diversion. "I've met one or two in my life," she supplied sweetly. "About last night."

I didn't miss the way she eyed me suspiciously. Of course, she thought I was behind it. "You're referring to the husks in the city?"

She nodded but didn't continue, letting me lead the direction of the conversation. Smart girl.

"Holden already questioned me. But as you know, I don't stray from the manor or your side." I hoped she caught the coquettishness of my tone.

"I didn't mean to imply I thought you responsible. I only wanted to know what you thought of the matter."

"Haven't I relayed my thoughts already? That this would continue if the person responsible wasn't stopped." Kaya finally led me to the grassy plain.

"And you think they chose now to act so they could use you as a scapegoat?" Her eyebrow quirked.

"It would seem the most likely motive."

"You've seen something like this before." It wasn't a question, but she wanted my confirmation all the same. She waited, her foot tapping slightly on the dirt.

"I have."

She was quiet for a moment, thinking. "Can I trust you, Tynan?"

The question startled me so much that my breath hitched. I stilled, unsure how to act under her heavy gaze. Behind her was a fallen log. I skirted around her, my sights on the seat before me. When I lowered myself onto the trunk, I rested my elbows on my knees.

"I would very much like for you to trust me." It was the truth. Something about her spoke to some part of me I had never dwelled on before. That force inside me urged me closer to her, both physically and mentally. It was nearly impossible to tamp down that desire, though I tried as hard as I could.

"I know Holden has instructed you not to relay the details, so I won't ask that of you. If you're to be accepted here, you need to keep his trust. But if for any reason I suspect your intentions here aren't honorable as you say, I will not hesitate to enact justice."

She was so exact. So straightforward and outspoken. Not like the women I had known back home, who had been punished for such attributes.

"You remind me of my sister." The remark left my tongue without a thought.

"You have a sister?" she asked, her eyes sparking with interest.

"I did. Once." Though we never got along, I smiled at the memory of her.

"I'm so sorry for your loss." I could hear the sincerity in her tone. Heartache etched her features. "I had a brother. Once." She offered me a sad smile.

My smile deepened. "It's a hard thing to lose one's family, isn't it?" I stretched out my legs and placed my hands behind me. "I had many brothers as well. Some have passed on. Some are still out there."

"I just had the one brother. I never knew my parents either." Kaya plopped onto the log next to me, her hands resting upon her lap.

"My father wasn't a good man. My mother was too demure for him. Most women of my realm were that way. Even my wife—"

"You have a wife?" she asked, her voice raising a few octaves in alarm.

"Yes. And a child on the way. Well, I suppose it would have been born by this point."

"Then why did you leave?" Her tone was almost accusatory.

"That's something I'm not supposed to say. Just know I would have stayed had I the choice." I turned pensive. "I'm not sure if they made it."

"I am so sorry, Tynan. I can't imagine that pain." She sidled closer to me, and my heart rate spiked when her hand landed on my forearm. Of its own volition, my power latched on to her. Because it was still so weak, she didn't seem to notice the invasion. I allowed that force to explore her inner depths, all while she remained unaware. Her finger trailed along my skin, circling a path through the hair growing there. I wasn't sure if she was aware she was doing it, but all the same, I watched as taut bumps speckled beneath her touch.

"I try not to dwell on what I cannot change," I said as my power continued its search. Our eyes connected, her copper irises softening immensely as she found something within my own. Perhaps there was, in fact, sorrow, there that she saw. I willed the feelings to show, willed her not to notice my onslaught.

It worked.

She remained intent on whatever she saw in my eyes, and I poured my focus into her innermost depths. And when I found what I was looking for, I latched on to it, sending my will into it. *Acknowledge me. See what I'm showing you. Trust me.*

I watched as Kaya blinked a few times. Her grip remained steady on me, though. With reddening cheeks, she flashed me a shy smile. I returned it, lowering my head just slightly closer to hers. I didn't miss the way her eyes tracked to my lips for a fraction of a moment.

My smile widened. Though she would never admit it, I knew she watched me when she thought I wasn't looking. Perhaps I was making something out of almost nothing, but even if it was just a scrap, there was something between us.

"We should get to work. If something is indeed about to happen, we need to be ready to stop it." Her hand dropped from my arm as she stood and headed out into the clearing, effectively breaking our small connection. I smothered any lingering smile I had and followed after.

Minding one's own business was hard when that person was constantly being trailed. I couldn't step into the trees to relieve myself without feeling the overbearing weight of an eye upon my back.

This boy either had attachment issues, or he wasn't as easily fooled as everyone else. I couldn't blame him either. If his intuition was that good, then he was a smart boy indeed.

I only wondered if he saw through my façade that easily or if he saw the way I'd set my sights on *her*.

Just as I couldn't blame him, he couldn't blame me for wanting her. She was perfection personified. And if what I'd gleaned from those histories was correct... Well. I wouldn't say there was a lot more to her than met the eye. If only these people could see it.

One of them had; that was certain. And it was only a matter of time before they came for her—for her ability.

Luckily, I had gotten here first.

I fastened my pants, rolling my neck to work out the kinks from my early morning training with Kaya. Stepping further into the forest, I called over my shoulder to my shadow. "A moment of peace would do me wonders. I'm sure you could use the break as well."

A soft thud sounded behind me, the impact of boots as Cillian dropped from one of the many trees. I turned, catching the annoyance in his one good eye as I flashed a rueful grin.

"Enjoying the show, are we?" I asked.

He didn't deign to respond. Chuckling to myself, I continued deeper into the forest. I hadn't done much exploring on my own, and I greatly wanted to get my bearings on this new land. If this was to be my forever home, I needed to get heavily acquainted with the terrain and atmosphere.

Cillian was no longer trying to hide as he followed me on my journey. We didn't speak for a long while as I meandered through the trees and took in everything this land had to offer. It would undoubtedly take weeks for me to travel the entirety of the place, but I was in no rush.

"What's your intent here?"

The question put me on edge. I stopped walking so that I could face him head-on. His hands were tucked in his pockets; his brow furrowed as he awaited my response.

"Well, to make a new life, of course."

"What does that new life look like?"

It was an effort to keep my face open and inviting. I did not like this boy. "Quiet." I leveled a look at him before I turned on my heel.

He snorted, and I ground my jaw in response. He was a pest—a tiny, insignificant insect. I would not let him get under my skin.

I continued, ignoring the intrusion as he followed my every move. There were so many caves on this land that it was almost alarming. It made me wonder just what might have been buried beneath the surface of this place, what other secrets this island might have held.

The sun was sinking ever faster as I kept up my search. It wasn't until near dusk that I happened upon the field of wildflowers.

Their burial ground.

The expanse was impressive. Even with the oncoming autumn, the flowers held true. An undeniable sign of strong power within not only the people of this land but within the land itself.

I heard the faltering footfalls of the boy behind me.

"Does this place make you uncomfortable, Cillian?" I asked caustically.

He didn't respond for long enough that it piqued my interest. When I faced him, his eye was solely on the flowers before us. Curious indeed.

He cleared his throat, and it looked like it took effort for him to meet my gaze. "I haven't been here since…"

His voice trailed off as his eye once again landed on the graves around us.

"I'm surmising that someone you cared deeply for is out here."

His eye tracked back to mine. His arms crossed over his chest, and I got the feeling that it was to comfort some sort of ache within him.

"Kaya's brother was killed over six years ago. I buried what was left of his body just over there." His head nodded in the direction of a large pine tree.

"And you're telling me this because?"

"If you're going to be spending time with her, you should know some things about her." He stepped closer to me, his scowl heavy. I stood my ground, unwavering. "That death nearly broke her. I've never seen her in so much pain."

"We've all suffered loss, haven't we?"

"Yes. Ezra was my friend, and I failed him. I failed Kaya." He was towering over me, so close that I could feel the heat of his body. Feel the weight of his eye on me. "I won't let anything like that happen again."

He watched for my reaction, but I gave him none. "What is it you think I'm going to do here?" I asked innocently.

He wasn't fooled. His lips curled into a smile as he looked down at me. "I'm not sure, but know I'll be watching your every move." His hands dropped from his chest as he took a step back. His eye didn't leave my face as he walked backward, step by step, before disappearing between the trees and into the surrounding blackness.

The weight of his eye still weighed on me as I made my way back into the city.

Chapter 26

Kaya

I couldn't make up my mind. One minute, I held utter distrust for Tynan. The next, I found nothing alarming within him. I wasn't sure if he was simply a man who was down on his luck or if he was someone to be feared.

The idea didn't sit well with me. After everything, I prided myself on being able to spot a person's innermost identity—their truest self.

But Tynan was something else altogether.

And I didn't miss the way his eyes lingered on me when he thought I wasn't looking. When I noticed, I wanted to reach out a hand and slap him. However, at the same time, I was utterly flattered by it.

That was another thing that completely unsettled me about him. I had never let anyone's scrutiny affect me in that way. Other than Cillian's. But Cillian looking at me in that way was completely different.

Wasn't it?

I hated that I was even questioning myself at this point. Cillian had finally kissed me the other night. It was a step in the right direction since coming home. Something I had been yearning for. Yet it was being clouded by Tynan worming his way beneath my skin. The fact that he was making me even second-guess myself pissed me off to no end. I didn't endure what I'd endured to be set back into the past.

But I did know one thing for sure. He wasn't behind the mess we were in. It had started long before he'd washed up here. Yes, the attacks had conveniently started again. But all of that could be easily explained.

And that force in me told me that he had been telling the truth. That it wasn't him, and he wanted to help. How he'd help us, I wasn't sure. But if Holden was correct when he said we'd experienced similar things, Tynan could be a valuable asset.

If he'd experienced a power-hungry tyrant as well, maybe he could spot the culprit. See the signs.

He was undoubtedly still hiding something, though.

It was an issue for another time. Someone in our realm wanted unending power. With this power, they could rule over us without contest. Without anyone to stand in their way, they'd be able to take anything and everything from us. They would destroy our home. It was a disgrace.

As a girl, early into my life within the guild, I had felt a pulling within me. Not unlike that pull I felt toward Cillian. But this was different. It wasn't leading me to another person. It was leading me to *them*—a pulling toward power.

I'd ventured into the forest, unbeknownst to those around me. No one paid me much attention when I was so young and so small. I'd slipped into a tree, following that urge and heeding that demand. I didn't know what it meant back then. And it was lucky someone intercepted me when they did, for I was about to break our land's most sacred law.

No one was to touch the tree. *The* tree. The original entity from which all of our lands were said to have come from. Our powers were gifted from the source, from its life force.

It was said that the forest was sentient, able to force its will upon us all. We bent to its desires, even if we didn't realize what was happening ourselves.

I hadn't felt that pull since I was a young girl.

And then I'd landed back on the island after years away.

It grew each day I was back and was getting harder and harder to ignore. I'd nearly forgotten about that childhood excursion until I'd made it back to this land. The memory hit me with a pang in my stomach, and the feeling of having experienced it before was so overwhelming. I wondered if the person responsible for the husks had that same feeling. Or something similar.

Perhaps I should give in to it, I thought as the water in my tub began to cool. I sent out a surge of heat from that fire inside me, blushing as I thought of Cillian and when he bestowed it upon me. The water warmed around me, the scent of lavender swelling up with the newfound steam. I sent the nagging thoughts swirling away with it.

Readjusting to life in Farehail wasn't easy. I found myself wanting to revert back to my naïve ways, wanting to reclaim my innocence from before. But I knew in my heart I wouldn't be allowed that reprieve. I wouldn't be allowed a quiet life with Cillian. Something truly was coming— was here already—and I was caught in the middle of figuring out what it was.

Sighing, I heaved my heavy limbs from the water. The air inside the bathing room was chilled, but I didn't bother wrapping myself in a towel. I let the water drip from my skin, still standing in the bath as the water slowly drained. All my energy had been siphoned from me all at once. I was beyond tired.

When the water was gone, and my skin was mostly dry, I stepped from the basin and wrung out my hair. It was late and I'd had a long day. My bed was calling my name, so I hurried to my room for some warmth and rest. My skin was still slightly damp, and the nightgown clung to me, water from my hair dripping trails down the back.

A light tapping sounded, and I looked toward the window, expecting to see Cillian.

Instead, Tynan stood just outside. It took me a moment to collect myself and realize he was gesturing for me to meet him at the door. I didn't dwell on what he might have seen as I stepped from the room to unlatch the front lock. I was too confused as to why he was there, to begin with.

Tynan stepped around from the side of my cottage, his form not quite filling the doorframe, though that didn't make his presence any less commanding. In his hand, he held a small bundle of wildflowers. I cast him a questioning look. He was waiting expectantly. Patiently. He wanted me to invite him in, I realized.

I took a step back, allowing him access. A slight bow of his head and quirk of his lips was the only gratitude he gave me. The chill from the autumn night wafted in, sending a shudder down my spine as I closed the door behind him.

I hoped Cillian wasn't watching from somewhere in the shadows. He would be absolutely livid not only with Tynan but with me for allowing him into my home. Alone.

Honestly, I didn't know why I did.

Tynan walked to the middle of the living space. He paused, then made a show of spinning in place, inspecting every nook and cranny of my home.

"Why are you here?" I asked, unable to keep the edge from my voice.

"I brought you these," he said. His hand extended the bouquet toward me.

"Why?" I made no move to accept the offering.

"I ran into Cillian in the forest the other day. He graciously directed me to where your brother was laid to rest. I thought you might like these from atop his grave."

Silence, both inside and outside of my body, that was all I was capable of as I looked at the flowers. My brother. Ezra. These were a piece of him. I hadn't had the chance to ask Cillian about his burial and hadn't wanted to seek it out just yet.

"Thank you." I wasn't sure if Tynan heard the whisper as he gave no acknowledgment. I stepped closer, grasping the stems. Our hands brushed as he handed the flowers off to me. "Thank you," I said again, my voice sounding slightly raw.

"Of course. As I said before, it's hard losing those you love." His voice was quiet, reminiscent. "The pain never heals. It just becomes easier to manage with time."

I didn't miss the way his index finger traced mine as he finally relinquished the flowers. I tried to stave off the blush but instead became uncomfortably aware of my attire. My silky nightdress did nothing to hide my body, breasts peaked from the night's chill. Tynan was aware of that fact as well. I slipped past him, still feeling the heat of his gaze as I stepped into the kitchen in search of a vase. Procuring one, I filled it with water with half a thought. Tynan watched my little trick with a hint of smugness. I sat the vase on the counter.

"I thought you were a healer." It wasn't a question, only an observation.

"I was forced to learn some new tricks during my… stay in the South."

"Is that so?" he asked with a hint of amusement. "From what I know, our powers only manifest in one way. Unless…" He didn't continue, and I didn't offer him an explanation. He knew as well as I that Holden had forbade me from doing as much.

"I won't tell," he said, his voice conspiratorial. But not unkindly so.

"I shouldn't have done that in front of you."

"Then why did you?"

I paused, deliberating. "I'm not sure." I felt as if I wasn't completely in control when I was around him. I didn't like it.

He closed in on me, his eyes darkening just a fraction. I felt my power squirm in his presence, but I couldn't tell if it was uneasy or... intrigued.

"My guess is that you were in the South against your will." He stepped closer, and I made a move to back away.

"Not initially." My voice sounded faint, too breathy.

"And you saw horrible things," he breathed. "Things you can't... unsee. I've seen those things too, Ky." He purred my name as he leaned above me. His sage eyes speared me through; the lashes rimming them fluttered partially closed. His hand reached out, so slowly. My attention snagged there, my body unable to move while I waited to see what he would do with it. Flexing his fingers, he inched closer and closer to my waist.

I was barely breathing. I couldn't think straight as I watched that hand make contact with my body. It was warm, the touch light as he gripped my side, just below my ribs. A shiver crept up from where he touched me, the expanse of my skin pulling into taut bumps beneath my nightgown. I was wedged between him and the counter, nowhere to run even if I wanted to. I wasn't sure I did.

He dipped his head lower, his breath assaulting my face as he said, "I know what this person is capable of." His face lowered bit by bit. My eyes flicked closed; my mouth parted as he hovered over me.

But then he pulled away, straightening his clothes and taking a step back. I blinked a few times, questioning what had gotten into me, wondering why I had allowed him to have that sort of effect on me. I didn't stop him as he headed for the front door.

"Can you help me find out who it is?" I asked, only if to cover up how flustered he'd made me.

He smiled across the room at me as he reached for the handle of the front door. "I'll do everything in my power to help you bring them to justice." He hesitated, his smile faltering slightly as he watched me.

Uneasy under the weight of his watchful eyes, I crossed my arms over my chest, waiting.

"Good night, darling," he said, then disappeared through the door and into the dark night beyond.

A shaky sigh loosened from somewhere deep within me. What was happening to me? Power hummed beneath my ribs, the feeling foreign and mystifying. I could still see the bumps that littered the lengths of my arms and could feel them along my legs. My body felt strange.

Alive.

I glanced behind me once more, admiring the flowers that were resting on the counter. Before I went to bed, I double-checked that my locks were secure and blew out all the candles.

Lying down, I stared blankly at the ceiling. My eyes wouldn't close. My mind wouldn't stop. I just kept replaying the interaction I had with Tynan, how he had leaned in as if he was about to kiss me—how I had almost let him.

Luckily, Cillian didn't show up after Tynan left. I wasn't sure how I'd explain the exchange we had. I wasn't even certain if I knew what really had happened.

Surely, I would have never allowed him to kiss me. I was certain that if he had truly tried, I would have shoved him aside and given him a proper tongue-lashing. Though, he didn't know the history I shared with Cillian. He didn't know what we meant to each other. He thought I was free for the taking, I guessed, so I couldn't entirely blame him for trying.

I had done the same once and pursued what I wanted relentlessly.

I tried not to think about Tynan and Cillian and whatever mess I was in as I compiled a list of possible culprits. My desk was littered with parchment, and ink marred the surface with near-incoherent scribbles and scratches. Alas, I was getting nowhere. If I was being honest, I had nearly nothing to go on. Other than the fact that I knew those in positions of power often craved *more* power. Both Asher and Cillian were revered for their fire abilities, but I didn't even bother putting them on any of my lists. There was Lucy with her ability to influence, but she was pure of heart, so it was unlikely to be her behind the husks. Holden and Sloan were the heads of our city, the ones trying the hardest to rid us of this problem, so they were out as well.

That left very few names on my list. Perhaps one of the guards who was tired of their low-ranking job? Maybe someone who had been taken from their family because of their powers and were bitter about our way of life. I wasn't quite sure if any of the names I'd come up with had anything to do with it, but I had compiled evidence along with it. I'd have to shadow them to find out more about their day-to-day lives. Slowly, I would cross them off or be led to the truth. It was just a matter of time before this person slipped up. I would be waiting.

I had little doubt that the person at fault would eventually be brought to justice. How that would take place, I wasn't sure. Part of me hoped it was by someone else's hand than my own. Maybe Tynan would prove himself useful in that regard.

I crumpled the paper I had been using to tally up what little I knew. Because really, I knew little. Holden had kept everything from us before, and then I had left. While I was gone, the person was dormant. Until I'd returned...

Surely that was a coincidence.

Tap, tap, snick.

The window directly before me began swinging inward, startling me from my internal spiral. Cillian stood just outside the cottage, a bemused look on his face.

"What are you doing?" he asked as I tossed the parchment ball onto the floor.

"Oh, you know. Trying to save our land."

"Is that right?" He quirked an eyebrow, then hopped through the window frame. I scrambled backward, giving him additional space to fling himself into the room safely.

"Why don't you just use the front door? Don't you have a key?" I was pretty sure he had a spare that Ezra gifted to him long ago.

"Yes. But I much prefer this method of entry. Straight to the point." He winked at me—actually *winked* at me. I wasn't sure if I'd ever know Cillian to be so… playful.

I smiled broadly at him, my heart warming at his apparent acceptance of my return. I met him as he righted himself. His arms swept around me, pulling me into an embrace as his head dipped to touch my own. I couldn't keep the smile from stretching further along my lips as his breath tickled my face. I nestled closer, clinging to him.

"So, did you solve the mystery, then?" he breathed onto the top of my head.

"Sadly, no. I have nothing to go on. Do you have any ideas for me?" Cillian pulled back slightly to study my face.

"Well, the only thing I know that you don't is what your brother thought."

"Ezra thought he knew who was behind it?" My brow scrunched as I pondered this. Ezra had mentioned nothing to me about who he thought was behind these atrocities. Yet I wasn't surprised he had confided in Cillian.

"I guess I should say who *I* thought that he thought it was. He never actually voiced it, simply heavily implied."

I was thoroughly confused now. Apparently, Cillian could see as much because he elaborated further.

"He said he wanted to be sure before he came forward with his theory. But he indicated to me that he knew who it was."

"Okay, are you going to tell me what he thought or not?" I asked. I'd broken from his arms and moved back a step.

He winced before saying, "Asher."

The laugh that boomed from me was so genuine and surprising that I ended up laughing more because of it. Cillian studied me, a slight smile of his own on his face. "He seriously thought it was Asher?" I wheezed.

"Well, you have to admit that Asher didn't really have a good reputation."

"But he isn't even here anymore."

"Could he have followed you back?" he asked, his voice growing somber.

"No. He stayed. He was happy serving his new king." I left no room for argument. My best friend, Asher, wouldn't trade what he had built for himself there to come back to this place. Not when everyone here thought the worst of him. As apparently my own brother even had.

"Then I have nothing for you to go on either."

"It was really that quiet while I was gone?"

"As a ghost." Cillian turned about the room, his face turning contemplative as I mulled over what I had missed during those years. "It was eerie, actually. The second you were gone, it was like nothing had even happened. The husks stopped appearing, and everyone here just forgot about it altogether."

His hand skimmed across his jaw, his mask resting around his neck. I drank him in. I didn't realize I was staring until he shot me a questioning look.

"Does it hurt?" I asked before I let my cowardice win.

"Does what hurt?"

"The scar."

I watched as his eye bounced over my face, weighing his next words very carefully. "Sometimes it... twinges." I watched his jaw tighten over the word. He was lying to me, trying to protect my feelings.

"Can I see if I can do anything to ease the *twinges*?" I asked, almost silently.

"Kaya, if you feel guilty—"

"Please, Kill." Before he could protest, I was before him, reaching my hands toward his face. His eye closed, and he nodded once, taking a step back to sit on the chair I had vacated moments ago. His chest rose slowly as he drew in a deep breath. I felt myself doing the same as I slowly inched my fingers across the skin of his face.

I trailed my hand along his slightly stubbled jaw; the rough patches of new growth there scratched the pads of my fingers slightly. I paused, delving my power into the hurt there. My eyes fluttered closed as I focused on the inner workings of the scar. I could feel that downward tug on his muscles, forever twisting his lips into a slight frown. The wound felt hard, unmoving against my efforts. Surrounding that hardness was something prickly and needlelike. I sent my power in that direction instead. There, it made quick work. It smoothed the barbed edges into something more even and smooth.

From that point, I worked my way toward Cillian's eye. I traced both my fingers and my power up the ridge of his scar. When I reached his lid, I swept my pad over his lashes. My power sank down deep. It took everything in me not to gasp, not to cry out at what I felt beneath the surface.

His eye was completely gone. The tangling web of nerves left over was a muddled mess of agony. I could feel the excruciating ache almost like it was my own wound. The pain pulsed in waves, some spiking higher than others, but each one was incessant. I sent calming ripples of power into that tangle, focusing on dulling the ache while I tried to work through the mess beneath the surface.

I didn't know how long we stayed like that, Cillian unmoving beneath my touch, me rigid with my power so entangled within him that I couldn't differentiate my body from his. His pain was a puzzle that I refused to give up on. With each thread I unwove and redirected, I could feel that stabbing becoming less and less.

It would never be entirely painless.

I tried to swallow down the shame and regret that knowledge left, twisting in my gut. It wasn't until Cillian's finger wrapped around mine that I finally pulled my power free of him.

I looked down into his face. He peered up at me in wonder.

"Did it help?" I asked, unable to raise my voice above a whisper.

Cillian pulled my hands lower, dragging the rest of me down with them. His lips met mine, and the feel of them was soft and comforting. He moved them languidly over me, his tongue flicking out to taste me as I kissed him back. I opened for him, drinking him in as he explored my mouth.

I supposed my power had worked for him. I smiled, kissing him fiercely in return as he pulled me so that I was seated atop him. I crushed him between my arms, deepening our kiss as my need for him grew in strength. I wanted him so completely that the feeling almost consumed me entirely.

But his kisses began to slow, our pace along with it. His hand gently pushed against me, though he didn't stop kissing me. I got the message well enough.

He wasn't ready to take this any further. And I couldn't blame him for that.

When we finally broke apart, he was smiling. I noted how the side of his mouth was still downturned, but maybe not as much as it had been. I could see the dimple on his other cheek, though, and almost cried out in joy.

"Thank you," he breathed into my mouth, kissing me one last time before slipping me from his lap. He stood with me, scooping me into another embrace. "I didn't realize how much it still hurt me until you took all that pain away."

"I'm sorry I didn't stay to fix it. When it happened."

His face fell a fraction before he said, "Kaya, I don't blame you for how you reacted. I wish you hadn't left me. But I understand why you didn't want to stay here."

"I didn't want to leave you." I knew my words didn't make sense, and I cringed as I said them.

He didn't contradict me, though; he only nodded his head, understanding. "I should get going," he said, and my heart sank. I didn't want him to leave. I didn't want him to be keeping this bit of distance between us still. But I couldn't tell him as much. I couldn't force him into anything he wasn't ready for. And he obviously wasn't ready for this.

"I'll walk you to the front door," I said, and nudged his side. He chuckled but followed me from the room.

It wasn't until it was too late that I remembered the flowers.

Cillian halted almost instantly once he noticed them. He stiffened, and I wondered if he knew exactly where they had come from. But how could he?

"Did you pick those?" he asked, but something in me suspected that he knew the truth. Either way, I couldn't lie to him. Not when I was trying my hardest to win him back.

"They were a gift," I said, not wanting to give everything away, not wanting to have to admit to the truth and the injustice of it.

He turned. Slowly. So slowly, in fact, I thought for a moment that time was standing still. My stomach plummeted with every second that passed until he finally faced me.

"From?" he asked, his voice like ice. A stark contrast to the fiery power lurking beneath his surface.

As if summoned by my own thought, candles lining the room flickered into flames one at a time.

I swallowed and hoped he didn't see how guilty I felt. "Tynan dropped by earlier." My voice was weak. There was no way he didn't notice the slight wobble in it, either.

"Why was Tynan here? Or was it just to ply you with flowers?" He was definitely irritated. I could almost taste his annoyance as he choked out Tynan's name.

"To offer his help in finding out who our assailant is."

"And you turned him down." It wasn't a question. Cillian watched me with piercing attention. I squirmed. His eyes narrowed. "Tell me you turned him down, Kaya."

"Well." I couldn't form the words. But I didn't need to. Cillian's face dropped in utter disbelief before I even opened my mouth.

"This guy is bad news, I can feel it." He ran a hand through his hair. "I hate you being around him already. I don't want you spending any more time than necessary with him." The agitation in his voice grew as he spoke.

"If Holden trusts him, why shouldn't we?" I asked, pleading with him. "He's been through some of the stuff I have. Who better to help me—"

"Why do you think *you* need to be the one to figure this out? That way of thinking got your brother killed." Cillian was inches from my face now. He was furious.

"I feel like I'm the only one who can," I said, my voice quivering slightly. "I feel like something is telling me that it *has* to be me."

Cillian shook his head and turned his back to me. Once more, he stared at the flowers. I could almost see waves of frustration leaking from him.

I couldn't imagine how he'd react if I told him what Tynan had tried to do. No. I couldn't do that, at least not right now. It wasn't the right time. Not when he was so worked up already.

"I just need to see what he knows. His insight could help me figure everything out. And if it's useless information, what is it going to hurt?" I asked.

Cillian's shoulders rose and fell in tandem with the sound of his breathing. As he calmed, so did the flames atop the candles. His anger was ebbing, and I released a silent sigh of relief.

"You need to be careful, Ky. I know you won't listen when I tell you it's a bad idea." He turned to face me again. His head hung a little lower as he continued. "If I can't stop you, let me help you."

The smile that slowly spread across my lips was the most genuine one I'd ever given.

Chapter 27

Cillian

Would have bet my life that those flowers had come from Ezra's grave. The idea of that odious man atop my best friend's resting place sent my muscles locking up. I wanted to kill him.

Not only for defacing Ezra's grave but also for bringing such a gift to Kaya. I should have been the one to present her with his flowers. I wasn't sure if Tynan understood what that meant or if his homeland had the same customs as ours, but he had beat me to it.

The slight was intentional, meant to get under my skin. He was pissed that I'd been following him. That wasn't the entire reason, though. He wanted Kaya. And somehow, he knew that she was already mine.

I wondered if we were that obvious, thinking back to Shepard and Nash after Kaya's return. They had all been aware of our… spark. I wasn't sure if they realized how deep that connection went. I would hazard to guess that they could assume well enough.

So maybe Tynan wasn't interested in Kaya at all. Maybe this was simply another ploy to irritate me.

It was working.

I hated it. I hated how stubborn Kaya was even more. But that was how she'd always been, so I wasn't surprised when she showed reluctance toward staying away from Tynan. I knew that the harder I fought, the harder she would cling to the idea that he might be able to help.

He might actually have been able to, though I preferred that he didn't.

Tynan and Kaya were sitting on the dock together while I hid in the tree line. I knew that she knew I was there, but there was no point in going out to greet them. She would get more information from him alone than with me lurking about. And ultimately, that was the goal. Dissect every bit of information he had about his similar situation and apply it to ours.

Kaya was a smart woman and didn't need me holding her hand. Even though I knew this was true, I stayed poised and at the ready. At even the slightest hint of distress, I wouldn't hesitate to rush onto the dock and whisk her away.

Kaya's laugh reached my ears from even this distance, and I was glad she couldn't see the effect it had on me. What could he have been saying to her that was so damn funny? They were supposed to be discussing power siphoning and death, not soaking up the sun and chatting about their passions.

I wished I could hear better from my vantage point. I strained my eye as well as my ears, watching for anything amiss.

Though I couldn't hear well from this distance, I could see just fine. And I didn't miss the way Tynan trailed his finger down the side of Kaya's hand where it rested against the dock. Nor did I miss the faint smattering of red as it crept up her neck.

She pulled her hand away from his touch, and I let go of my breath. I was reading too much into this. He could try all he wanted, but Kaya wasn't going to fall for it.

I took a step back, not wanting to witness anymore. It was working me up too much, and that was exactly what Tynan wanted. I wasn't going to allow him that win. Turning away from the pair was harder than I thought it would be, but I managed it.

Sunken eyes in sallow skin stared back at me as I faced the forest. The figure stood a mere ten feet away, eyes unseeing. Body still. Cold dread washed over me, freezing me in place as I stared into the empty eyes of a husk.

I wasn't breathing, but then I was breathing too fast. My hand fumbled for my daggers, fingers slipping over the clasps holding them in place. But still, the husk didn't move.

Well, it swayed slightly but made no move to advance on me.

I choked on a gasp as I tried to regain control. I wasn't inherently in danger, not with it frozen in place as it was. Reason was winning out, and I steadied my hands. I lifted an arm, waving my hand back and forth in front of the figure's face as my other poised to strike should it make a move.

Nothing.

I had caught it off guard. It seemed to have been searching for someone else, but had found me instead. And it had no interest in me whatsoever.

I'd never known a husk not to go after someone living that stood before it. I made an easy target, with my attention solely focused on Kaya and Tynan. How long had it been standing behind me while my back was turned?

I sidestepped, hoping my jarring movement might snap at its attention. Its focus remained forward.

Not on me, I realized. But on the two figures sitting on the dock. Now that I was out of its viewpoint, it began moving, its limbs breaking free with jerking motions, a sickening moan emitting from its throat.

I stalled, hanging back just to be sure of its target. I began trailing it once it broke from the tree line and onto the beach. It didn't stray from its intended path as it purposefully stepped onto the dock.

The creaking of the wood jarred both Kaya and Tynan. They leapt to their feet, eyes widening as they looked between me and the husk.

I didn't miss the fear Tynan so carefully tried to hide as he looked at the creature. Or as he looked at me. As if—

"Cillian, what's going on?" It was Kaya who asked the question. She slowly drew her blade as the husk closed in on them.

"It was behind me in the forest, but made no move to attack me. I followed it out here. To you." I had to nearly yell over its moans. The husk picked up its pace, seeing its prey was within reach.

Kaya. It wanted Kaya.

But she was too skilled. With one swing of her arm, her dagger was embedded into the skull of the husk. It crumpled to the ground at her feet.

"You just let it come after her?" Tynan accused. I refused to give him the satisfaction of a reaction.

"I had to see what it was after since it made no move against me." I leveled a glance at Kaya. "Who."

"Why would it come after me? *How* could it come after me? It's not like they can control themselves." She toed the carcass at her feet.

"Actually..." Tynan gazed at the shrunken body on the ground. His brow was furrowed. "Hmm."

"What do you know?" I demanded. Kaya shot me a look that said, *be nice.*

"Back home, the person who did this to our people could somehow push their own will into the bodies once they were... drained." He looked at Kaya, who waited patiently for him to continue. "They could essentially force them into doing their bidding. For example, killing someone for them, as this one seemed to be trying to do." He looked at me then, expecting me to contradict him.

"Similar to Lucy's ability." Kaya's eyes met mine as she said it. Was she accusing Lucy of being behind this? She looked away before I could ask her. It wasn't the time nor place for that anyway.

"There's someone here with the ability to command others?" Tynan asked. He sounded a little too intrigued for my liking. Kaya didn't seem to notice.

"Yes. One."

"Then perhaps we have our culprit."

"I wouldn't make any rash conclusions," I interjected. Kaya eyed me suspiciously. "What would Lucy have to gain? Kaya, you know her too. All of this would be so out of character for her."

"Cillian isn't wrong. Plus, Holden would have seen an uptick in ability." Tynan looked at her then, utterly bewildered. She mirrored his look and asked, "Did Holden not tell you his power?"

"No, he did not. Enlighten me if you would."

"He can sense the powers of others and how they manifest. How powerful they are. So, if anyone could find the culprit, it would be him. And he hasn't sensed any change in those around us," Kaya explained.

"I see," Tynan said. He rested his chin between his thumb and forefinger, lost in thought. I found his pensive reaction rather odd.

"Holden could have always missed something. Or maybe she's using her powers against him," Kaya suggested.

My gut clenched. I didn't like Kaya accusing Lucy. Lucy had been... Well. She had been a good friend to me when Kaya was gone—a very good friend. Kaya didn't know that, of course, but I couldn't help but feel like it was an attack against me.

"We need to be sure before we say anything to him about it. The last thing we want is for someone innocent to be killed because of pure speculation." Tynan surprised me by being completely levelheaded about the situation.

My appreciation was short-lived when I caught the knowing look he sent my way.

How was the man so observant?

Kaya was reluctant to listen to either of us, though. She gained a hard look as she acquiesced. Choosing not to press the issue further, she crouched low to get a better look at the body lying on the dock. She flipped it over and assessed their facial features thoroughly.

"I've seen this one before. I think he was one of ours." She gestured for me to have a look.

I crouched lower, recognizing them now that my fear had worn off. His skin was sunken, but I could still see some of his defining features beneath the gray-washed tone. "Greyson," I breathed. I'd only known him in passing, mainly from when he'd ratted Kaya and Asher out to Ezra some years ago.

"That's what I thought," She nodded absently.

"Is that abnormal?" Tynan asked.

"Most of them have been people we didn't know. Either not of our land or not within the guild. It is rare to have it be one of our own targeted." Kaya stepped over Greyson's sunken form and marched up the dock. She headed for the tree line, but Tynan and I made no move to follow. We eyed each other warily instead, silently waiting for Kaya to return from wherever she was heading.

I couldn't hold my tongue when I noticed him smirking at me. "What?" I demanded.

"Lucy?" he asked suggestively.

I couldn't control the burning that stung my face but was thankful for the mask hiding most of my exposed skin. "That's none of your concern."

"But I would guess it would concern our darling Ky." He gave me a toothy grin, his face contorting into something snakelike.

"*Kaya* is also none of your concern. And I would appreciate it if you would back the *hell* off." I was before him before I realized I had moved, my hand instinctively reaching for my dagger.

His eyes danced with amusement as he flicked them down to where my hand rested upon my blade. "Do you plan on hurting me, *boy*?" It was almost a snarl.

"I'm not sure yet," I admitted.

"I think that would be a poor decision on your part." His words were clipped.

The knocking of three sets of boots against the dock had us splitting apart, moments from drawing blood.

"Back up," Holden commanded. The two of us obliged, making room for Holden as he crouched over the husk.

"Why does it always seem to be you two when something like this happens?" Sloan asked as she went to join Holden. She cast a threatening look between me and Kaya, then landed her gaze upon Tynan.

I chose not to respond to the slight.

"They've been showing up around them?" Tynan asked, startling us all.

"It's a new development," Kaya offered. "When they were in the city, it was right outside my cottage. And now this one." She paused before asking, "Have those been the only two occurrences since I came back?"

"It would seem that way," said Sloan. Holden remained silent beside her as he studied the corpse. What he was looking for, I wasn't sure. Perhaps some telltale sign, some calling card left behind? It was hard to say because then he stood, signaled for some guards to collect the body, and disappeared without another word to any of us.

Sloan followed shortly after, and I didn't miss the sneer she sent toward Tynan. Maybe she sensed something just like I did.

"Well, Kaya, would you like to assist me in keeping watch over Lucy?" Tynan's words sent my blood boiling, but before I could protest Kaya spoke.

"So you think she might be the one?" Kaya asked, completely ignoring me.

"I think she might have reason to send these creatures after you both." Tynan smiled at me but didn't elaborate more.

"You aren't going to tell me why, are you?" She shot me a look, but the question was for Tynan.

"I don't want to make any assumptions or spread falsities without knowing anything for sure." A simple shrug of the shoulder, and he, too, sauntered off down the dock. Kaya watched him leave until he was out of sight.

"Are you going to mention your little side quest to Holden?" I asked, trying to keep the uneasiness from my voice.

"Not yet. As Tynan said, we shouldn't spread any falsities." She rolled her neck, then stretched out her arms. "We need to get some evidence before we act."

Kaya skirted past me, making quick work of the length of the dock. I watched as her boots slipped through the sandy beach. It wasn't until I couldn't see her anymore that I moved from my place.

I wasn't sure which aspect scared me more. Us trailing Lucy and her discovering that Kaya suspected her.

Or Kaya finding out about my relationship with her.

Chapter 28

Tynan

The best part about agreeing to assist Kaya with hunting down the culprit was that I got to spend even more time with her. Not only did we spend our days together, but our reconnaissance of Lucy had us together well into the nights.

It didn't even bother me that Cillian lurked somewhere in the dark. He was far enough away not to be that big of a problem.

Kaya and I sat on the roof of a busy tavern, waiting for Lucy to make her appearance. This was the second night we'd watched her as she visited the establishment. She was no stranger to the place, it would seem. Everyone greeted her by name, and the steward knew just what she wanted, thrusting it into her hand the second she got settled.

She stayed for hours as she drank, talked, and participated in many strange drinking games. I'd never seen something so... relaxed as this place. I was almost envious of the lives these people lived.

But then I remembered this place wasn't much different than the one I had recently escaped.

Tonight, she was in extra high spirits, which meant Kaya and I would be sitting here a while.

Cillian was stationed farther away with a good view of Lucy's cottage. If, by chance, she evaded the two of us, Cillian would be able to see her coming. Kaya wasn't going to give up on this manhunt until she found out who was behind the creatures, who had caused her brother's death.

I couldn't blame her in the slightest. I, too, would want justice. I had never lost anyone I'd cared about as deeply as she did her brother, but I could imagine the feeling well enough. I'd lost people, yes. But their relationships ran deeper than any I'd had. And I wanted that justice for her. I wanted her to gain that peace in knowing the truth—the why of everything.

She would get that answer soon enough.

The wind picked up, jostling her dark waves over her shoulder. We were sitting close enough that her loose ends wrapped haphazardly around me and tickled my face. I laughed softly and brushed them away, collecting the pieces in my fist and returning them over her shoulder. Even though it was dark, I didn't miss the shy smile she tried to hide.

"What do you think we're going to see by following her?" I asked quietly.

Kaya didn't speak initially, her eyes dancing over the stragglers along the street below us. "I don't know, really. Maybe she'll sneak out somewhere. Maybe take someone home with her. Or we could be wasting our time completely."

After a moment's debate, I decided that if I was going to tell her the truth, now would be the time. "Do you really think it's her? Or are you suspicious because of her and Cillian's relationship?"

I felt her stiffen beside me, and I tried not to let any bit of my satisfaction come to the surface.

"What relationship?" she asked.

"Oh, I thought you knew." I feigned my surprise.

"How could *you* know? You just got here." She'd become almost defensive.

"Well, I don't actually *know*. But I've noticed the way he looks at her. And when you mentioned her being a suspect on the dock, he clammed up quickly."

"So that means they're together?" She sounded like she wasn't convinced.

"Maybe they aren't right now, but they have some sort of history." I folded my arms behind my head and lay back against the roof. I decided to settle in, seeing as it was going to be a long night.

Kaya was quiet for a long while. I wasn't sure how much time had passed, but I could feel her silently stewing beside me.

"Do you know about us, then?"

Startled by the sudden noise, I sat up. Her arms were crossed around her legs, her eyes staring blankly in the direction of Cillian. "That you have some sort of history together?"

She nodded, not daring to take her eyes from the black abyss before us.

"Yes. I could tell from that first moment in the cave. But things are rather." I searched for the right word. "Tense between you two."

She looked at me then. Or I guessed she was looking at me. I couldn't really make out her eyes in this darkness. Clouds blocked out the only light from the stars. "Things have been different since I came home. I arrived not long before you washed up, actually."

"Why did you leave?" I had a pretty good guess, but I wanted to hear her story.

"Because Ezra died, and I couldn't face what had happened."

"You loved him dearly." I dared to loop an arm over her shoulders. She didn't brush me off.

"I did. But it wasn't just that." Again, she became silent. I could sense she was debating how much she wanted to tell me. "Part of me blamed Cillian. I hated myself for it because it wasn't his fault. But some awful part of me hated him for letting my brother die."

I felt her forcing her breathing to remain even, but I knew tears dripped down her cheeks. I could almost smell the saltiness of them. My power swirled within me, straining to get closer to her.

I felt my heart rate quicken, confused by the sudden change in the force inside me. It had never reacted in this manner, and it was quite unsettling. But I allowed it what it wanted, sneaking that bit of power through our connection and into her. I encouraged it to be undetectable as it slipped past her defenses.

Again, she didn't seem to notice my intrusion.

"Finding somewhere to place blame is a normal part of grieving. You were angry that he died, and you needed somewhere to direct that anger. Cillian was the logical choice at the time." I slid closer to her, drawing my arm tighter around her shoulders. My fingers stroked along the arm of her jacket. "Don't beat yourself up about it, darling."

I nearly stopped breathing when her head dropped onto my shoulder. My power delighted in her proximity. It took everything in me not to tilt my head toward hers and plant my lips upon her skin.

A slight thumping from behind kept me from acting on those impulses. I drew my power slowly from Kaya so that she wouldn't become aware that it had been inside her at all. Her head left my shoulder almost immediately as that thumping loudened.

"Did you not see her leave?" Cillian asked by way of greeting.

Kaya stood so that she was facing him. "We got to talking, and she must have slipped past. Did you see anything?" Kaya was good at compartmentalizing her emotions. She gave no indication that she knew of Cillian's little secret.

I smiled to myself, knowing she was going to bide her time until the right moment arose to spring it on him.

"Nope. She came straight home."

"Was anyone with her?" I asked, ever helpful.

"Yes. One of the guards." Even I could hear Cillian swallow uncomfortably from where I stood.

Kaya snorted, and I couldn't stop the laugh that choked from me.

"Well, Cillian. I think you were right. I'm pretty sure she isn't who we're looking for," Kaya said. She lowered herself from the roof, using the rough sides of the building to climb her way to the ground. I followed, though not as gracefully as she. Cillian dropped to the ground a heartbeat later.

"What now?" he asked.

Kaya let out an exasperated sigh. The noises she made were music to my ears. I could listen to her antics for the rest of my life and die a happy man. There was just something about her that made her... Well. Perfect.

Apparently, my power sensed it as well. It was restless in her presence since the moment I laid eyes on her. At first, I thought it was a response to her beauty, then because of my suspicions about her. Both of which were true. But now, I was beginning to think it was something else entirely.

"Have you given much thought to Holden and Sloan?" I asked, trying to regain my focus on the task at hand.

"They're our leaders. The ones who've been trying to stop this since the start," Cillian said angrily.

I didn't look at him, which I knew just made him angrier. Instead, my eyes stayed pinned on Kaya. Hesitantly, she met my gaze. I simply quirked an eyebrow, knowing she would understand my meaning. *Who usually craves power?*

Her lids lowered, and I wondered if she'd actually heard my question. Could she... Certainly not. She was a healer, and yes, she could manipulate water. But another ability?

"You can't be serious," Cillian said, exasperated. "Kaya, don't tell me you're going to listen to him." He'd closed in on her, leveling himself so that she was forced to look at him.

"We can't rule it out, Kill," she said, and I could tell she regretted having to admit it to him.

"I can't be a part of that. If he finds out—"

"Then you can sit out from now on. Surely you have other duties you've been neglecting," I offered. If looks could kill, I'd be dead. Cillian wasn't remotely happy about being put aside, but if he was unwilling to trail their precious leaders, then this wasn't the right job for him.

"Cillian, I understand. Don't feel obligated to follow my decision blindly." Kaya placed a reassuring hand on his shoulder. He softened beneath her touch as if it were the tether keeping him alive.

"Perhaps we should call it a night. Emotions are high. We can think more about it after we rest," I said. Kaya smiled sweetly at me. Offering her a slight bow, I turned on my heel and disappeared down the alley. I didn't look back as I turned the corner, knowing that Kaya and Cillian still stood there, talking quietly together.

Ultimately, it didn't matter. Kaya would heed my advice.

And Cillian's honor wouldn't allow him to go against the order of things.

Sleeping in the manor was the best place for me to watch Holden and Sloan. They both lived within its wall, though on separate wings. But I had been learning their patterns since the first night I had stayed here.

I knew when and where they took their meals, when they held meetings, and when they usually went to sleep. Hell. I even knew when they went to relieve themselves.

It was easy to relay all this information to Kaya, as well as the gaps of time that I couldn't account for. Sure, they could have been dealing with their duties. But they could also have been completing other transgressions. It didn't take long for a person to siphon another's power.

That would be up to Kaya to decide—to uncover. I was just along for the journey. It had started out as a game. But now, I genuinely thought she needed to do this on her own. She needed to discover the truth on her own. This was her journey, and I was simply here to witness it.

Those gaps in time were what intrigued her the most. Because of them, we'd spent the last week together trailing the two wherever they went. Some days, we would follow Sloan, while others, it was Holden we shadowed.

I'd seen only glimpses of Cillian, the boy too afraid to step a toe out of line. I wasn't upset about his lack of presence one bit, though I knew it weighed on Kaya. It was evident in the way she held herself and in her stiffness when he confronted her during our off time.

She had left him early this morning. I was aware of this simply because of her sour mood when we met by the fountain—that and the fact that I had been watching her from afar. Honestly, I had been no better than the boy himself.

She'd been quiet most of the day.

"It has to be one of them, doesn't it?" she asked.

"That seems to be how these instances work," I offered noncommittally. She shot me a sideways glance.

"What if it isn't?"

"Then we haven't gained nor lost anything. We start over. Start checking elsewhere." I nestled my back against the trunk of a tree, crossing one leg over the other.

"I just want this to be over." Her head tilted to the evening sky, her eyes fluttering closed as a light, chilly breeze brushed through her hair. Her black waves danced behind her, and I admired the way each strand shimmered beneath the setting sun. Then the scent of her hit me. She smelled of lavender soap as if she'd just stepped out of the bath.

"You don't find this all exciting?" I asked her. Apparently, it was the wrong question to ask because she shot me a disgusted look.

"My brother is dead. Because of whoever this power-hungry mongrel is. No, it's not exciting." She flopped back into the grass and closed her eyes against the waning sunshine. "I just want to be at peace again. Like I was when I was young. Naïve." It was a whimsical wish. One that I hoped dearly she would see to fruition.

"One day it will be over, Ky. Then we can put this behind us and move on." I tried to keep any hint of hope out of my voice. The last thing I wanted was to unsettle her with my own wishes for the future.

Our future.

A flash of red had me flipping onto my hands and knees, the movement jarring Kaya from her meditation. She rolled into a crouched position, scanning the forest as I was.

A scratching at the back of my head had me looking over my shoulder. Nothing was there. I felt it again, realizing something was trying to get *in*. Kaya watched me expectantly, senses still trained on the surrounding forest.

I opened my mind, knowing it would be her voice that floated between the cracks of those carefully crafted walls I'd placed decades ago.

Show me what you saw, she demanded in my mind. I obliged, too shocked to refuse even if I wanted to. Without warning, she was on her feet and racing into the forest before us. Numbly, I hefted myself up and stumbled after her.

I couldn't keep up. She was out of sight before I'd made it ten feet. I strained my ears, listening intently. A snap of twigs far in the distance had me pivoting and careening into the darkening forest.

We were heading deeper into the trees. In the direction of the burial ground, if I wasn't mistaken. What an odd place to be led.

My breath was wheezing out in giant puffs, my chest aching from the strain of running. Just when I thought my lungs would burst, I broke through the tree line and stumbled into a field of wildflowers.

Off in the distance, I could see two shadowy figures racing toward something out of sight. Kaya's hair flowed behind her, easily identifiable even in the oncoming blackness of night.

Cursing, I started up my pace once more. My side was in stitches, but I silently thanked Kaya. If she hadn't been working with me these past few weeks, I wouldn't have made it even this far.

I felt Cillian next to me before I saw him.

"Where is she?" he demanded. I couldn't breathe, let alone speak. I nodded my head in her direction, and before I could blink, he'd passed me, leaving me in the dust.

With three figures in front of me, I could easily see where it was we were heading. It seemed to be an enormous tree in the center of the field. It was so out of place, a lone entity towering over the graves of their people, keeping watch over them even after death.

But before that figure at the front of our procession could reach the tree, they were thrown to the ground beneath the force of Kaya's lunge. Screeching met my ears long before I closed in on them.

Cillian reached them first, but I wasn't as far behind as I expected. Bodies flailed in a tangled mess amidst the flowers, and Cillian tried to insert himself into the fight. Kaya barely let him reach a hand between them before she pulled her dagger and held the tip against Sloan's throat.

"Explain," Kaya hissed with such vehemence that even I flinched internally. The tip of her blade dug deeper with every second Sloan chose not to defend herself. A small bead of crimson trickled beneath the metal, and I watched the bobbing of Sloan's throat as she swallowed her nerves.

Still, the woman beneath Kaya's wrath said nothing.

"Cillian, get Holden. *Now.*" Cillian didn't hesitate like I thought he would. Instead, he turned around and raced back across the field, disappearing into the first tree he came into contact with. I wondered to myself why he didn't just slip inside the giant tree right before us. A question for another time, I supposed.

Sloan's eyes stared vacantly at Kaya, trying with all her might to hold in the truth—to keep her vicious reasonings a secret for a moment longer. When her eyes found mine, I offered her a smug smile.

"You can tell me, or you can let Holden pry it out of you. Your choice." Kaya slipped her second dagger from her belt, readying that one above Sloan's prostrate form.

Sloan mashed her lips tighter together in defiance.

A heartbeat later, the frantic voices of Cillian, Holden, and others breached the night around us. They sounded hurried and distressed as they quickly came to where the three of us were locked in this stalemate.

"What's the meaning of this?" Holden barked at Kaya.

Kaya didn't so much as flinch, refused to take her eyes from Sloan's writhing form as she said between gritted teeth, "She was heading toward the tree."

I looked up at the tree before us. Was it something special? Why would it matter that Sloan was coming here?

Holden, too, looked at the tree in the center of everything. His eyes held a horror I couldn't understand, as did Cillian's and those who had joined them.

"End it, Kaya."

My body went taut and loose at the same time. A chill skittered down my spine as I looked between Holden and Kaya. I surprised myself by looking toward Cillian.

Utter fear coated the air around him as he gazed, horrors truck, at Kaya.

"Lord Holden?" Kaya's voice wobbled slightly, and I almost thought I'd imagined it.

"We've found our miscreant, Kaya." His voice had softened as he gazed at his second-in-command. Remorse mixed with pain was what I saw on his face as he gave the command to Kaya a final time. "End it now. That's an order."

This time, Kaya didn't hesitate. She slipped the blade into Sloan's neck as if she were gliding it through water. Sloan's mouth went slack, a gurgling gasp slipping free.

More crimson began spurting from her throat as Kaya withdrew her dagger and dismounted her waning form. Sloan's hands came to clutch at the wound, but they were unable to staunch the bleeding. No one moved; they simply watched as the life slowly faded from her eyes as blood sputtered from her gaping mouth.

Chapter 29

Kaya

I t was too hard to think, too hard to breathe with that rhythmic pounding inside my head—inside my soul. Being that close to the tree had everything inside of me screaming to touch it. Fighting against its will was nearly impossible.

Holden had given me the order to dispatch her. I didn't mean to hesitate, but that otherworldly force surrounding me seemed to hold my hand in place, frozen. Like it was begging me not to kill Sloan.

But everything had been because of her. She had been the one behind the husks all along. Tynan had been right. I didn't want it to be the truth, but I knew there was no other plausible explanation.

As he had asked me the other day, *Who craves more power?*

I couldn't stand the look of pain in Cillian's eyes as I turned from Sloan's lifeless form to await my next order. Tynan only watched me with compassion, like somehow he understood the pain I was working through.

Still, that otherworldly throbbing radiated through me.

Holden didn't speak for some time. Finally, he gave the order for Sloan's body to be collected and for us to return to the city.

"No one speaks a word of this," he hissed at us. Not that I wanted to relive this moment ever again.

My heart ached.

As we stepped away from that tree, the yearning depleted immensely. I let out a sigh of relief as I once again could form a complete thought.

I'd killed Sloan. Sloan had been the one behind the husks. She had been the reason for my brother's death. The reason I'd left for the South. I shouldn't have been as broken up about it as I was. I had my retribution. Why didn't I feel relief after all this time?

I needed to wash her blood off my hands. I couldn't even look at them for fear of getting sick. Normally blood didn't bother me. But this blood felt different. Heavier. Tainted.

Night as black as pitch surrounded us as we filed into a tree, emerging just before the city gates. The guards on post watched our procession as we silently made our way back into the city's embrace. I refused to acknowledge their questioning stares, refused to so much as look back at Cillian or Tynan as I broke from the group and trudged home.

My cottage was dark, and I left it as such. I only wanted to fall into my bed and never get back up again. But a bath would have to come first so that I could wash Sloan's drying blood from my skin. My eyes pricked, but I refused to cry. I'd done enough crying over my brother's death. I wouldn't waste a tear on his murderer.

I filled the tub, heated it to a near-scalding temperature, and stripped naked. I dropped into its depths and sat back, intent on a long, sorrowful soak.

But the familiar sounds of Cillian coming through my window wouldn't allow any of that. Inwardly, I groaned. I didn't want to face him and that disappointment I knew he held for me.

The candles within the bathing room flicked to life one by one as Cillian slipped through the open doorway. His one eye fell upon my body, his attention slowly trailing up every inch until he finally found my face.

His fingers pinched the fabric just under his chin, slipping that mask from his nose, then his lips, and finally from his face altogether. His tongue darted out briefly, running over his bottom lip before he said, "I'm sorry he made you do that, Kaya."

"Someone had to," my voice scratched out, and I looked to the wall as my throat tightened over the words. He noticed my struggle anyway. Coming to crouch over me, he plunged his fist into the water to grab my hand. His fingers laced with mine, and he brought them to his lips. Pressing a kiss to each digit, I could feel the water growing warmer. I wasn't sure whether it was from his power or the need I always felt when I was close to him.

"How do you feel?" he asked.

I slipped my fingers from his and grabbed the soap. Scrubbing myself, I took inventory of my emotions.

They were in such disarray; it was hard to tell just how I felt about it all. Relief. Despair. But also... anger. I was angry that it had been her who had torn my brother from me. Angry that Ezra wasn't here, partly because of Cillian. It wasn't his fault, but I was also angry at Cillian for an entirely different reason.

I dipped my hair beneath the surface to wash the bubbles from the strands. Still, Cillian kneeled just beside the tub and waited.

When I was satisfied with my cleanliness, after all the evidence of earlier had washed down the drain, I motioned for Cillian to grab me a towel. He obliged, holding the fabric out for me to step into. When I did, he wrapped it securely around my body, his hands lingering a bit longer than necessary against my sides.

I stepped from his grip without giving him a second glance, that small kernel of anger simmering into something more. His footfalls matched my own as he trailed me into my room. Slipping my nightclothes onto my body,

I scrunched the water from my hair and discarded the towel. When that anger was too much for me to hold in, I finally let the words fly.

"When were you going to tell me about Lucy?" I hissed.

He winced like I'd struck him. But he didn't deny anything. He chewed his lower lip, and for some reason, the innocence of that movement made me regret confronting him.

"How'd you find out?" he asked.

"Tynan."

"Of fucking course, Tynan told you." He rolled his eyes, throwing his head back for emphasis.

"What is that supposed to mean?" I shrilled.

"It means the man has been trying to force a wedge between us since he opened his eyes," he nearly shouted back.

"Oh, grow up. He hasn't done anything wrong. You're the one hiding things from me." I was seething. All Tynan had done was offer his help and his insight. But I didn't dare mention that night he'd brought me those flowers. Not when Cillian was this upset. Because what had actually happened anyway? He'd simply leaned closely to me, then left.

"Don't pretend you haven't noticed those looks he gives you." His jaw clenched. I could tell he was angry, but I couldn't stop myself from pushing him further.

"Is that how you looked at Lucy? While you were *missing me*?" I scoffed. "You had me in anguish, thinking you spent the last six years in agony, pining after me. Yet, in reality, you were cozied up with her."

"Yes, just like you and Asher. What's the difference, Kaya?" He was really yelling now. So, I matched his volume.

"The difference is I told you *everything*. Even when Holden ordered me not to. I told you everything, and you told me *nothing*."

Cillian went very still, and if I didn't know better, I would have expected him to strike me. But Cillian wasn't that low of a man. No. He'd never lay a hand on me outside of the training field; of that, I was unwaveringly sure.

"If you need to yell at me, then yell at me. Hate me. Do whatever you need to do to get over it because I can take it. What I *can't* take is losing you again, which is why I felt like I couldn't say anything about it earlier. What we had was already so broken; I didn't want anything to hurt our chances at mending any more than what was already there." He stormed closer to me, that anger in his eyes turning molten, evidence of that fire beneath his surface.

"I love you, Kaya. Nothing you can do will change that. You can scream at me. You can strike me. You can put thousands of miles between us again, but I swear to you *nothing* will change this. Not Asher nor Lucy. Nor *Tynan*." His face was inches from mine, but I refused to relinquish a step. His breath assaulted my face, saliva speckling my cheeks as he seethed, "And I vow that I will never let you throw away what we have ever again. Where you go, I go. If you fall, I fall. You are *mine*."

He leapt from my open window before I could even form a response or even process everything he'd said.

I didn't sleep well after that.

I refused to talk to Cillian out of pure stubbornness. Part of it was because I was still reeling from Sloan's death and the idea that Ezra's memory could now rest in peace. It had opened old wounds, and I needed to process them before I could sincerely apologize to Cillian.

Wasn't closure supposed to feel good? Peaceful? That was not what I felt.

Since I was still Tynan's mentor, we'd been spending a great deal of time together. Tynan hadn't mentioned the ordeal in the forest, but I caught hints of concern when he thought I wasn't looking. But he gave me the space I so obviously needed.

Cillian had made himself scarce, though I felt him everywhere I went. It was both a comfort and an annoyance.

Holden had announced Sloan's betrayal to our realm. Our people were shocked but had since started healing. It would be a long, hard journey for everyone to forgive and trust each other again. But I had faith that we could do it. All of us, together.

Everything should have been going back to the way it was before. Yet, something felt off.

Perhaps it was that persistent thrumming I could feel in my veins. Fight it as I might, I couldn't stave off that yearning. I was torn because I knew what it was swaying me to do, but it defied everything our realm stood for. Our laws—our order—would be upended if I gave in to that building need.

But I knew it wouldn't stop until I did just that.

"Are you alright?" Tynan startled me by asking, his brow furrowed.

"Fine, why?" I tried to play off my nerves, but I could tell he saw through the farce.

"You seem preoccupied."

We were in the training field, and we had long given up on our workout. We were alone, but I scanned our surroundings just to be sure. I couldn't even feel Cillian's eye on me, so even he was tied up elsewhere. "Can I trust you?" I asked him, mirroring those words from weeks ago.

He smiled at me, undoubtedly remembering that very same moment. "Yes, Kaya. I would never betray you. I fear you're my only ally on this island."

Sliding my body closer, I lowered my voice as I said, "Our land has many legends. One of which is that all power originated here." I paused, gauging his reaction.

"I've been reading up on your tales in the library," he offered.

"Well, those powers are said to have come from the forest. One particular tree, to be exact." Again, I waited, seeing if he would make the connection. When his eyes brightened and landed back on me, I continued. "Yes. The one Sloan was heading for. It goes against our laws to get close to it. That's why our people are buried around it. In offering, and as a reminder."

"What happens if someone were to touch it?" Tynan asked.

I shrugged a shoulder. "No one knows for sure. It's said that one can draw immense power, much like siphoning. Others surmise that if someone touches it, they dry up. Much like one of those husks." I lay back into the grass, bending my arms beneath my head like a pillow.

"Why are you telling me this?"

I didn't know how to word it without sounding insane. How could I tell this man anything, and why did I even want to? He was nearly a stranger, and if I was to tell anyone, it should certainly be Cillian. I drew in a few deep breaths, debating.

"Because I think the forest is telling me to go and touch it."

He didn't speak, but I felt him stretch out next to me. "In what way?" he finally asked.

"Like it's speaking to me, influencing me. I'm not really sure. I feel like there's a tether within myself that's being yanked in the direction of that tree. When we pursued Sloan, I almost couldn't breathe. I almost couldn't control myself."

I dropped my head sideways so that I could see him. He was already watching me. "When did this start?"

"When I got back from the South. But it's been growing since. And." I stopped, unsure if I should divulge everything. I decided it made no difference at this point. "It happened when I was a child as well."

Sensation brushed along my fingers. Tynan slid his hand along mine briefly before covering my hand with his own. "Why don't you do it, then?"

I blanched. "Were you not listening? I could die."

"Or you could gain power. Either way, I don't think you have much choice. If that need is growing, why are you fighting it?"

He had a good point. Our legends did say that the forest had a will of its own. If that will was encouraging me to do this, then who was I to deny it what it wanted?

"If someone finds out, I'll be put to death. Just like Sloan." I shuddered, remembering her waning life beneath my fingers.

"Then don't get caught." I could hear the smile in his voice. I laughed at the simplicity in his thinking. We let the conversation die, both of us lost in our thoughts. Really, we should have been training. That was what we had set out to do. But I had spent my entire life building up that endurance just to have lost it while I was away. It was so hard to get back to that place, and I didn't really want to put in the effort.

Tynan was older than I and had spent his life in the exact opposite way if the softness of his body told me anything. Even the skin of his hand was soft, callus-free against my own. His warmth leached into me, and the feeling pulled buried thoughts to the surface of my mind.

My eyes roved over his body, down his shoulders, over his broad chest, and onto his soft, slightly rounded stomach. I wondered how that softness would feel beneath me, what sounds he would make while I rode atop him—

I sat up, ripping my hand free from his. What the hell was I thinking? My face heated, and I could have sworn he knew *exactly* what I was thinking.

Maybe he was thinking about something similar.

"Darling?" he asked as I got to my feet.

"We should head back." I hoped I didn't sound as flustered as I felt.

Luckily, he didn't question me. I couldn't stop replaying the thought over and over again as we walked through the forest and back into the city. What had gotten into me?

Chapter 30

Cillian

I kept telling myself that she was just upset about everything, about having to be the one to end Sloan. About finally having closure. I, myself, didn't know how to feel about finally knowing who was behind those attacks. I couldn't believe Sloan had it in her.

It was a lot to digest, and I understood why Kaya wouldn't be handling everything so well. If she needed to use me as an outlet for her anger, I would let her. If that meant she was giving me the silent treatment, I would suffer through that as well.

But I wouldn't lie to myself. It hurt to see her with Tynan. Spending time with him, no doubt confiding in him instead of me.

She would come around. I had to keep assuring myself of that or else I would break apart altogether. Not having her here was one thing. But having her right in front of me and not being able to hold her, talk to her, touch her… It was agony.

And I wanted to kill Tynan. She might not have believed it, but he was intentionally putting a wedge between us. I knew if I kept trying to prove it to her, though, I would only be playing further into his game. But it was infuriating to sit idly by until she realized it for herself.

I swore I was going to be staring up at my ceiling for the entire night. I sighed and rolled onto my side, tucking a hand beneath my pillow. Images swirled within the blackness of my room. After a moment, those shapes turned into the writhing forms of Kaya and Tynan.

I threw the blanket off my body and placed my feet on the cold floor.

No, I was definitely not getting any sleep tonight. Even though the autumn air was chilly, I wasn't cold. My power pulsed beneath my skin, eager to be released. It felt restless.

Half a thought had the candles in my room aflame. I stepped into my pants and pulled a shirt over my head. After making quick work of my bootlaces, I shut my cottage door behind me, not bothering to lock it.

Where I was headed, I wasn't sure. A long stroll through the empty streets might be enough to settle my nerves. It was beautiful out, at least; the stars high above were twinkling and glittering as far as I could see.

Before I knew it, I was standing a few buildings down from Kaya's home. It surprised me that there were candles flickering in her windows. Apparently, she couldn't sleep either.

I set my sights on her bedroom window, quite used to creeping through the frame even though it wasn't necessary. But when I reached the area just outside her room, I saw that she wasn't alone.

Though her room was, in fact, empty, I could still make out two shapes seated in her living area. Kaya was perched atop the counter, Tynan leaning a hip against it.

If she hadn't noticed my presence thus far, she did shortly after. Every candle within her cottage that wasn't already lit burst into flames. Each dancing speck of fire climbed higher than was natural.

Her eyes found mine the next instant. She wasn't quick enough to cover up the look of guilt she held, either.

I stormed my way around the cottage and through the front door without knocking. Tynan stood stoically as Kaya dropped from the countertop as if it, too, had caught fire.

"What are you doing here?" she accused.

"I could ask him the same thing," I hissed back, my tongue dripping acid. It was then that I realized I'd forgotten my face covering. It was hard not to let my embarrassment show as Tynan studied the features he'd never before seen, as his eyes snagged on my ugly scar.

"I was invited in," he said as he smirked at me.

I could have sworn my teeth would break from how hard I was clenching my jaw. The candles jumped even higher. But then they tamped themselves back down to a normal glow.

Tynan looked at Kaya in wonder. "You have a bit of fire inside you, too. Is it from that boy?"

Before I could let my anger take hold of my tongue, Kaya chimed in. "Cillian isn't a boy."

"When you get to be my age, darling, everyone is a child." He smirked at her.

"You're what, five years his elder? That isn't a big difference." Kaya only seemed mildly annoyed at Tynan's dig. I didn't understand why she was even entertaining his antics.

"Looks can be deceiving, Ky," he mused.

"Well, you look as if you've never held a sword in your life. Can you prove me wrong?" I jabbed, not hiding any bit of distaste I held for him. Kaya scowled at me.

"We aren't doing this right now," Kaya reprimanded. "Tynan couldn't sleep, and neither could I, so we were just talking."

"Well, I couldn't sleep either. So, I came here to talk with you." I gave Tynan a pointed look. I tacked on, *"Alone."*

Kaya looked annoyed, but she turned to Tynan and said, "We can pick this back up tomorrow. I need to see what he wants."

She said it as if it were a chore to talk to me. I hated the idea of being a burden to her. What had changed over these weeks since she'd returned home? She had been clinging to me that first night, and now she seemed to want nothing to do with me.

Thankfully, Tynan headed for the door without any objection. I nearly bit off my tongue when he said, "Good night, darling," as he closed the door behind him.

A blush crept up her neck and stained her cheeks. Did she actually enjoy that?

When the reverberations from the door closing finished echoing through the room, Kaya dared a look at me. I couldn't cool the hardness of my features, too pissed off about her being alone with that creep.

"I'm not doing this right now, Kill," she said before stomping off to her room. Chasing her probably wasn't the right move, given the situation, but I did it anyway. I was done caring, done skirting around everything.

"Leave," she hissed as she tried to shut her bedroom door in my face. I knocked it back a little too forcefully, sending her stumbling backward a few steps. More candles flickered to life, and I wasn't sure if it was from my power or that kernel I had given her when—

I grabbed her hand, yanking her closer to me. When our skin met, her face softened immediately. Whatever hold Tynan had her under had snapped. She melted into me then, like wax solidifying as it dripped down the side of its pillar. I felt her body loosen into my touch, her curves forming against me.

I wanted to claim every inch of her. To prove to her that I wouldn't let her fall through my grasp again. Prove that I had meant every word from the other night.

My lips connected with her and the way she eagerly reciprocated made every last drop of anger leave my body. I stepped further into her, edging her toward the bed. Her body made contact, and I gently shoved her down. Our kiss broke, her mouth still hanging open as she settled back amidst the tangle of blankets.

I unfastened my shirt, each button popping free beneath my expert touch, all the while never pulling my eye from hers. The trembling in her hands was minute, but I tracked the unintentional tremor regardless. They were frozen in the air before her, waiting for something to grab onto.

After throwing my shirt to the floor, I balanced myself with a knee on her bed. Wrapping a hand around her ankle, I pulled her back toward me, eliciting a surprised gasp that caused me to smile. Her eyes darkened when I looped my fingers beneath the waistband of her trousers.

Lifting her hips from the bed, I pulled her legs free and threw the fabric in a heap with my discarded shirt. I wasted no time in taking what I wanted. My mouth was against her, my tongue darting out to taste the skin of her leg before she could pull the shirt free from her arms. She struggled with it after I started kissing the inside of her thighs, climbing higher and higher. Her body vibrated beneath me, her legs spreading farther apart as I sought out what I truly wanted.

The way she weaved her fingers into the hair at the crown of my head while moaning my name had my hardness pulsing. I ran my tongue up her center, flicking it around that bundle of nerves just at the apex of her thighs. Her grip on my hair tightened as she bucked her hips against my face. That last tether holding my sanity in place snapped as I devoured her.

You're mine, you're mine, you're mine. I must have been shouting the silent mantra because I heard her voice inside my head echoing, *I'm yours, I'm yours, I'm yours.*

I slid myself up her body, unable to stifle my need for her any longer. Edging myself against her, the slightest pressure had me slipping inside. I groaned as I seated myself completely. Swallowing her gasp, I kissed her fervently as I moved inside her. With each thrust, a piece of myself fell back into place. As if what I'd been missing all these years was finally fitting itself back together.

Kaya clamped her mouth around my tongue, sucking gently and pulling a moan from my throat. I was ravenous. I couldn't drink down enough of her, push myself inside her deep enough. My need was unquenchable.

Thrust for thrust, Kaya met my urgency with her own. Our breathing came in opposing waves so that whenever she exhaled, I inhaled the taste of her. It wasn't enough.

Unmatched force had me rolling onto my back, Kaya seating herself atop me in a swift movement. Her weight pressed against my hips as she ground herself against me. Taking her pleasure into her own hands, I watched as she writhed atop me. I was nestled so deeply inside her that I could barely see straight, my nerves sending shock waves rippling through me.

Her fingernails dug into the skin on my chest, but I didn't notice the pain behind the pleasure. Trapped under her like this, all I could think was that she was a goddess given form. Candlelight reflected off her glistening skin. Her hair tumbled in waves down her back, tickling the skin on my upper thighs behind her.

My body began shuddering in tandem with each of her thrusts. Try as I might, I couldn't stave off that building sensation. Kaya's head tipped to the ceiling, more of her hair collecting against my skin as she pressed more firmly into me. She rocked against me, grinding into me as her own pleasure built. I could see it in the blushing of her skin, in the way bumps erupted along her arms, in the hardness of her peaked nipples.

With her cry of ecstasy came my undoing. My fingers dug into the soft flesh of her hips, working them through her climax as her body clenched around me.

After she was spent, her head crashed into my chest. My heart pounded wildly beneath her cheek, and I could feel hers racing as well. I kissed the crook of her shoulder, tasting the salty sweat where it misted her skin.

Time passed as our breathing slowly returned to a normal rate. Her heart began to settle as her hand stroked circles into my neck, another into my arm. I gripped her back, too afraid to let her go, afraid that she would fly away at any moment should I relinquish my hold on her.

When I noticed she had fallen asleep, I pulled a blanket around us. Unwilling to push her away, I left her atop me as I remained snuggly inside her. I savored every second she remained at peace, every second she remained fused to me in this way until I, myself, slowly drifted off into darkness.

Chapter 31

Tynan

Kaya was a step closer to being mine, and she wasn't even aware of it yet.

Once she worked through this ordeal with Sloan's death—this remorse she held over it—we could confront the other issues at hand, like the fact that some ancient force was trying to tempt her. Trying to tell her something.

I was especially intrigued when she confided in *me* about it. Knowing that she hadn't even told Cillian made it all the more enticing. That said something about our connection.

The fact that they'd fucked after I'd left meant little.

Once Kaya discovered the true depth of her power, she would want me to stand by her side. I was someone who wouldn't look down on her for how she'd have to obtain it and what she'd undoubtedly done to obtain as much as she had. She needed someone who wouldn't balk at everything she could be, everything she was meant to be. This *will* that was being pressed upon her was there for a reason.

Kaya was in an uncharacteristically chipper mood when I met her midmorning. There was no way that boy knew enough about a woman's body to have fully satisfied her in that way. I chose not to comment on that fact, though. Instead, I focused on the anger that had been dwelling in Cillian. The anger I was sure he had let out as soon as I'd been far enough away not to hear.

"I hope Cillian wasn't too angry with you last night," I said with mock remorse. I didn't feel guilty in the slightest about being alone in her home, knowing damn well Cillian would know about it.

She blushed, then shook her head quickly from side to side. "I think we worked everything out rather well." A secret smile graced those beautiful lips, and my mood soured.

"Have you told him about—"

Her hiss cut me off, a command to be silent. I looked around, noting the few people in the shop. No one had been listening. She threw me a reprimanding look anyway. I smiled back at her, darkening my expression slightly in a playful manner.

I leaned in closer, my mouth nearly brushing her ear in the process. "If you follow through, they're all going to find out anyway."

Who said I was going to follow through? Her voice in my mind had me tensing, an ugly, unpleasant memory floating into me. I had hoped I'd imagined that moment in the forest, but I couldn't deny the fact of Kaya's capabilities now. I tamped it back down before she could notice my unease.

Well, well. You are full of tricks, my darling.

My power hungrily swarmed around her intrusion, greedily dancing in her presence. I watched a blush deepen along her neck. Whether it was from my compliment or my own power's obvious obsession over her, I didn't know.

How did you become so adept? I asked as I steered her back into the streets. She could see the thoughts I had about her, my assumptions about how she'd managed to obtain so much power.

It was her turn to stiffen in discomfort.

I only took what was... left. After. She wouldn't elaborate more, wouldn't show me what had occurred, or how she was put in that sort of situation. I thought it best not to push her for fear of scaring her off. The last thing I wanted was to push her back to Cillian when I'd worked this hard. *Took actually doesn't accurately describe it*, she went on. *It sort of leapt out at me as if it were seeking some sort of safe harbor. I couldn't deny it even if I tried.*

Our arms looped together, a measure to keep us from veering from one another as our minds were otherwise occupied, the connection almost like a tether connecting our bodies in a more intimate way than I'd ever known. Most unlike the last time I'd felt an intrusion such as this. It was such a foreign feeling that I didn't even notice where we were going until I registered the silence around us.

We were in the forest but still within sight of the city wall.

"That's quite..." I paused, unsure how to describe the situation. I'd never known magic to go to another person willingly—scraps left in a corpse or not. Most powers were firmly planted within their host and content to stay. But even my own power seemed to sing in her presence. "Interesting."

She raised a brow at me as a smile erupted across her cheeks. "I know. I can't explain it either." Her hair swayed with the shaking of her head, the glow of the waning sun catching the strands and sending them shimmering. How black could ever look so candescent, I didn't quite understand. I'd never known a color so alluring yet so reminiscent of a wretched past.

I assessed her more closely then. I took in her features, an obvious reflection of their ancient queen. Did she truly not know? Did she truly not see that connection? Feel it? It would have explained so much if only I could have shown her. If only I could have convinced her. But I wasn't sure how to do so without overwhelming her.

Confusion scrunched her face, discomfort at my heavy attention.

"You've told me the tales of your land. But is there more?" I asked, my voice hedging.

"More, how?"

"That once powerful queen. The statue in the library? Is there more about her?" I didn't want to make her uncomfortable, but I had to push her toward the truth, at least, even if it was only a step at a time. Give her enough of a rope to lead her in the right direction. And hope she didn't hang me with it.

"She was the most powerful queen our land had known. That was why her lover betrayed her. It was all a ruse, or so they say. That lover only sought her queen's power. Her realm, not her love. And in the end, they both suffered."

"What if someone else turned them to stone? Not this *will* that you keep telling me about. What if it was someone's ability?" I tried to ask the right questions. The ones that would get her thinking. Have her questioning what she'd been told.

"Someone turned them to stone for what?" Her arms crossed over her chest, an obvious defense mechanism. She didn't like not knowing the answers to these questions.

"Well, maybe there was someone else who also wanted her kingdom," I said simply. It was a tale as old as time. Something we'd both seen before. Something we were seeing now.

She thought about it for a moment before responding. "Why wouldn't we have been told that?"

"Maybe no one knows the truth anymore. Or maybe." I feigned that the thought had just come to me. "Maybe the person who did it did a good job of covering their tracks. Maybe they're still running the show."

"We've had different lords leading us since then. Holden, himself, has only been in charge for—"

She stopped talking, the thought falling flat before us. Her eyes had gone wild, lost in confusion, but also struck through with fear.

The look of utter dread on Kaya's face when she noticed the creatures wandering through the trees behind us was almost heartbreaking. The realization that it had not been Sloan behind those atrocities dawned within her copper eyes. Her face went suddenly pale, which was quite concerning since her skin was usually a nice honey brown.

Her body swayed slightly, and she clung to the tree beside her, trying as she might to stay standing upright. She was frozen, it seemed, perhaps in shock.

I cursed inwardly, annoyed by the dreadful intrusion when Kaya was finally making headway on the truth. But I supposed this was another truth that we had to deal with as well. I went to her, resting a hand along her shoulder.

"Ky, we need to do away with them," I offered as gently as I could. "Warn those within the city as well."

She only stared at them in horror as the beings weaving through the trees, heading in our direction. Heading toward Kaya.

They picked up speed.

"Ky," I snarled. She needed to move. Needed to fight, or run, or scream. *Something* before they got to us. And they were closing that little bit of distance now that they'd spotted her.

I drew my dagger, praying she'd snap out of it before they were upon us.

Two, three… eight. There were eight of them in number. Still, Kaya wasn't moving, seemingly frozen in place by fear. But that didn't make sense. She hadn't hesitated before, nor did she hesitate in pursuing Sloan. Fear didn't seem to be an emotion she knew—until now.

I had no choice but to act when they descended upon us. Ky remained flat against that tree, her face growing more ashen by the second, her breathing coming in short puffs. I pulled the sword at my back free, the weapon mostly decorative until this point.

Letting out a final, slow breath, I began to slash through the tangled mess of husks with sword and dagger. Each seemed distracted enough by Kaya's mere presence that hacking through them proved easier than I thought. They only had eyes for her and didn't even register my presence until my blades were digging into their carcasses.

Three were on the ground, forever unmoving, before I even broke a sweat. My weeks of masquerading as a weak, insolent fool were completely undone in an instant. Though, I wasn't sure if Kaya would even remember this moment. Her horror-struck face wasn't even focused on me. What was wrong with her?

I cut down another two before Cillian appeared beside me, sliding his dagger into the skull of what looked to have once been a woman. He took out another with little effort. Not to be so outdone, I raised my sword, ready to slice the head from the remaining one's shoulders.

"No." The guttural cry was almost unearthly as it ripped from Kaya's throat. I halted immediately at her command, turning to see her staggering forward, utter devastation on her face. She reached a hand toward me. "No," she sobbed. I looked to Cillian for an answer, but his eye was solely on Kaya; that devastation echoed upon him as well.

This last husk must have been someone of importance to her, I realized.

Sheathing my blades, I stepped back as Kaya approached the remaining husk. Her shoulders jerked as she pulled her dagger free from her belt.

A peculiar thing happened then. My heart constricted, a sort of pain shooting through my chest as I watched Kaya step within reach of that remaining husk. Was this sorrow?

One word was all that met my ears, snapping me from myself as she plunged the blade into the creature's chest. One word—one name—was all she sobbed over and over again as she gently lowered the body to the ground, cradling it in her arms.

I wasn't sure who this boy Nash was, but apparently, he meant a great deal to her.

Chapter 32

Kaya

Finn's body was curled around mine in the way it had been curled around Nash's after he'd lost his sister. But now, it wasn't us comforting each other after he'd lost family. No. It was two of us mourning our third. Mourning a piece of us that we'd never get back.

I had never seen Finn in such anguish, never heard those guttural cries of grief emit from him. Not as they had poured from Nash after his sister. Not as they had ripped from my throat, alone in the Southern Kingdom.

Finn had so far been untouched by the presence of death. There had always been a degree of separation from him. Until the moment I had to plunge my dagger into the heart of his best friend.

His lover, apparently, which I'd just recently discovered upon my return to this realm.

The mere thought of losing Cillian sent a pain so unending, so aching and raw, through me that I couldn't breathe. I held Finn just a little bit tighter.

We'd just buried Nash, sending our sparks of power to stay within his resting place forever. We'd watched the flowers as they bloomed over his grave despite the biting cold of the day. Autumn was fully upon us, and just as the terrain around us was dying, as was any bit of hope I'd had left.

Sloan had been it. Holden had been sure. Tynan and I had caught her encroaching on the tree like she was about to siphon more power. Yet, more husks had shown up. These weren't made prior to her demise either because Nash had been happy and carefree the day before I'd plunged my dagger into his chest.

That pounding was steady in my veins as Finn and I remained close to Nash's grave. In the distance I could see that enormous tree, its presence overwhelming me. Its will was a separate heartbeat beneath my flesh as it coaxed me forward.

But I was too numb, too dead inside to heed its call.

When we finally left, we did so quietly. That undeniable need lessened the farther we got from it. The closer we got to the city, though, the more painful our loss became. To live in this place without Nash, after I'd finally healed just enough after Ezra…

It was almost too much, all the loss and emptiness that kept befalling our realm. Within that emptiness grew a hopelessness I couldn't shake, no matter how determined I wanted to be.

Finn shook off my offers to stay with him; he and I parted ways as the sun disappeared beyond the wall. I understood the need to be alone after such a loss. I'd put an entire sea between us when I'd lost my brother. And Wren had…

"Finn!" I yelled without thinking before he disappeared from my view. My sudden call startled him, causing him to whirl to face me. I rushed over to him, my heart racing, tears streaming freely.

"Promise me, Finn," I said, the tears still coming incessantly. I couldn't choke the words out, though. I couldn't explain my need with all the pain strangling me from the inside out. My throat was too tight, my eyes burning.

"What, Ky?" Finn's arms consumed me, folding me between them.

"Wren," I breathed, the word gargled between wet cries.

Finn stilled around me. His hands went from smoothing across my back to digging into me. His heart thundered beneath my ear, which was pressed against his chest. I heard the breath he sucked in and held as he realized what I was trying to say.

"Ky," he breathed as he pulled back. He leveled a serious look at me. "I won't leave you. I promise." He was crying now, though not as messily as me. His tears flowed silently from red-rimmed eyes, but the pain behind them was all the same. As was the truth of his words.

Appeased, I stepped away from him. With that promise, I felt content enough to give him his space. He smiled solemnly before departing. I tried not to think about it, tried not to dwell on it. But it was hard to keep the thought from creeping in.

If Nash had died any other way besides being drained of his essence, Finn would have been able to save him. He would have been able to bring him back with that tiny kernel of Nash's power he held within his soul.

I sent an internal finger brushing along that place where Cillian rested within me, thankful that I had that piece of him. Always.

My cottage was quiet and dark. I'd hoped Cillian would be waiting for me, but I knew he'd be receiving new orders from Holden now that our threat had resurfaced. Now that we knew it hadn't been Sloan. Well, it hadn't solely been Sloan. Whether she was working in tandem with someone else or at someone's will was unclear.

I shuddered as I lit some of the candles in the main room by hand, remembering in great detail when I'd been unable to take charge of my own life. It had been a fate worse than death. If Sloan had been manipulated in that way, it was a mercy that she was no longer suffering, even at the cost of her life. I remembered begging for that death myself, just to escape the torment.

That led me back to Lucy. She was the only person in this realm who could command people in such a way. Though, if someone was indeed siphoning powers, it was not unfeasible that they might have taken some of hers without her knowing.

Honestly, that was most likely the truth. Lucy was a sweet girl; she had always been a sweet girl. She didn't have an unkind bone in her body. Plus, we'd followed her for over a week and ruled her out. I was confident enough in my reconnaissance to know that we hadn't missed anything.

My head spun. And I could still feel that pounding beneath my skin, though it was light. Softer than it had been in the forest. But it was still there, radiating through my body and into my skull, humming beneath my skin. I pressed my hands over my ears, pushing against that pulsing pressure in my mind. I felt like I was going insane.

It wasn't until the sound whooshing in my ears loudened that I realized it was someone pounding at my door. The wood of the door reverberated beneath each fervent thud.

Who would be coming to my house at this hour? After such a long, long day. My body deflated as I went to the door, wanting to do anything but pull it open and see who was waiting on the other side. I knew it wasn't Cillian, as he would have let himself in without question.

When the door swung open and revealed Tynan, I wasn't actually surprised. We hadn't talked since the incident in the forest, so it was only a matter of time before he'd come to check on me.

I supposed that time was now.

I stepped backward, allowing him room to enter. He did, resting a hand on my shoulder for a moment before he swept past me. I stilled beneath his touch, noting how calm his presence seemed to make me. An aura of reassurance surrounded him and saturated his touch. I secured the door behind him, not taking any chances on someone or something coming into my home uninvited.

It was becoming harder to deny that these husks were somehow associated with me. I just wasn't sure how. Or why.

"Are you alright?" Tynan asked by way of greeting.

"No," I replied honestly. My heart throbbed, and I could do nothing to stop it.

Tynan didn't bother to sit down. He simply stared at me from a few paces away. I watched him with just as much intensity, again noticing how he carried himself. Everything about him screamed regality. The way he held his chin high, the way he laced his fingers together as he stood stoically in my tiny cottage. Even the way he dressed—in clothes that weren't even his, nonetheless. Everything looked as if it had been made for him.

He studied me with those viper eyes.

"Who are you?" I asked the question that had been eating away at me from the moment I'd found him nearly lifeless in the water.

"I've told you, Kaya." He prowled closer, his eyes transfixing me in place. My heart raced faster with each step he took, knowing when he reached me, something would happen. We were on the precipice of something life-altering. I could feel it, but what?

"You've barely told me anything," I breathed. "You had brothers. A sister. A wife." I swallowed hard, trying to keep my voice steady as he closed that distance. "You knew Olen but won't say how." Though not as tall as Cillian, he towered over me. "You seem so detached from your past."

He looked down upon me, the heat from his body sinking its teeth into my flesh as I stood motionless. My body felt like it was frozen in place. I couldn't move.

"My wife hated me. Many of my siblings tried to kill me." His hand latched on to my arm, though gently, before I could process his words. "And Olen was an open book when it came to me, even when it wasn't his

- 278 -

intention. With everything in disarray in my own realm, I thought it best to leave when I had the chance to keep my life."

Though his words should have frightened me, I didn't feel afraid in his presence. No. I felt oddly at ease, comforted by his touch. My skin pricked beneath his palm, an icy bite anchoring me in this moment. My eyes were still stuck on his, the light green of his irises forever stamped in my vision. He was beautiful. Enchanting.

And then his lips were upon mine, soft and light at first. Once he pressed them further into me, used them to part mine, his tongue dipped into my mouth just enough to taste me.

I sucked in a breath, unsure how I'd managed to be put in this situation, how he thought it would be okay to pursue me like this. But still, my body wouldn't move. It wouldn't separate from his. It didn't move closer, either.

I was thankful for that much because all I could see swimming in my mind was Cillian.

My eyes remained open as his fluttered closed. I watched the candlelight dance across his skin if only to distract myself. I counted his eyelashes as he pressed further into me, corralling me toward the empty expanse of wall behind us. My back connected with a soft thud. His mouth worked, and mine mirrored his movements of its own volition. He took what he wanted, bruising me and brushing his tongue along the roof of my mouth as I kept my lips open for him.

One hundred and thirty-seven lashes sprinkled his left eye.

Sensations pressed over my shirt along my ribs, gliding up and manipulating my breasts. I felt the touch, but it was foreign and didn't reach my soul in the way it did when Cillian caressed me. It was a pressure more than a feeling—a stale thought being inflicted upon me.

His tongue moved in my mouth, and I could feel the reverberations as he grunted in need, the compression on my breasts intensifying. But still, I felt nothing. It was as if this were happening to another person and not to me. I was void of emotion as he freed my shirt from the waistband of my trousers.

The icy skin of his hand connected with the bare skin of my stomach. He slipped that hand beneath the fabric around my hips. Then lower.

His fingers slipped between my thighs.

One hundred and nineteen hairs fluttered on his right eyelid as his fingers entered me. My hands were limp at my side, and a quiet part of me wondered why they weren't pushing him away. I couldn't understand why they weren't reaching for the dagger on my belt and slamming it into his throat.

Another more foreign part of me silenced those questions. They didn't resurface again as the weight of Tynan pressed me harder into the wall. As I felt the length of him pulse against my thigh.

"Darling," he breathed, and the word flowing into my mouth almost made me gag, the only sign that something wasn't right. The sudden tension in my body had his fingers faltering as he worked them inside me. He pulled back a fraction, his mouth finally parting from mine.

His dilated pupils bounced back and forth, dancing over whatever expression I held. I wasn't sure what I looked like because I still couldn't feel anything.

Not liking what he found, he slipped his hand free from my trousers and stepped back. Righting himself and clearing his throat, he said, "I apologize. I let things get away from me."

He wouldn't look at me. Why wouldn't he look at me? I wasn't sure if I wanted him to look at me or not, but it was rather odd after he'd just been so intimate with me. My mind was swimming, the thoughts swirling in thick mud.

He brushed his hair back from his face, still not meeting my eyes from where I remained rooted against the wall. Shuffling his weight uncomfortably, he adjusted the sleeves of his jacket, which had run up during his exploration of my body.

"I should leave." He said it as if he wasn't actually sure. Did he want me to object? I opened my mouth, then shut it again. Words wouldn't form around the rising feeling of nausea, the panic spiking through me. It felt like something inside me was giving way, an internal war being waged. It gurgled in my gut as my head became very light and dizzy.

Tynan furrowed his brow. He hesitated as if he was going to ask if I was okay.

Instead, he nearly ran from my cottage and slammed the door behind him.

I remained plastered in place for so long that the candles nearly extinguished themselves, their wax running over and wicks withering to nothing. My body was locked up, my joints frozen and mind still and quiet. The first rays of morning light began peeking through my window before, my stiff bones began to crack free. It was then that I fully comprehended what had happened to me, what he had done both to my body and my mind.

And I vomited across the floor.

Chapter 33

Cillian

When I'd gotten to Kaya's, Tynan was already there. He hadn't yet arrived at Holden's manor by the time I had been dismissed, so I knew what had held him up. Peering through the window, I saw how they had been pressed so closely together, his mouth against hers. Everything in me had screamed that I needed to intrude. My mind had been raging to turn him to ash.

But I couldn't hurt her in that way. If she truly wanted to be with him, I'd let her have that. So, I just watched in horror as a few heartbeats passed, then ran home.

I agonized over it for the rest of the night. The betrayal didn't feel quite right—like I was missing a key piece to the puzzle. I just didn't know what it was. Kaya and I were tethered; we were in love. We had made a breakthrough. Something wasn't adding up.

Until I figured it out, I planned to keep my distance. I didn't want to tear into the rift—no matter how small—that was still present between Kaya and me, especially if there wasn't cause to. Maybe I didn't see what I thought I did.

One thing was certain, though. Sloan hadn't been behind the husks. It didn't feel right even when Kaya and Holden were sure, even when she'd been caught in the act of defiance of our laws. Now, we just needed to figure out the true culprit.

Easier said than done. This person was at fault for not only Sloan's death but Nash's, too. With more of our loved ones falling victim, it was pertinent now more than ever that we stop them, especially since they'd set their sights on Kaya.

Holden had instructed me to stay close to his side. Since Sloan had been targeted—used as a tool and discarded—he had his suspicions about what this person was after. His position within our realm, that power over our people. To do what with, one could only guess. Because of this, I was to stand guard within the manor. I knew part of this was to keep me within his reach just in case something bad happened. It was for my protection as much as his.

I should have been grateful for his concern for me. It only annoyed me because I'd rather be watching over Kaya. Those husks had been coming for her, just as the one on the beach had. Either Holden didn't believe that, or he didn't care about her well-being as much as he did mine.

Both could have been true.

Holden was in a meeting, instructing some of his peers on the procedures following the encounter of late. I knew this was my only opportunity to stretch my legs. Lucy was also sequestered in the manor, and she gave me a pointed look as I left my post and headed for the library upstairs. I gave her a dismissive wave, to which she rolled her eyes.

She knew only I could get away with this sort of dereliction.

I could feel him before I even finished opening the door to the library. The wood groaned as it completed its inward swing, and Tynan peered over a shoulder at me as I entered. His mouth set into a hard line before he brought his cup to his lips and sipped from it, all while turning away from me. He was staring intently at the statue in the center of the room, almost like he was waiting for it to come alive.

"Sleep well?" My simple question was full of accusation. I wanted him to know what I saw. I watched his shoulders tense as he surmised its underlying meaning.

"No." His knuckles were white as he grasped the handle of his cup and sipped the steaming tea. He shot me a sideways glance but wouldn't acknowledge my accusation head-on. He also looked like he felt guilty.

Confident I was projecting my own feelings, I stopped beside him and cast my eyes upon the statue. I'd always thought the rendition was beautiful, something familiar in the set of her mouth and the arch of her brow.

"When she finally opens her eyes, she'll see she was made for greater things than this."

I stilled. Tynan still stared at the statue, his face set in concentration, as if he was trying to look through the stone and into the soul beneath.

"The old queen?" I asked, thinking the man had officially lost his wits. Was he truly talking to a statue, or was he referring to Kaya?

He smirked and threw me a sideways glance. Some knowing secret danced behind his eyes. I was sure he had many of them, but what did he actually know of this land that I didn't?

"Our Kaya."

My blood chilled in my veins at the way he said her name, claimed her as if any part of her belonged to him. My hand reacted first, my mind slowly catching up as it curled around his throat, all before I could think about what I was doing. The cup clattered from his hand and onto the floor, shattering on impact.

"She is nothing to you," I seethed, saliva splattering his face as he clutched at my arm. I didn't let up on my grip even as his face reddened slightly, his fingernails pricking at my skin.

He truly was weak.

"Cillian, let him go."

Holden had appeared in the entryway of the library. I heard his boots stomping against the floor as I clung tighter to Tynan.

"Cillian." Holden's voice was commanding, closer now. My fingers loosened of their own volition. Cursing inwardly, I took a step away from Tynan as he sucked in breath after ragged breath.

Holden's hand squeezed my shoulder. "I don't know what's gotten into you," he said to me, a look of absolute bewilderment on his face. "Accept my apologies on his behalf, Tynan."

I could have strangled Holden as well for his concern over the scoundrel. Tynan was slimy, a snake ready to strike at any moment. Why was I the only one who saw him for what he truly was?

"It's no matter, Lord Holden. I think everyone's emotions are running high as of late." He rubbed at the raw skin on his neck, shooting me a condescending look. I didn't miss the gleam of triumph in his eye either. "I suppose I should return to my duties as well."

Tynan bowed at the waist before he turned from us. Holden grasped me by the back of the neck, ready to scold me, when Tynan added, "I'm sure Kaya will be wondering where I've gone off to."

Dread washed over me as I whipped my head in his direction, breaking from Holden's grip. His smile was serpentine as he disappeared around the doorway. My gaze landed back on Holden, his look measured as he waited for me to ask the question he knew was simmering.

"What do you have him doing?" I demanded, knowing I wasn't going to like what he had to say.

Holden dropped his hand and sighed in exasperation. "Now, don't get all worked up, Cillian. It's just a precaution."

"Tell me. Now." My hands balled into fists, fingernails digging into my palms as I waited. The chandelier above us grew ever hotter as my temper rose.

Another sigh as he scrubbed a hand over his face. "These husks are targeting her, which raises my suspicion of her. They stopped before when she left. They started once more when she came back. And what she showed me while she was away… Well, Cillian. Kaya isn't the innocent girl you think her to be."

"What are you saying?" I wanted to shove him, wanted to throw him to the ground, and make him take back what he was saying. Kaya wasn't behind this. I knew it in my heart.

"She's done things that would chill your blood." He tried to convey unsaid words through his eyes, but I refused to accept them. I knew what had transpired while she was gone. She'd shown me everything. Holden wasn't aware of that, though. And I couldn't tell him, or else Kaya would be punished for breaking his orders. But he seemed to be trying to imply something sinister about her that I knew wasn't true.

"So, you have Tynan watching her? Someone foreign to this land?" I spat.

"He's given me no reason not to trust him. I've seen his past. His intentions. We need not fear him." If only it were that simple.

"If you suspect her, have me watch her."

"You're too close to her for me to allow that. Too compromised. That's why you're *here*."

I couldn't believe what I was hearing. Holden seriously thought it was Kaya behind this madness. Kaya, who had drained Nash. Killed Ezra. I felt like I was going to be sick.

"And if you find any speck of evidence? Will you give the order against her without proof, as you did *Sloan*?" I didn't hide my anger. The room was nearly sweltering. I needed to get out before I set the entire manor aflame.

"Sloan was a calculated move, it seemed. Whoever was behind that knew what they were doing." His brow hardened. "Don't for one second think that my affection for you will cloud my judgement when it comes to our land. And I won't stand for you intervening."

Numbness radiated through me. He would kill her, given enough evidence. No matter what I did, what I said, I could do nothing to stop it. And Tynan knew of this. He knew it was his job to collect the evidence against her.

And he was taking advantage of his position over her.

I stormed from the room, not bothering to give Holden a response. He didn't want one anyway. My silent acquiescence was all he'd ever wanted. All he would ever have accepted.

I was out the front door to the manor without a second thought, without looking back.

I had visions of sinking my blade into Tynan's belly, of sinking my teeth into his neck—that was how badly I wanted to end him. It wasn't just for what he'd been doing with Kaya but for what he'd been doing behind her back as well.

That two-headed snake was on my last nerve. And Kaya was about to find out just how untrustworthy he really was. I would make her see it.

Luckily, he wasn't with her as she tossed daggers in the training field. Where he'd gone after Holden dismissed him, I couldn't bring myself to care. The less I saw of him right now, the better it was for him. However, I didn't see my rage calming anytime soon.

"Where were you last night?" Kaya asked without turning around. She seemed preoccupied but still sensed me almost instantly. Her tone was soft, almost dreamlike, but there was a sadness to it.

"Holden had me under lock and key." I didn't want to mention how I'd tried to visit her, but she was otherwise engaged. The memory left a foul taste in my mouth.

And when she turned to me, I understood why. Her eyes were rimmed in red like she'd stayed up the entire night. It looked like she'd been crying for hours.

"What is it?" I breathed, meeting her embrace as she reached for me.

"I don't know what's happening to me." She sobbed into me. I tried not to tense, but she felt the hesitation all the same. "Tynan came to me last night," she whispered. I tucked her head into the crook of my neck—that piece of her falling neatly into place against me—unable to face her as she relayed what had happened. "I let him do things to me. I couldn't stop him."

I blanched, putting her at arm's length. Looking at her anew. "Did he force himself on you?" I asked through gritted teeth. If I'd been angry before, my temper was roiling now. Something new and raw radiated beneath my skin, sending my limbs quaking in the wake of that rage.

Tears sprinkled from her lashes. She opened her mouth, but no sound came out. She was choking on the words. She tried again, this time admitting, "I don't know. I didn't stop it. But it was like I couldn't stop him." Her lip trembled, and the movement broke my heart. "I didn't want it."

My hands were gripping her a bit too tightly. I tried to control that tightening so I didn't harm her. "Tell me."

"He cornered me, but I didn't move. Didn't stop him. I let him touch me. I even questioned why I was allowing it, but still did nothing to stop it." She gaped at me as if she was realizing the same thing I was. That moment of realization pounded through us both, strong and undeniable.

"He was controlling you," I breathed. The dropping in my gut told me it was the truth. I knew Kaya would have never betrayed me if there were any other options. I should have stormed in there last night. Should have stopped it—

She didn't look convinced. "It didn't feel like that." Her brow furrowed, and she looked down toward my chest. She was lost within her mind for a moment, grasping at something. "It didn't feel the same."

"Kaya," I pleaded, because I could tell she was wavering. That hold he had on her was influencing her even at this moment.

Fuck. He was probably influencing Holden as well.

Who else had he gotten his venom into?

"Kaya," I called louder, this time because she had stepped from my hold. Her head shook from side to side, trying to make sense of it all. I could see the unspoken battle behind her eyes.

"It was different than that, Kill." Her voice had gone too quiet. Something switched inside her instantaneously. She was bereft, morose, and then suddenly, her face was contorted in agony. I lunged for her as her hands pressed against the sides of her head. She crumpled to the ground, out of my grasp, crying out in pain.

When I pressed a hand to her neck, her heart rate was beating so rapidly I thought it would burst from her chest. I didn't realize I was screaming her name until my throat became raw. She writhed on the ground as I hovered over her, unable to do anything to stop the hurt. The stillness that followed had my stomach lurching.

"Kaya," I rasped. With her chest rising and falling—stuttering as it was—I knew that she was still alive. "What's happening?"

Another breath. Then another. A deeper one.

"She's being called," Tynan said from somewhere in the forest.

Chapter 34

Tynan

I f looks could kill... Oh, I would have been a dead man. But I'd gotten very adept at avoiding death during my life. If I were that easily destroyed, my sister would have done away with me years ago. And her daughter after that.

Yet here I stood on another land altogether, moments from finally getting what I knew I deserved. The last months had culminated in this point, this moment when Kaya wouldn't be able to deny her destiny anymore.

"Help her up. We need to go," I said as I emerged from between the trees. Cillian again gave me that scathing look as he reached for his blade.

"I'm not letting you near her," he hissed. His one eye was steady on me as he ripped off his face covering. With his teeth bared like that, he actually looked a bit frightening. But he was nothing but a simpering child.

"Whether I go near her or not is beside the point. She's being called, and it's a call she needs to heed. It won't stop until she bends to its will."

I could tell my words were falling flat from the look of confusion on his face. Luckily, Kaya began to stir. Her eyes flicked a few times before they finally opened. Her brow furrowed in pain—excruciating by the look twisting her features—before she sat up and looked between us.

"Stop," she said, though I wasn't sure if she meant to.

"Kaya." Those copper eyes snapped to mine when she heard my voice, unable to deny my pull. "It's time."

She didn't move, still intent on fighting every step of the way. I dared a step closer. Cillian was on his feet in a flash, dagger raised to my chest. I held my hands level with my shoulders, trying as I might to assure him I wouldn't harm her. That wasn't my goal here. He, on the other hand, I would gladly make a casualty of the situation.

"Darling," I encouraged. "You can't keep fighting it." I kept my voice light—coaxing a frightened animal before me. Cillian allowed me to pass, sure that if I tried anything, he'd have the upper hand. I let him think it as I offered my hand to Kaya.

"What if it kills me?" she asked. Her large eyes stared up at me, making my breath catch at their beauty. Oh, she was something to behold.

"You don't have a choice, I'm afraid. You know that as well as I do."

Her eyes flicked to my hand before she placed her own atop it.

"A choice in what?" Cillian snarled. His blade was still angled toward me, but I ignored it.

"The will of the forest," I said simply. If I'd been told about something like this during my first day here, I would have laughed and thought these people were mad. But after reading their histories, seeing that damned statue and its uncanny resemblance to the beauty before me, listening to Kaya's firsthand experiences, I couldn't deny their truth.

"It's calling to me, Cillian," she said to him as I helped her from the ground. Her hand was limp in my own, and I knew it was a consequence of last night's mistake.

I hated myself for it.

"You can't be serious," he said in disbelief. I began leading Kaya in the direction of the forest, walking toward a tree I knew would take us where we needed to go. It would guide us in the right direction for Kaya to fulfill its will.

Before we could disappear into that void, however, she reached a hand back for Cillian.

He was swallowed up with us.

Chapter 35

Cillian

We emerged on the outskirts of our land's burial ground. Kaya had a death grip on my hand, her other lying limply within Tynan's. He looked perturbed that I was with them but didn't insist Kaya send me back.

He acquiesced to her as he led her between those flowers and toward that ancient presence in the center of it all.

I felt it then. There was a pulse igniting the air around us. The night was alive with a need I couldn't quite explain. My hair stood on end as I clung to Kaya's sweaty fingers and my heart synced up with that ominous rhythm.

I swore Tynan's eyes pulsed in time with that beat beneath my skin, the rhythm in the air around us. Kaya was entranced, her feet moving almost in a dance as we stepped over the flowers, and we silently made our way closer.

Closer.

"Kaya," I breathed, and couldn't hide the dread that drenched each word. She wouldn't look at me. She couldn't tear her eyes from the tree that was just before us. "He's doing this."

Tynan scowled at me, his lip curling in disgust. But it was Kaya who said, "No. He isn't."

With trembling limbs, she stepped ever closer. I refused to drop her hand.

"I was skeptical myself. But this." Tynan turned and raised his hand before the entity. "This is something to fear. Something to behold. This is where it all started." His voice had taken on a dreamlike quality.

"Where what started?" I asked, knowing good and well that he was insane.

"Everything." It was so quiet I thought I'd imagined it. But I heard it in the air around us, in my soul, as I rotated in place. That pulsing was almost deafening at this point as we stood unmoving together, waiting.

Waiting for what? Kaya glanced nervously around, taking her one free hand and reaching it toward the peeling bark. My heart leapt as her fingers stretched out.

"Kaya," I reprimanded as I yanked her back. "You can't."

"I must." That dreamlike tone coated her words as well, as a film slipped over her irises, casting them with a far-off look. "It wants me to."

"If anyone finds out, it will be the end. They'll kill you." I'd planted my hands on either of her shoulders, shaking her gently, trying to coax her from this trance. But when our gazes clashed, I saw nothing but coherent determination beneath that insufferable need. She was there. She was in control.

Tynan pushed me sideways as Kaya stepped forward.

"Why?" I asked neither of them in particular, not even trying to defend myself at this point. Kaya didn't answer, but I watched her shoulder rise and fall in a shrug.

I looked at Tynan. Monster he might have been, but he knew something we didn't.

His smile was demented. He'd officially lost that carefully crafted mask he'd worn since he arrived. He looked upon Kaya in wonder as he proclaimed something that couldn't be the truth. Yet every fiber of my being felt that snippet of information click into place as if I'd known it all along.

"Because she's the queen."

And then Kaya stepped through the most ancient tree in our land, thus breaking every order and law we'd ever known.

It swallowed her whole.

The second she disappeared into the dark, that ominous pulsing silenced. And in its wake, a horrible feeling settled. That silence in the forest was too loud. Tynan and I looked at each other in disbelief as the moment ticked by, and Kaya didn't reappear.

Mirroring my movements, Tynan drew his sword as I drew mine. Both of us were ready for a fight. Neither of us was keen to start.

"You hurt her," I accused. Now that Kaya was off *somewhere*, I could finally confront the sadistic man beside me.

Sadness ghosted across his face, but he didn't deign to respond. He didn't confirm nor deny the accusation.

"It was never my intention to cause her any pain." Perhaps he did have a heart somewhere deep down. We circled each other, and each of us zeroed in on our prey.

"Then what is your intention?" I barked at him.

He looked at me as if I should already have known the answer. "Well, to rule at her side, of course."

I stopped in my tracks, realizing what his other admission had meant. Kaya was the queen. Or, meant to be the queen. I wasn't sure of the specifics, but the knowledge was unwavering in me regardless. She was meant to rule this realm. The knowledge felt... right.

But not with him.

I lunged, disregarding the rules of a fair spar. My intent was to kill him as quickly as possible. I'd kill him before he could sway my Kaya any further, control her any more than he already had. It should have been simple, given how inept he had proven at fighting since he'd arrived.

Except he met me blow for blow. The ease with which he moved with me was unsettling, though I wasn't surprised to find one more thing he'd lied about. This man was a snake.

Without the ancient pulsing resounding around us, the clashing of metal was nearly deafening. His smile had my teeth snapping together in frustration.

"How long?"

He understood what I was asking. "I've known since my first few days here. How you've never seen it is beyond me."

But I did see it now, clear as the wildflowers around me. Kaya's resemblance to that statue of our ancient queen was uncanny. Which begged the question...

Tynan's blade nearly struck the side of my head as the realization had me faltering, the knowledge of who had been taunting us, hunting us all this time.

"So, you've figured it out?" He smirked, backstepping only slightly as I righted myself. I realized he was toying with me.

"You've known that too, I assume?"

His smile broadened, causing my anger to lash out. Fire erupted around us, the dry foliage singeing into nothing as I focused that power. If he'd only acted, we could have avoided all the unnecessary deaths.

Power ran up the length of my blade.

My sword was aflame, my brow sweating when I next lashed at Tynan. I sent a surge of flames toward him.

But they fizzled out before they got close enough to do any damage. The little fires around us hissed as they were slowly smothered out by ice.

Even my sword chilled against my skin, though my will alone kept those flames from extinguishing.

"It's quite amazing how this land can restore what was once lost." His fingers flexed theatrically. "I was near useless until I washed up here. How lucky," he mused.

Our powers counteracted one another's then. Great.

I wouldn't give up, though. Kaya needed me now more than ever. She needed someone who wouldn't take advantage of her power, someone who wouldn't use her for their own gain or try to control her. I wondered where she'd ended up after she'd slinked through the tree. Was she safe?

The thought cost me. Tynan closed in, his blade nearly knocking mine from my grasp. I recovered quickly, forcing every bit of that anger, fear, and uncertainty into my sword—into each slash I sent his way.

It was no use, though. Not when he procured a dagger from nowhere, throwing it in my direction as I swirled from the downward cut of his sword. As it soared closer, I saw that it was made strictly of ice. Its crystals shimmered as it moved—almost slowly, as if time had paused—piercing the air with an accuracy I didn't know he was capable of.

The last thing I felt before my world turned to blackness was the cold stinging of Tynan's blade sinking into my chest.

Chapter 36

Kaya

Time slowed to a near standstill as I trudged through that inky blackness. This darkness wasn't as light and freeing as the void within the other trees. This was harsh, all-consuming, and thick. As I moved through the muddiness of it, I got the feeling that I could go anywhere. Venture to any realm. But I allowed that ancient force to guide me where it wanted me.

I wasn't sure how long I was in there. It could have been seconds. It could have been years. When I came to, I was lying on my back, the world spinning around me. My surroundings were swimming, my head dizzy as I tried to right myself once more. Debris covered the ground around my body, the stones looking as if they'd just been smashed under intense pressure.

The ground beneath me was actually a floor made of wood. Confused, I pushed myself onto my feet, brushing remnants of that rocky debris and dust from my clothes. When I placed my surroundings, I stopped cold.

I was in the manor's library and had just emerged through the statue that rested there.

My unceremonious arrival must have been deafening because Holden came careening through the door a moment later, blades raised. Ready to fight.

The uneasiness on his face as he assessed me—scrutinized me—had the truth unfurling from my gut. My journey through the tree had somehow impressed upon me all the memories of this realm, all the truth I once could not see.

"You." It was a realization and accusation in one. Holden knew what I'd meant without explanation, though. His face fell, but not in defeat. Fell in a way that said I was ruining all his fun.

"Me," he confirmed. The guards that rushed in with him looked between us in confusion. Before any of them could decipher what we'd meant, though, their eyes were befallen by a vacant expression I knew all too well.

I had no weapons; my blades were still stuck in a slat of wood at the training ground. Cursing inwardly, I settled myself into a fighting stance regardless. Cillian had taught me combat without weapons, and I was trying with all my might to ready myself for that fight. I'd need to disarm Holden first. Possibly his guards as well. He would use anything he could to defeat me. To cover up his mess.

"It was always you," I accused, trying to buy myself time while I came up with a plan. "Ezra died because of you. Sloan. Nash." I choked over their names, the pain still raw, especially from only days ago.

"Yes. Your brother and Sloan were unfortunate causalities." He actually smirked at me. Rage coursed through me, and I wasn't sure I could contain it without acting. But I needed to wait.

"Nash?" I asked, trying to keep him talking. Something new was slithering beneath my skin. A gift, it seemed, from this realm—from that tree.

"I didn't have any of that darkness yet. And, well. I wanted it." He said it as if he'd simply bought a new pair of trousers from the shop.

Icy rage overtook almost every other emotion I held. It was a cold stinging in my chest, the wound raw and open.

"You had the chance to stay gone. You realize that, right?" He was talking down to me like I was an insolent child.

"You know I couldn't do that."

He smirked at the mess on the floor. "You've discovered the truth, I presume?"

I didn't bother answering. I still couldn't make sense of it, honestly. The truth had been here all along, but I'd chosen not to see it. The truth that I could no longer deny after my journey. When that urge first came to me as a child, I should have realized I was different.

"How long has it been going on?" I asked instead.

"What? The siphoning? That's new." He finally dared to creep closer, his sword dropping slightly. He was trying to throw me off my guard. It wouldn't work.

"Why?"

He threw me a bemused look as he began to circle me. "Because after centuries of the monotony, I'd grown bored. And the rush it gave me." He smiled to himself before turning back to me. "You should be familiar with that feeling as well."

I ignored his jab, my mind hooked on one word. "Centuries?"

"Oh. I thought you'd figured it out." His toe kicked at the rubble on the floor. "When I took this kingdom from *her*, I was content to play puppet master with everyone she left behind. But since then, I've realized my ambitions were far too low. With the North in disarray, it'd be easy to take them for my own. After that, what would be stopping me from going south?"

His teeth gleamed in the sunlight that filtered through the windows. I thought I was going to be sick. Asher was still in the South.

"Your brother had nearly figured it out, you know." His head tilted to the side as his blow landed. He was waiting for my pain, but I wouldn't show him that weakness. "Tynan knows, of course. He figured it out on his own. Though, I'm not sure what he intends to happen. I've left him alone for now."

My breath hitched slightly, and he narrowed in on the tell. "Maybe he thinks he can take this land from me. He's mistaken if that's the case. Or perhaps he thinks he can take it from you." He pointed to my chest with his sword. "After all, even I did it once."

His move came quickly, but I'd been waiting. I dropped to the ground, grasping a piece of the statue and throwing it toward his face in the same moment I plunged a mental knife into his mind, through the crack he'd so carelessly left wide open.

He shrieked in pain, unable to dodge the stone cascading into his nose, not with the pain in his mind. He slashed at me blindly, but I rolled from his strike. Guards descended, undoubtedly stirred forward by his will—his command. That power he'd stolen from Lucy, though luckily not every drop she had.

I sent spirals of darkness and fire wrapping around their limbs, holding them in place. I'd silently thanked Nash for that kernel of power that leached from him and into me when I'd slid my dagger into his chest. It wasn't enough for me to slip into darkness as he did, but it was enough to hold those who'd harm me at bay, if only for a moment.

"Kaya." Tynan's shout echoed through the library as he rushed between the writhing guards. He paid them no mind as he raced to me. I didn't realize I was waiting for Cillian until he didn't rush in after. Panic seized me, but Holden asked the question that was evading me.

"Where's Cillian?" Was that genuine concern I heard in Holden's voice? Tynan didn't answer, but I couldn't dwell on it. I had to keep my focus on the problem at hand. I wouldn't worry about things I could not change. No. Not yet.

I saw my opening and took it once more, spiraling a rope of fire in Holden's direction. He had been distracted slightly by Cillian's absence. He skirted around it, but narrowly so. I lashed out again, this time with Tynan's help.

Shards of ice began flying through the room, coming from various directions and giving Holden too much to effectively dodge. It worked, though. My tether found him, curling up and around his body as he ripped at it to no avail. That flaming tether was fueled not only by Cillian's power, but by Asher's and another just like them. I pulsed my will into that power, sending it looping around Holden's neck. With one thought, the remaining end was snagging around the chandelier above him, hauling him from his feet and into the air.

My binding tightened, that fire blazing against his skin. Angry red blisters swelled up around his neck, along his hands, where he dug relentlessly on that hold. Gargling and gasping, he tried to suck in a breath. But no, I wouldn't allow that. I tightened my hold, blocking out the sound of Tynan behind me. What he said didn't matter; it would be his turn soon enough.

Holden's eyes bulged as he realized that this was his end. His feet kicked out around him as they searched for purchase, something to alleviate the pressure of his body's downward pull. He found no relief.

That fiery rope held firm even against his ugly thrashing. His body began to sway as his struggles became halfhearted. I didn't take my eyes from his as the light slowly drifted from them, and his hand slipped from that flaming tether around his throat. He stopped moving altogether, and I let his body drop from the chandelier with the jerk of my neck. He remained unmoving in a crumpled heap at my feet. My foot kicked forward, impacting with the dead weight that was once the head of our realm. I kicked again, the memory of my brother surfacing before me.

He'd stolen so much.

"Ky." It wasn't a reprimand or an admonishment. It was a praise. I stopped my debasing of Holden's body, the air burning in my lungs. I turned to find Tynan kneeling behind me, his eyes alight with wonder. Falling onto his hands, he lowered his head in a low bow before me.

The cracking that emitted from his face when my boot connected with his nose shattered through the room, echoing off the walls of the otherwise silent library. He was too shocked by the assault to recover quickly. I delved into his mind, searching for any sign of Cillian. I found what I was looking for... And more. His true name was hidden deep in his mind, buried under so many images I could never unsee.

When I beheld the image of Cillian's bloody body, I leapt upon Tynan's writhing form. He moaned in pain, but I paid him no mercies.

"Pray he's still living, Tynan. Because if he isn't, what I did to Holden will be nothing in comparison to what I inflict upon you." And then I summoned every bit of that darkness I could, dissolving myself and Tynan into nothing and willing myself to appear at Cillian's side.

The blood spilling around him was sinking into the dirt, fresh flowers erupting in its wake. It was still flowing, which told me that I still had time. I discarded Tynan's crumpled form somewhere he wouldn't be a bother. My hands were ripping the shirt from Cillian's chest, searching for that death below before it could consume the rest of his soul. My heightened power sank into him with little thought, searching for everything that had been split in two by Tynan's icy attack.

My power stitched him back together, but still, I felt his essence waning. Searching within myself, I found that spark of power that had once belonged to him. I collected it with a thought, with my will. I sent that kernel flowing from my fingers into his very heart.

I shut my eyes against the agony that was trying to tear me in two; the thought of Cillian slowly fading from this world was nearly blinding. That agony was almost too much for me to ignore. My grip on him, on his soul, was hard and unwavering until I felt that life force inside of him begin to grow and swell beneath me. The flames that were Cillian began to burn brighter.

Relief replaced my agony for only a second before I finally let go of him and turned on Tynan. Another problem to extinguish. He was crawling toward me, one hand still cradling the place where his nose used to be. Blood spewed from his face, but his eyes still held longing as he slowly made his way toward me.

Fueled by my hatred, by rage and betrayal, I was above him in an instant. I braced a foot on either side of his body, looking down at him as he rolled onto his back. He choked on his own blood as he tried to speak.

Then, I did something I knew I would regret until my dying day.

"You have until sundown to leave my realm. I don't care where you go, but if I see you again, I swear I will kill you." Maybe it was pity, maybe it was something else entirely, but I couldn't bring myself to inflict more death today. "Do you understand?"

He nodded, the only answer I would get from him with the blood that was running down his throat.

He should have died, but I couldn't bring myself to do it, even though he'd betrayed me—tried to kill my tethered—he led me to my fate. Someone someday would get that luxury, but it wouldn't be me. With Cillian stirring just behind me, my attentions were needed elsewhere. I was confident that he couldn't go home to the North. He'd have to hide out somewhere in the South. He was a worm and letting him go free condemned him to a life of living as one.

I stepped away, ignoring Tynan altogether as the rise and fall of Cillian's chest deepened and leveled out. I dropped to my knees beside him as he flicked his eye open partly. The relief I saw when it focused on me sent my heart tearing in two.

My love. My life.

Cillian's hand reached for my face, his sticky fingers lightly dragging down my cheek, checking to see if I was real. I smiled, ignoring the shuffling from behind as Tynan—or was it Ansel?—scurried off to some other hole somewhere.

"Kaya," Cillian croaked. My name from his lips broke me and healed me all in the same breath. I fell forward, my lips searching for his. As they met, I felt his power surge up beneath me. A shriek ensued from off in the forest, and I knew it was the sound of Tynan succumbing to Cillian's flames. But I didn't care. The way our bodies melded together was like the spring after the harshest winter. It was a new beginning after the darkest of nights.

He was my tethered, my king, and together we were one.

Epilogue

F arehail hadn't known a queen for hundreds of years. With the turning of the tide, however, came a new reign. Though it was a time for change, that change brought about a new light to the once-darkened realm.

The queen of the island was something to be revered. Her rule was fair and exact, never to be contested after so long in the shadows. Her will was their will, and she was relentless in her duty to the land. That force within the forest was something to fear, and she did not falter in her ability to uphold its desires.

Her tethered was her equal in every way. He was unparalleled in his skill, unwavering in his commitment, and unmatched in his affection for his love. Wherever one was found, the other was not far behind, lurking just out of sight, enveloped in the shadows.

The pair ruled together in harmony, the land having been rid of those who would see it turned to ruin. With order restored, peace like never before was bestowed upon the once-derelict island.

They mended.

They prevailed.

They cherished.

Fin.

Acknowledgements

Once again, I would like to thank my readers for their unwavering support. Without each and every one of you, these books would not be possible. I hope you enjoy these stories just as much as I enjoy writing them. There is so much of my heart wrapped around each word, set into each page, and inside every character. These books mean the world to me.

A special thank you to my cover artist and graphic designer. The two of you are the best, and I value the hard work you do for me immensely. Along with those two amazing ladies, my sisters are ever supportive as well. I appreciate your honesty and eagerness when it comes to reading my work. You're both the first set of eyes I allow on each draft because I know I can trust you to hurt me when I need to be hurt.

Lastly, but never the least, a special thanks goes out to my formatter—also known as my husband. You make my clusters of words in a document into an actual book, and without your hours of research and work, this thing would be unsightly to say the least.

Not only that, but your essence in wrapped into very book boyfriend I write—from Zale to Oran, from Ender to Cillian—you are the best qualities of each man I put to paper. You love my violence; you always have my best interest in mind; you push me to do the thing. And yes, you were my brother's friend first.

You'll forever be the light in my darkness.

Always.

Made in the USA
Columbia, SC
24 February 2025

54314203R00195